ONCE UPON an Achingly Beautiful KISS

#5 The Whickertons in Love

BY BREE WOLF

WOLF PUBLISHING

Once Upon an Achingly Beautiful Kiss by Bree Wolf

Published by WOLF Publishing UG

Text by Bree Wolf
Cover Art by Victoria Cooper
Paperback ISBN: 978-3-98536-030-7
Hard Cover ISBN: 978-3-98536-031-4
Ebook ISBN: 978-3-98536-029-1

WOLF Publishing - This is us:

Two sisters, two personalities.. But only one big love!

Diving into a world of dreams..
...Romance, heartfelt emotions, lovable and witty characters, some humor, and some mystery! Because we want it all! Historical Romance at its best!

Visit our website to learn all about us, our authors and books!

Sign up to our mailing list to receive first hand information on new releases, freebies and promotions as well as exclusive giveaways and sneak-peeks!

WWW.WOLF-PUBLISHING.COM

ALSO BY BREE WOLF

The Whickertons in Love

The WHICKERTONS IN LOVE is a new series by USA Today bestselling author BREE WOLF set in Regency-era England, portraying the at times turbulent ways the six Whickerton siblings search for love. If you enjoy wicked viscounts, brooding lords as well as head-strong ladies, fierce in their affections and daring in their search for their perfect match, then this new series is perfect for you!

#1 Once Upon a Devilishly Enchanting Kiss

#2 Once Upon a Temptingly Ruinous Kiss

#3 Once Upon an Irritatingly Magical Kiss

#4 Once Upon a Devastatingly Sweet Kiss

#5 Once Upon an Achingly Beautiful Kiss

More to follow!

Prequel to the series: Once Upon A Kiss Gone Horribly Wrong

ACKNOWLEDGEMENT

A great big thank-you to all those who aided me in finishing this book and made it the wonderful story it has become. First and foremost, of course, there is my family, who inspires me on a daily basis, giving me the enthusiasm and encouragement, I need to type away at my computer day after day. Thank you so much!

Then there are my proofreaders, beta readers and readers who write to me out of the blue with wonderful ideas and thoughts. Thank you for your honest words! Jodi and Dara comb through my manuscripts in an utterly diligent way that allows me to smooth off the rough edges and make it shine. Thank you so much for your dedication to my stories! Brie, Carol, Zan-Mari, Kim, Martha and Mary are my hawks, their eyes sweeping over the words to spot those pesky errors I seem to be absolutely blind to. Thank you so much for aiding me with your keen eyesight!

ONCE UPON *an* *Achingly* *Beautiful* KISS

PROLOGUE

Whickerton Grove, Spring 1797
Six Years Earlier

At the sound of her father's voice, Lady Juliet Beaumont, eldest daughter to the Earl of Whickerton, pulled to an abrupt halt outside his study. She had never been one to eavesdrop on other people's conversations and she did not mean to do so now; however, there had been a chilling edge to her father's voice that rooted her to the spot, forcing her to listen whether she wanted to or not.

"What do you mean?" her mother inquired, a cautious tone in her voice as she moved toward her husband. "What has happened?"

Juliet swallowed as she peered through the small gap between door and frame, only catching a brief glimpse of her parents standing with their hands linked.

Her father inhaled a deep breath, as though he wished he did not have to speak the words that lay upon his tongue. "I've just received word that," he cleared his throat, his voice thick with emotion, "Sebastian Hurst...was killed in a riding accident."

"No!" Juliet's mother exclaimed, a desperate plea in her voice that echoed within Juliet's heart. Her own breath lodged in her throat and tears shot to her eyes, blurring her vision. This cannot be true! Oh, please, this cannot be true!

Utterly unaware of her surroundings, Juliet stumbled down the corridor, barely able to see where she was going. She knew she ought to collect herself—her parents would need her—but she could not. All she could think about was Kit! What would this do to him?

As she staggered out the terrace door into the cool spring air, Juliet breathed in deeply, willing her tears to subside. Only they would not. Her emotions continued to rage in a way she had never experienced before, and so she continued onward, her slippered feet carrying her down into the gardens until she came upon the small pavilion where they had spent many happy moments together.

Of course, Sebastian had never been one of them. As the eldest son and heir to the Earl of Lockhart, he had rarely spent time at home with his family and the Whickerton siblings on the neighboring estate. Instead, he had enjoyed the diversity of the season in London as much as traipsing from one scandalous house party to another. Juliet knew very little about such things, but over the course of her two-and-twenty years, she had overheard whispered words here and there and knew that throughout his short life, Sebastian had acquired a bit of a reputation.

And now he was gone.

Although Juliet had rarely seen him, her heart broke at the thought of such a loss. She knew she ought to think of his poor parents. She ought to think of his little sister Nora, barely eighteen—the same as one of Juliet's own sisters, Leo. Yet her thoughts lingered with Christopher—Kit, as she called him—Sebastian's younger brother...and Juliet's dearest friend.

Leaning her forehead against one of the smooth columns of the pavilion, Juliet closed her eyes. Fresh tears slipped out and rolled down her cheeks. Her hands clamped around the strong pillar as she felt herself begin to sway upon her feet at the thought of what Kit was going through at the moment, for the thought of losing her own brother almost made her knees buckle.

Ought she go to him? Her head rose, and she tried to blink back her tears. "Perhaps he needs me," she mumbled, remembering the pain in his brown eyes whenever his parents overlooked him in favor of the more important son, the heir. For despite his tall stature and strong physique, Kit had always been a sensitive man, one who cared, who felt emotions deeply. Juliet loved that about him!

Inhaling a deep breath, she determinedly brushed away the last of her tears before turning to—

Stilling mid-step, Juliet stared across the pavilion toward the wide expanse of lawn beyond it, her eyes settling on the man who had been her dearest friend for as long as she could remember.

Leading his bay mare by the reins, Kit moved toward her, his steps slow and somehow weighted as though iron shackles had been fastened to his ankles. His shoulders were slumped, and his head was slightly bent; his gaze, however, held hers, such sorrow and misery in his eyes that Juliet felt fresh tears stream down her cheeks.

The need she saw in his eyes propelled Juliet forward, her feet hastening down the few steps to the lawn before large strides carried her to him. Without stopping, without a single word leaving her lips, Juliet threw herself into his arms, her own wrapping tightly around his shoulders as she balanced herself on the tips of her toes.

For a moment, Kit seemed as still as a stone column. Then, however, she felt his arms come around her, holding her tighter with each moment that passed, as though he could no longer bear the crushing pain. His forehead sank to her shoulder, and she felt the soft wetness of tears fall upon her skin.

"I'm so sorry," Juliet whispered then, her voice choked. "So very sorry." Saying these all but meaningless words made her feel even more helpless, and so she simply held him tighter.

It was all she could do.

If only she could take his pain away.

If only.

More than ever before, Christopher Hurst, now only son and heir to the Earl of Lockhart, was grateful for the slender young woman who held him in a tight embrace that threatened to squeeze the air from his lungs. He, too, hugged her with every bit of strength he had left in him, fearing the moment he would have to release her.

Nowhere in the world did Christopher feel more at peace than when Jules was with him. He had always felt so. Even as a little girl with pigtails and freckles, she had had a way about her that had completely disarmed him. Her warm moss-green eyes always shone with kindness and compassion, her heart always seeing the good in everything and everyone. She never spoke much, but whenever she did, he knew to listen. She was his conscience, his compass, guiding him through life with a steady and kind hand.

And Christopher had needed her last night...

...when they had received news of his brother's death.

...when his world had come crashing down.

...when he had seen fear and regret in his parents' eyes at the thought of the earldom now resting upon his shoulders.

Christopher had never been good enough. Never. He had always known that. Although he had never known why. Even as a child, he had done his utmost to please his parents, to make them proud, but the look upon their faces had never changed.

Disapproval.

Disappointment.

Regret.

Fortunately, Christopher had only been the second son, and so his parents had lavished most of their attention—good or bad—on Sebastian. No matter what scrapes his elder brother had gotten into over the years, in their parents' eyes he could do no wrong.

Even though Christopher had never been able to understand Sebastian's roguish ways, he had loved his brother. The thought that he would never see him again, never again hear him chortle in that way of his or spot him lounging on the settee after a night out at the local tavern almost brought him to his knees.

"I'm so sorry," Jules mumbled, her voice full of sorrow and anguish. Her hands brushed up and down his neck as he held his face buried in the crook of hers. "So very sorry." The warmth in her voice made

Christopher crush her against his chest, certain that she would object at any moment.

She did not.

Oh, how he had needed her last night! Only it had been too late to call on her. Christopher almost had, before his father had called him back, reminding him in a stern and disapproving way to show proper manners. And so, Christopher had sought solace elsewhere, following his dead brother's example and headed down to the village tavern.

Quite literally, he had drowned his sorrows.

Christopher cringed at the thought of what he had done. He had not been himself, and yet that was no excuse. If Jules ever were to find out—

Even more than before, Christopher recoiled from that thought. He could not bear it. Although he was used to seeing his parents' disappointment, he could not bear the thought of seeing the same upon Jules' face. He needed her to look at him the way she always had with those big, green eyes of hers.

As though he were a wonderful man.

As though he were worthy of this life.

As though he deserved to be loved.

Forcing his arms to release their crushing hold on her, Christopher looked down into Jules' tear-streaked face. Her eyes glistened with sadness, with compassion as she reached out to cup his face with gentle hands. "What can I do, Kit? Please, tell me," she sobbed, biting her lower lip as her teeth began to chatter. "What can I do?"

Christopher wished that there were something—anything!—she could do, that somehow, she could squint her eyes or snap her fingers and rewind time. Swallowing, he shook his head. "I need to go," he croaked, his voice raw as though he had spent last night screaming at the top of his lungs.

"I understand," she replied as the pads of her thumbs gently traced the line of his cheekbones. "Send word if you need me," she dipped her head to look up into his lowered eyes, "and I will be there. Do you hear?"

Christopher nodded, even though he knew he would not. Until the end of his days he would remember the way she was looking at him now, and he would not risk that changing.

Ever.

He knew he should not see her again. Not while he stood so close to the precipice, her belief in him the only thing keeping him from falling into that black pit.

He needed her to be his conscience, his compass.

Today more than ever before.

He was no longer the second son.

Now, he was the heir.

Heaven help them all!

CHAPTER ONE

A BLAST FROM THE PAST

Laurelwood Manor, Autumn 1803
Six Years Later

"Where could she be?" Juliet mumbled to herself as she hastened down one corridor after another, eyes wide and searching. "It's her wedding day. She can't simply..." Juliet swallowed as she peeked into yet another chamber, only to find it empty.

"Juliet!"

Turning upon her heel, Juliet found her cousin Anne hastening toward her, her cheeks slightly flushed and her eyes wide with joy. "You made it!" Juliet exclaimed with relief and rushed to embrace her beloved cousin.

Giving Juliet a tight hug, Anne nodded, then heaved a deep sigh. "Oh, I wouldn't have missed this for the world." Wide, wondrous eyes looked into Juliet's. "Our little Harry getting married? I never thought I'd see the day."

Juliet chuckled, but the sound was strained. "Neither did I; however..." Again, she let her eyes sweep up and down the corridor of Laurelwood Manor—her little sister's future husband's favorite estate—as though hoping Harriet might come climbing out of a painting or reappear out of thin air.

"What is it?" Anne asked, a slight crease coming to her forehead. "What's wrong? You look worried."

Briefly closing her eyes, Juliet heaved a deep sigh. "I don't know where she is."

Anne stilled. "You...?"

"She's not in her chamber," Juliet clarified as she began to pace once more, her skin crawling with unease. "She's gone!" Staring at her cousin, Juliet shook her head. "Do you think she...?"

"No!" Anne exclaimed, a horrified expression coming to her eyes as she stepped forward and grasped Juliet's hands. "You don't think she... she left, do you? That she changed her mind?"

Juliet shrugged. "I don't know. She never wanted to marry. She's always made that unmistakably clear. She—"

"But she fell in love," Anne interrupted, reluctant to believe Harriet would do something so heinous as leave the man who loved her at the altar, "didn't she?"

Juliet nodded, thinking of the many moments she had observed between Harriet and her fiancé. They were opposites in every way. Where Harry was impulsive, Jack was cautious. They were like night and day, complementing one another in an endearingly perfect way. Never had Juliet seen her sister so happy, so at peace.

"I'm certain this is nothing but a misunderstanding," Anne counseled, her face suddenly pale, and her hands tightened upon Juliet's as she began to sway on her feet.

Juliet's eyes widened. "Are you all right?" Supporting her cousin, she guided her to an upholstered chair by the window overlooking the drive. "Here. Sit. I'll fetch you a glass of water."

"No," Anne replied with a hand on Juliet's arm, stopping her in her tracks. "It is nothing. I'm fine. I'm..." She inhaled a deep breath before a radiant smile slowly spread over her face. "I'm with child."

Staring at her beloved cousin, Juliet felt something in her stomach flit...and her heart ache with longing. "Oh, I'm so happy for you!" she exclaimed, blinking back the tears that shot into her eyes. She embraced Anne, reminding herself that she ought to be happy for her cousin.

And she was.

Truly.

If only...

The sound of hooves on gravel drew her attention to the window. The autumn sun shone brightly, and Juliet had to squint her eyes, momentarily blinded. Then she could make out the outlines of a rider charging up the drive before pulling to a halt just outside the front stoop. The moment he swept his hat off his head, Juliet froze.

She could not say what it was about him that stilled her heart and stole the air from her lungs. She could barely make out his form, let alone his face. Yet...

Deep down, Juliet knew it was him.

Him and no other.

She would know him anywhere.

But why was he here today? Why had he come? Long years had passed since they had last spoken, and yet it seemed her heart still longed for him with the same intensity it had the day after his brother's passing.

Everything had changed after that. He had changed, and to this day, Juliet did not even know why.

"Are you all right?" Anne inquired, a bit more color back in her cheeks. "You look as though you've seen a ghost." She rose from the chair and came to stand beside Juliet. "Who is he? I can't see his face."

Juliet swallowed. "A...An old acquaintance." Gritting her teeth, she turned from the window. "No one important." Reminding herself of their current predicament, she met Anne's eyes. "Do you feel well enough to help me look for Harry? I do not wish to alert her fiancé. This might all just be a—"

"Yes, of course I am," Anne assured her with a smile. "Do not worry. Between the two of us, we shall find her."

Juliet breathed a sigh of relief, and the two cousins headed back down the corridor they had come. "I'll search downstairs while you—" Anne broke off as Juliet lifted a hand.

"Do you hear that?" she asked, straining her ears to listen.

"What?"

"Voices."

"Voices?" echoed Anne as they slowly moved past the stairs leading to the ground floor.

Juliet nodded, her gaze moving down the corridor and darting from door to door. "I thought I heard—"

In that moment, a door at the opposite end of the corridor opened and Grandma Edie stepped out into the hallway. She spoke to someone over her shoulder before Juliet spotted not only Harriet but also their three other sisters, Louisa, Leonora and Christina, exit the chamber as well.

Beside Juliet, Anne chuckled. "It looks like a war council, don't you think? I wonder why we were not invited."

Indeed, Juliet could not deny that the expressions upon her sisters' faces held something secretive, their eyes widening in a semblance of alarm the moment they spotted Juliet and Anne standing there. Only Grandma Edie seemed to possess the ability to hide her thoughts, the look upon her face almost innocent as she smiled at Juliet and Anne. "Oh, how wonderful that you could make it, Annie dear." She embraced her granddaughter warmly.

"I'm happy to be here," Anne replied, beaming at her cousins and hugging them each. "I wouldn't have missed this for the world." She grinned at Harry.

"How was...well, England?" Louisa asked with a bit of a frown. "Where did you travel again? I'm sorry." Shrugging her shoulders, she sighed a bit exasperatedly. "I've found myself to be a bit scatter-brained ever since..." She patted the bulge under her gown gently.

Harriet laughed. "Are you certain you've not always been like this?"

Louisa feigned an outraged glare in her sister's direction. "And here I thought brides were sweet and polite." Her brows rose meaningfully.

This time, Christina broke out laughing. "Oh, bride or not, Harriet has never been sweet or polite."

Before Harriet could retaliate, Grandma Edie rapped the end of her walking cane on the floor twice to catch their attention. "As much as I'd love catching up with you," she grinned at Anne, then patted her hand, "there is a wedding to take place within the hour." She looked from one granddaughter to the next. "Leo and Chris, would you help Harry get ready? Jules, I could use a bit of help getting down the stairs." She chuckled, as though there had been something humorous to her words. "Lou and Annie, find somewhere comfortable to sit and have your husbands fetch you something to drink. In your condition, you should not be on your feet too long."

Juliet smiled as her sisters' eyes moved to Anne, their jaws dropping. "You're with child?" Louisa was the first to exclaim, one hand still resting upon her own bulging belly while the other reached for Anne as though she feared her cousin might be a mirage.

Blushing most becomingly, Anne smiled. "I am." After a myriad of hugs and well-wishes, she turned to their grandmother. "How did you know?"

Grandma Edie merely chuckled in that mysterious way of hers before slipping her hand through the crook of Juliet's arm. "Help an old woman downstairs, dear, will you?"

"Of course, Grandmother." As they descended the stairs, Juliet glimpsed Harry, Chris and Leo disappear into Harriet's chamber while Lou and Anne followed them to the ground floor. "What were you all doing?" Juliet inquired, exchanging a look with Anne over her shoulder. "I was worried because I couldn't find Harry. I half-expected her to have—"

"Run off?" her grandmother supplied with another chuckle. Then she patted Juliet's hand reassuringly. "Don't worry, dear. All is well." Juliet was glad to hear it; however, that did not answer her question. She could not help but think that something was going on...and that everyone was determined to keep it from her.

Had it simply been some kind of pre-marital talk for Harriet? Although Juliet was the eldest Whickerton sister, she was the only one yet unwed—not counting Harriet, of course—which would explain why she had not been invited. Still, if it had been about her youngest sister joining the ranks of married ladies, why had their mother not been there?

"Ah," her grandmother suddenly exclaimed with a wicked-sounding chortle, "the Earl of Lockhart returns to these shores!"

At her grandmother's words, Juliet almost tripped, her heart clenching at the thought of pulling her grandmother down the stairs along with her. In the last moment, however, she managed to catch herself before her head swiveled around and her eyes fell on a familiar face.

The Earl of Lockhart.

Christopher.

Kit.

His brown curls were windswept, and his eyes shone with something akin to excitement. Still, he moved with grace and decorum, unlike the eager and impulsive young man Juliet had once known. He truly had become the new earl, the expression upon his face reflecting his parents' expectations rather than his own heart.

But what did Juliet know of his heart?

Nothing.

Bowing to her grandmother, Kit greeted her sister and cousin before his gaze finally found hers. "Lady Juliet." His eyes seemed darker than she remembered as they looked into hers, and yet they were undoubtedly his. An odd ache came to her chest, and for a shocking moment, she feared she might throw herself into his arms.

The truth was, though, that the man standing only a few steps in front of her was a stranger.

"Lord Lockhart." Juliet politely inclined her head before turning away and urging her grandmother along. "Grandmother, perhaps you should sit."

Fortunately, her grandmother did not argue, and so Juliet exhaled the breath she had been holding the moment she could no longer sense those dark brown eyes upon her. Oh, why had he come? Never would she have expected to see him today!

Yet, try as she might, she could not ignore the little dance of joy her heart had performed at the mere sight of him. Stranger or not, he was Kit...

...and he would always be Kit.

No matter what.

CHAPTER TWO

OLD FRIENDS REUNITED

Christopher's palms were sweating, and his pulse thundered like a stampede charging down a hill. Of course, the hard ride to Laurelwood Manor could have caused it. Christopher had been hard pressed for time and feared that he might not arrive to see the youngest Whickerton sister married. He was uncertain why he had been invited. What he did know, however, was that one did not disregard an invitation from the dowager countess. Grandma Edie—as everyone tended to call her—was a force to be reckoned with, and if she called upon one, one was well-advised to answer.

And in a timely fashion.

With a deep sigh, Christopher watched Juliet escort her grandmother out of the entrance hall. A part of him wished to follow. It felt like a tug upon his heart, urging him onward. How long had it been since he had last seen her? A year perhaps?

In truth, he knew the answer. He knew the answer down to the exact day. He remembered every moment he had spent at Whickerton Grove last year. Then, too, it had been the dowager countess calling him home, back to England. She had had his steward forward a letter to him in Ireland, urging him back into her grandson's life, and

Christopher had been glad for it. Once, he and Troy had been good friends, the best of friends even...before Christopher had made yet another mistake.

One had cost him Juliet.

The other had cost him Troy.

"Christopher?"

At the sound of his old friend's voice, Christopher turned around and found Troy standing in an arched doorway, a look of utter surprise upon his face.

"What are you doing here?" Troy inquired; his gaze slightly narrowed as he tried to make sense of this unexpected reunion. Measured steps carried him closer, and his gaze swept over Christopher. "I assume this is not a coincidence." The right corner of his mouth quirked slightly, as though he wished to smile, but was not quite certain whether he should.

Christopher did smile, for he was glad to see his friend, to be here, to feel this odd familiarity once again. "I received an invitation," he explained, stepping toward his friend, "from your grandmother."

Although Troy was one of the most serious-looking men Christopher had ever known, the hint of a smile touched his mouth as he shook his head. "I suppose I should've known." His gaze narrowed in suspicion. "She did not tell you why, though, did she?"

Christopher chuckled. "Does she ever?"

Troy inhaled a slow breath, his gaze upon Christopher's. "Welcome back...old friend." Although they had seen each other a bit more than a year ago, that visit had felt strained. They had been unable to return to that old ease that had once existed between them. Long ago, they had been like brothers, the other's heart as familiar to them as their own. They had shared everything, had talked about everything. In truth, Christopher knew Troy better than he had known his own brother.

Before.

"Thank you," Christopher replied, uncertain what to say, wishing they could somehow slip back into their old selves. How often had he wished for that to be possible? "It feels good to be back." He allowed his gaze to sweep over the hall. "Laurelwood Manor is a quaint little estate. Quite charming."

Troy nodded. "As far as I know, it holds great sentimental value for Harriet's betrothed. He is a good man, and I am happy for her."

A good man, Christopher mused, feeling as though that phrase taunted him. Was he a good man?

"Come." Troy gestured for Christopher to join him as he moved across the hall and then headed toward the door through which Juliet and her grandmother had disappeared. "Harry and Jack decided to forgo the small chapel and be married in the drawing room. It holds more people, and Harry was quite adamant in the number of guests she wished to see present." A small smile flickered across his face. "You might remember how strong-willed she is."

Smiling, Christopher nodded. "I remember well...and fondly. And her future husband, is he much like her?"

Troy snorted, and Christopher stopped in his tracks, turning to look at his friend. "I apologize," Troy said quickly, a look of dismay coming to his eyes at his less than proper reaction. "In fact, the duke is quite the opposite to our dear Harry. Yet..." Shrugging his shoulders, he sighed. "Somehow they are perfect for one another." A touch of sadness rang in Troy's voice, and Christopher gritted his teeth, knowing full well that he was responsible.

If only...

"Lord Lockhart," came the dowager's voice from across the room. "Would you care to join us?"

Troy placed a hand on his friend's arm and leaned in conspiratorially, reminding Christopher of days long gone. "See if you can find out why she invited you here." Something almost youthful twinkled in Troy's eyes. "Not that I'm disappointed she did, mind you." The ghost of a smile played over his face before he turned...but then stopped and looked back. "Your sister is not here with you, is she?"

Christopher saw hope and dread war with one another in his friend's eyes. "She's not. She is still...mourning her husband."

A muscle in Troy's jaw twitched. "Of course," was all he said before he spun on his heel and walked away.

Clearing his throat, Christopher turned toward the dowager, his eyes immediately moving past her and settling upon Juliet. She sat beside her grandmother, her head slightly bowed and her hands folded in her lap. She did not look up, not once, not even to acknowledge his presence, and Christopher felt his heart sink. What had he expected? After he had left all those years ago.

Without a word.

Without an explanation.

Without even a farewell.

Of course, Juliet had every right to be angry with him, to still fault him for what he had done. Yet as his gaze swept over her, Christopher could not help but think that she did not look angry. Nor did she look sad or regretful. Indeed, the look upon her face held nothing but indifference, the expression of a person whose heart had not been touched in any way. Had he been mistaken? Had he only ever imagined that he was dear to her?

"It is wonderful to be here," Christopher greeted the dowager with a nod of his head. "I thank you for your kind invitation." To his surprise, he saw Lady Juliet's head snap up at his words. Her eyes widened as they flew to her grandmother, her jaw tense and her breath suddenly quickening.

Christopher frowned. Had she not known? Did her reaction speak of nothing but surprise? Or...was it more than that? Christopher knew it was ill-advised, and yet he couldn't stop the feeling of his heart lightening, hope growing anew. Was it possible that he still held a spot in her heart?

"Come," the dowager invited him, gesturing toward the empty chair next to Juliet. "Sit with us and tell us of your travels. How did you find the Continent?"

Christopher did as she bid him, but he did not fail to notice the way Juliet tensed as he moved to sit beside her. She kept her gaze lowered; her head slightly turned away as though she expected her grandmother to speak to her at any moment.

Seating himself, Christopher recounted the tales he had recited more than once. Of course, they were falsehoods.

Lies.

Inventions.

After all, he had never gone to the continent. He had left England, yes, but he had not gone to the continent. It had simply been a story he had invented because that was precisely what society expected of a young man like him. One traveled to the continent, did one not? No one had ever questioned his tales.

Slowly, the room began to fill as more and more guests arrived and found their seats. Wildflowers decorated every available surface, reflecting Harriet's spirit perfectly, and Christopher wondered about the man she had promised to marry. In fact, he recalled how adamant she had been in her youth about never accepting the shackles of marriage. It still made him smile. Always had he admired her free spirit, that dauntless certainty that she was who she ought to be.

As Christopher continued to speak to the dowager of his imagined adventures, places he had never seen nor cared to, he felt acutely aware of the young woman sitting beside him. Her gaze remained fixed upon her folded hands, the look upon her face distant, as though her mind was somewhere far away. Yet every so often, a slight shiver seemed to dance down her spine, and Christopher could not help but wonder if it was because of him.

He hoped it was because he felt it as well.

To avoid staring at her, Christopher allowed his gaze to sweep over the other assembled guests. He saw familiar faces as more and more of Juliet's sisters arrived. They walked in arm in arm with their husbands, smiles upon their faces and their eyes aglow with happiness. Always had they been a joyous family, sharing in each other's lives in a way Christopher had never known in his own. He remembered that as a young boy, he had often wished he could be one of them.

One of the Whickertons.

Oddly enough, he could not help but notice that the moment the sisters' eyes fell on him, a quite unusual expression came to their faces.

All their faces.

Christopher suspected it could be surprise at his unexpected arrival, for it seemed the dowager countess had not informed her family that he would be in attendance. Although Christopher could not help but wonder why, he had learned long ago that the dowager's mind could not be understood by mere mortals.

He grinned inwardly.

Once more looking up from recounting his tales, Christopher found that Juliet's sisters were...watching him. Perhaps even observing him. Was that possible? Or was he merely imagining it? Yet time and time again, their gazes strayed to him before they turned to one another, whispering quietly.

"Are you all right, dear?" the dowager asked, gently patting Juliet's folded hands. "You haven't said a word since we sat down."

Lifting her head, Juliet smiled at her grandmother. "I'm perfectly fine, Grandmother."

The dowager nodded, then leaned heavily onto her walking cane and pushed to her feet. "Pardon me for a moment." Juliet was about to jump to her feet, but her grandmother pushed her back down. "You sit and talk. How long has it been since you've last seen each other?" And then she hobbled away, leaving them alone.

Alone in a room full of people.

Curious people.

Christopher swallowed, then allowed his gaze to move to Juliet, determinedly ignoring all those watching them with ill-concealed interest. What was going on?

Juliet was still looking after her grandmother as though wishing with all her heart that she could join her. Then, however, she inhaled a deep breath, no doubt to steady her nerves, and her head slowly turned back to him.

Inch by inch.

Christopher held his breath as he watched her lashes sweep downward, her head turning another fraction in his direction before her eyes rose to settle upon his.

Finally.

Christopher felt it like a lightning strike. Her moss-green eyes held him in place, barely allowing him to breathe. To look at her like this, so close, was something he had dreamed of for years.

He had been a fool.

In more ways than one.

The very day he knew her lost to him; Christopher had come to realize that he loved her.

Not like a friend.

Or not only like a friend.

"Are you all right?" Juliet asked tentatively, her voice barely more than a whisper, her eyes still hesitant as they looked into his.

Swallowing the lump in his throat, Christopher nodded. "I suppose I am. It...It's simply been a long time since..." Again, he cleared his throat, mesmerized by the dark green flecks illuminating the moss-green of her irises. "Last time I was at Whickerton Grove, we...we didn't..."

Juliet swallowed. "Speak," she finished for him, as she had countless times before. It was a small, almost insignificant thing, but it made Christopher's heart soar.

"We did not," he agreed, wishing he could think of something more to say.

Her eyes fell from his but only for a moment. "You did not seem to wish to." A hint of accusation rested in her voice; yet Christopher could not help but think that she mainly longed to understand.

"I did," he admitted out loud, feeling his heart skip a beat when her eyes flew open at his words and returned to meet his. "I did."

Her breath shuddered past her lips as she held his gaze. "But you did not," Juliet finally remarked, and her gaze once more fell from his as she turned in her seat, once more facing the front of the room.

Christopher closed his eyes. Indeed, he had not. He had not spoken more than a few words to her, nothing beyond a greeting or a polite remark. He had wanted to but had thought it wiser to keep his distance. Only after he had left, had he realized the moments he had lost. If only there was some way for him to explain. Would she understand, though? Or would the truth simply sever the thin thread still connecting them?

"Which one is Harry's betrothed?" Christopher asked, leaning closer, for he desperately wished to continue this moment.

To hold on to it.

Juliet's gaze flickered to his before moving to a tall, dark-haired man at the front of the drawing room. "Over there," she whispered. "His name is Bradley Jackson, Duke of Clements." A small chuckle escaped Juliet's lips, and she carefully glanced at him. "Harriet calls him Jack."

Christopher smiled at her, delighting in the warmth that shone in her eyes. "I assume *Jack* was not too happy about that?" Indeed, the man speaking to Lord and Lady Whickerton possessed a bit of a stiff and rather formal demeanor.

Another chuckle left Juliet's lips, and Christopher wished he could lock it in a box for safekeeping. "He was not...at first." Her gaze warmed as she looked at her little sister's betrothed. "But I think he likes it now. It's in the way he looks at her when..." Her voice broke off, and she seemed to retreat into herself.

Christopher swallowed. "And who is that?" he asked, nodding his chin to an equally tall and broad-shouldered man. This one, however, wore his brown hair unfashionably long; so long, in fact, that he could tie it at the back of his neck.

"His name is Keir MacKinnear," Juliet replied after a moment of hesitation. "Grandmother invited him. He's from the Highlands."

Christopher frowned, then tried to catch her gaze. "Your grandmother invited him?"

Juliet nodded.

"Do you know why?"

"She won't say," Juliet replied with a glance at the Scot. "Chris and Harry speculated it had something to do with Grandma's matchmaking schemes. They think she brought him here for m—" Her voice broke off, and her head snapped around, her wide eyes meeting his before they dropped back down to her folded hands.

Christopher swallowed hard. "For you," he finished this time. "You meant to say, she brought him here for you." His jaw clenched at the thought. "Do you care for him?"

Juliet's gaze remained so stubbornly fixed on the front of the room that Christopher wanted to grasp her by the shoulders and shake her. Instead, he followed her example and turned away, his eyes staring straight ahead as he fought the urge to strangle the unknown Highlander.

And then the wedding ceremony began, and a hushed silence fell over the room, allowing Christopher to force a few deep breaths down into his lungs as he watched bride and groom stand up together. As stiff and formal as the duke had appeared only moments earlier, Christopher could not deny that a rather besotted look came to his face the moment his eyes fell on his young bride. Harriet being Harriet, she winked at him; her smile luminous as she took his hand.

Christopher felt his own heart clench with envy. He wanted nothing more but to reach out and grasp Juliet's hand. Again, it seemed like such a simple, almost insignificant gesture. To him, however, it meant everything. He had dreamed of holding her, of seeing those enchanting green eyes looking into his.

Gritting his teeth, Christopher glanced at the Scot. Was it true? Had the dowager invited Mr. MacKinnear because she wished to see him matched with Juliet? And why had she brought him, Christopher, here? Again, for Troy? To see two old friends reunited? Although Christopher wished for it, it was not all he wished for.

Far from it.

CHAPTER THREE

FIRST KISSES

Juliet felt as though she had scarcely drawn breath since the moment Christopher had arrived at Laurelwood Manor the day before. Her memories of Harriet's wedding breakfast were a bit hazy. She dimly remembered speaking to her sisters, her parents, a few guests as well; however, she could not for the life of her recall what about.

All she remembered was the dark look in Christopher's eyes as she had blurted out her sisters' suspicions. Do you care for him? He had asked, his rough voice sending a shiver down her back. She had not known what to answer, her voice caught in her throat.

Of course, she did not care for Keir. She liked him, yes; how could she not? He was a very charismatic man with a smile that had the power to light up the world. She had liked him instantly, for he had such an honest, cheerful way about him that had endeared him to her. Yet she did not care for him. Not that way. But was that truly what Christopher had meant? Had she misunderstood him? Such a simple question, and yet it had stumped her.

Unable to sleep, Juliet rose early and spent a good deal of the morning pacing the length of her chamber. Her heart yearned to see Christopher again, and yet she dreaded the very moment. What ought she to say to him? Her limbs trembled at the thought of meeting him alone, of having that suffocating silence linger about them. Once, they had known how to speak to one another without thinking. Now, however, everything was different.

A lot had changed in six years.

They were no longer the two people they had once been.

Especially not to each other.

That morning, Juliet was one of the last to set foot in the breakfast parlor, afraid to find herself alone with Christopher if she were to arrive early. However, he was already there, his gaze instantly finding hers the moment she stepped over the threshold. Juliet felt it like a soft graze along her skin, and she instantly averted her eyes.

Fortunately, conversation was lively that morning, everyone reminiscing about Harriet's wedding, teasing the new couple and recounting the most precious moments of the day before. Juliet sat and listened; her gaze fixed upon her plate. Yet, deep down, she knew Christopher was looking at her. She could all but feel it. Or was she imagining it? Was that simply what she wished for? Proof that he still cared? That she still meant something—anything—to him?

After breakfast was finally over, Juliet found herself dragged along by her sisters. While the men remained behind in the breakfast parlor, the women retreated to the drawing room, yesterday's setting of Harriet's wedding once again looked as it had before.

"It is so wonderful to have you back with us," Juliet's mother exclaimed as she once more embraced Anne. "We've missed you dearly." After Anne's parents had passed on years ago, their beloved cousin had come to live with the Whickertons and been like another sister to them.

"I've missed you all as well. It feels as though ages have passed since we've last been all together like this."

Juliet helped Grandma Edie settle into a cushioned armchair by the fireplace and then took her place beside her. Leonora, Christina and Harriet managed to squeeze onto the settee next to Anne while their mother and Louisa occupied the other two remaining armchairs.

"This is a snug little drawing room," Louisa remarked with a grin, one hand draped over her growing belly. "It's not just me, is it? Because I'm getting larger with each passing day."

Everyone chuckled. "Don't worry, dear," their mother said gently, reaching out a hand to grasp Louisa's. "It is perfectly normal to feel like this."

"You mean like a whale beached on the shore?" Louisa demanded with a huff. Then she turned her head and looked at Anne. "Something for you to look forward to." A teasing grin came to her face, and everybody laughed again.

Everyone except Juliet.

Although she wished she could join in, all of a sudden, there was sadness and regret in her heart. She did not want to feel it, but the sensation remained, stuck and unable to leave like Louisa's hypothetical whale on the beach.

Never would Juliet be a mother. Never would she know the feeling of a child growing inside her. Never would she share this experience with her sisters.

With a sigh, Juliet reminded herself that she had accepted that fact long ago. Why was she lamenting it now?

Somehow, she had become Grandma Edie's companion, the task to ensure that their beloved grandmother was well and safe and taken care of every moment of every day had fallen to her. It was not a thankless task, far from it. Juliet adored her grandmother as they all did, and yet her acquiescence to her grandmother's wishes had kept her from pursuing her own.

With a heavy heart, Juliet sat among her family and listened as her sisters, her mother, her cousin, even her grandmother began reminiscing about marriage, about falling in love, about their first kiss.

Their first kiss with the man they loved.

The man they had married.

"Mine was most awful as you recall," Anne chuckled, her cheeks slightly flushed as she looked around their small circle.

Louisa laughed. "Yes, the worst mistletoe kiss I have ever had the misfortune to witness," she teased good-naturedly.

Anne glared at her in feigned outrage. "It was your fault. You forced Tobias and me under that dreadful thing." She shuddered at the memory. "Everyone was watching. I wanted to sink into a hole in the ground."

Louisa flashed her an apologetic smile. "Yet you have to admit that without that disastrous first kiss, there would most likely not have been a second one." Her brows rose in challenge.

Juliet saw Anne's blush deepen. "I suppose."

"And the second was better?" Christina asked as only Louisa and Leonora had accompanied Anne to the Hamiltons' house party that year. The rest of the Whickertons had been forced to remain behind after catching a nasty cold.

Anne nodded with a twinkle in her eyes. "Much better." She sighed. "Tobias found me the next day in the library. We were alone, with no one watching," she cast a meaningful look at Louisa, "and…it was wonderful." Another sigh left her lips before she turned to Louisa. "What about you? The day you kissed Phin as a dare, was that truly the first time you kissed him?"

Louisa chuckled, and Juliet remembered the hatred that had once existed between Louisa and her husband because of a misunderstanding years earlier. "It was."

"You kissed Phineas because of a dare?" Harry interjected. "How come I never knew that? Was he surprised?"

Before Louisa could answer, Anne nodded. "Oh, yes, he was," she exclaimed with a laugh. "She marched right up to him, told him not to read anything into it and kissed him on the mouth."

Louisa bowed her head, trying to hide a grin, and her sisters roared with laughter. "And then?" Harry pressed, now at the edge of her seat.

With a sideways glance at Louisa, Anne said, "He kissed her right back, far from satisfied with only one kiss."

Louisa threw up her hands. "All right, enough about me. Tell us about your first time kissing Jack!" Louisa wiggled her brows at Harriet meaningfully.

Harry sighed with a slight roll of her eyes. "Well, he argues it was when I tried to catch him off guard with a peck on the cheek." She shook her head. "But anyone knows a peck does not count."

Juliet swallowed, wishing she could neglect a kiss with such ease. If only she had ever received one; even if only just a peck on the cheek.

She felt her fingernails dig into her palms as she listened to her sisters—her younger sisters!—speak of the kisses they had shared with their husbands, knowing she could never join in.

Never.

Harry chewed on her bottom lip in thought. "It was some time later. We had discussed kisses and their effect at length—"

"Truly?" their mother asked, surprise in her eyes before she exchanged a meaningful look with Grandma Edie, who chuckled with amusement.

Harry nodded. "Why?"

Leonora grinned. "It sounds very scientific," she remarked. "Like something I would do."

Rolling her eyes in a somewhat exasperated fashion, Louisa laughed. "Very true."

Harry shrugged. "Well, we did. We spoke of want and wanting, and then Jack suddenly looked at me and said that," a mesmerized smile came to her lips, "he wanted to kiss me."

"Oh, that's sweet," Leonora exclaimed with a sigh. "I think I'm beginning to understand why you call him Sweet Jack."

"What about you, Leo?" Christina asked gently. "When did you share your first kiss with Drake?"

Juliet watched Leonora tense slightly. Although her sister was not shy by nature, she rather disliked being the center of attention.

"Well," Leonora began tentatively, her hands folded in her lap, "I...I asked him to kiss me."

Louisa's jaw dropped. "You did? Bravo, Leo." She squeezed her sister's hand affectionately.

Leonora offered her a bashful smile. "Well, after...er...you know..."

Everyone nodded, and Juliet could all but feel a dark cloud descend over their heads at the reminder of what Leonora had suffered.

It had been roughly a year and a half ago—before Leonora had even met her future husband—that Louisa and Leonora had sneaked away to a forbidden masquerade. There, Leonora had been attacked by a man in a mask, the experience shattering her trust in men and haunting her every step for months after. In the end, it had been Drake who had seen her fear and offered his help. He had taught her how to protect herself, and Leonora had slowly regained a part of herself she had thought lost for good.

"I knew I cared for him," Leonora recounted, a soft smile gracing her lips as she spoke, "and I wanted to know what a kiss freely given would feel like."

Juliet saw their mother's eyes mist with tears, her hands clamped tightly around one another as she listened.

"And?" pressed Grandma Edie from her seat by the fire.

Leonora smiled. "It made me realize I wanted him and no other."

Everyone cheered, and Leonora blushed crimson.

"Well, who's left?" Grandma Edie exclaimed, and Juliet swallowed as her grandmother's gaze passed over her to settle upon her younger sister Christina. "Chris, we all know that you married dear Thorne because you thought him an awful creature and wanted to protect your friend from being forced into a union with him." She chuckled loudly. "We can all see that your opinion of him has changed. Pray, tell how did that happen?"

Christina grinned at them. "Truthfully, our first kiss was a test."

"A test?" exclaimed Harriet. "What do you mean?"

Christina cleared her throat. "Well, frankly, I had never been kissed before and the thought of being married to him, being...his wife," her brows rose meaningfully as a slight flush came to her cheeks, "made me somewhat uneasy. I told him so, and he suggested a test."

"To see how a kiss would make you feel?" Harry asked, a teasing grin coming to her face. "And?"

Christina fought the wide smile that began to spread over her face and failed. "Let's just say that after our test, I no longer felt uneasy."

Another cheer went up, and Juliet wanted to weep. How exactly had this happened? How had life simply...passed her by? Nothing in her heart but regret?

No, that was not quite true. Of course, Juliet felt more than regret. She loved her life, considered herself fortunate to be part of such a loving and devoted family and yet...something was missing.

Silently, Juliet rose from her chair. She mumbled an excuse under her breath and then quickly left the drawing room, her sisters' joyful voices echoing after her. Closing the door behind her, she stilled, wrenching a deep breath down into her lungs as she closed her eyes and rested her forehead against the smooth wood.

Regret pulsed in her veins, and she felt sadness trickle down her cheeks.

"Are you all right?"

At the sound of Christopher's voice, Juliet spun around, her eyes wide with shock and humiliation that he should see her like this. She wished he would leave, simply turn and walk away. She expected him to do so—men felt uneasy around weeping females, did they not?

Instead, however, Christopher moved toward her, the look upon his face whispering of concern as his dark brown eyes swept over her. "Tell me what happened," he murmured a heartbeat before she felt his hands cup her face, the pads of his thumbs gently brushing away her tears.

Juliet stared into his eyes, shock freezing her limbs. He was a stranger. Years had passed since they had really spoken. Yet, here, in this moment, he suddenly felt like Kit again. "Would you kiss me?" The words left her lips without thinking.

Instantly, Christopher's features stilled, frozen in place as though suddenly turned to ice. His eyes were wide and unblinking; yet there was something in his gaze that...

Humiliation found Juliet like an arrow suddenly piercing her heart. Heat shot to her cheeks, and her breath lodged in her throat. "I-I'm s-sorry. I...I didn't mean—"

"Yes." The word flew from his lips, echoing between them.

CHAPTER FOUR

A BOLD REQUEST

Christopher did not know what had happened. One moment, his heart ached at seeing Juliet so distraught, and the next, it jumped at the thought of kissing her.

And he wanted to. Heaven help him, but it was all he could think about.

Trembling, Juliet stood before him, her eyes wide and tears clinging to their lashes. He felt her cheeks warm beneath his hands as she dropped her gaze in mortification. He could see that she had not meant to ask for a kiss, that the words had all but slipped from her tongue. But why had she?

A part of Christopher did not care, urging him closer, urging him to reach for what he had only ever imagined.

He moved then; what little distance remained between them shrinking. His gaze dropped to her lips, slightly parted, her rapid breath mingling with his own.

Her green eyes flew up to meet his once more, now wide and...fearful?

Christopher cursed silently. "Tell me what happened," he urged her, allowing his thumbs to sweep over her delicate cheek bones once more.

Deep down, he wished he knew her better...as he once had. Years ago, he only needed to look at her to know what was in her heart. But who was she today? What had brought those tears to her eyes? What had prompted her to ask for a kiss?

Her lashes swept downward as she tried to lower her head. "It is nothing," she whispered in a voice that sounded vulnerable. "I did not mean..." He felt her hands against his, urging him to release her.

Swallowing, Christopher complied, regret filling his heart as he took a step back.

Away from her.

"It is not nothing," Christopher insisted, unable to let it go. He wanted to know. He needed to know. Whether Juliet felt as he did did not matter; to him, she was still his best friend, his confidante...the woman he knew like no other.

The woman he had known like no other.

Wiping at her eyes, Juliet shook her head to chase away whatever had caused this emotional outburst. Christopher knew she rarely succumbed to tears; her heart stronger than one would expect from the delicate look of her. That, more than anything else, made him determined to understand what had happened. If something had affected her enough to bring tears to her eyes, he could not ignore it.

Christopher could see that she wanted him to leave her alone; yet he could not. He reached to touch her arm, and she slowly lifted her eyes to his. "What happened, Jules? Tell me."

At his use of her nickname, she stilled before a shuddering breath left her lips. Her eyes held his, and Christopher could see her thoughts traveling back to a time when he had never called her anything else. Indeed, it felt good to say it again. It had been too long.

Juliet flinched as a bout of laughter echoed through the door, immediately followed by Harry's voice. "You dared him to kiss her? Grandma, you're without a doubt the worst one of us!"

More laughter drifted to their ears as Christopher held Juliet's gaze, watched her turn such a dark shade of red that he feared she might burst into flames. "Is this what brought on your request?"

Her throat worked. "My request?"

Sidling closer, he dropped his voice. "You asked me to kiss you." He lifted his brows, his lips curling up into a smile. "Have you forgotten?"

Juliet's mouth opened and closed a few times as her eyes darted to his and then away and then back to him. "I…I shouldn't have. I'm sorry." A shy smile came to her lips. "It was only because…"

"Because?" Christopher pressed. "What are they talking about?" His gaze settled more firmly upon hers. "Kisses?"

Juliet swallowed. "First kisses," she elaborated with great reluctance.

"I see." Christopher could not help but wonder who had claimed hers. "And you do not wish to participate?"

Her eyes closed for a brief moment before she lifted her chin, her gaze now meeting his without flinching away. "I can't."

"Why not?"

Her lips thinned. "Because…I've never been kissed," she huffed out at last, a hint of a challenge coming to her face as though daring him to laugh at her.

Christopher blinked. "You've never…?" Each day he had spent away from her, he had feared that another would lay claim to the woman he had so carelessly set aside. Indeed, he remembered his shock when he had returned to English soil the previous year and found her still unwed. Were the men of England blind, deaf and dumb?

Not that he minded.

"It is why I asked you to…" Her words broke off, and a touch of mortification once more burned in her eyes.

"I see." Christopher could not help the stab of disappointment that went through him at the thought that he was merely a means to an end. Did she truly feel nothing for him any longer? Only moments ago, he could have sworn that…

"I should leave." She made to step past him. "I—"

"Why?"

Juliet frowned. "Why what?"

"Why have you never been kissed?"

"Oh!" Her gaze fell from his, and she began tugging on her left sleeve distractedly. "I…eh…" Closing her eyes, she inhaled a deep breath, then looked at him. "It simply never happened. No one ever cared enough, I suppose." A brave smile flitted over her features. "Not even you would want to..." The hint of accusation that swung in her voice surprised Christopher, as though she had asked him for a kiss, and he had had the nerve to refuse her.

He sidled closer again, a slow smile coming to his face as he watched her watching him, a touch of alarm coming to her eyes. "You do recall me saying 'yes', do you not?"

A nervous chuckle fell from her lips, and she retreated a step. "Yes, but...you didn't mean it. You only—"

"I meant it, Jules," Christopher assured her without a moment of hesitation as another step carried him closer, his gaze fixed on hers.

Juliet swallowed. "But only because—" Her back suddenly collided with the closed door to the drawing room, and her head snapped up as she found him towering above her. "I mean, it's kind of you to...to..."

Christopher had to admit that he rather liked this flustered look about her. She seemed wholly unaware of how deeply alluring she was.

A slow grin tugged upon the corners of his mouth. Perhaps he should enlighten her. "It has nothing to do with kindness, Jules," he whispered, then leaned closer and braced his hands against the door, one on each side of her head. "Nothing at all."

Her green eyes were wide as she looked at him, disbelief etched into her face. "You...You wish to kiss me?"

Slowly, Christopher nodded.

Juliet swallowed, her eyes blinking rapidly. "I...We...You..." She licked her lips, then swallowed again.

Christopher smiled. He could not help it. She was adorable. How on earth had he made it through the past six years without her?

Gently, he grasped her chin, urging her to look at him. He could feel a shiver go through her and knew that he would never forget this day. "Look at me, Jules."

After an agonizingly long moment, her eyes rose and met his. They shimmered with tears, and yet the way they looked into his spoke of a yearning that reflected his own. "I've missed you."

Christopher swallowed hard, guilt clawing at his heart. "I've missed you as well." He had stayed away for too long, but now he was here. They both were.

Here.

Together.

In this moment.

Christopher's gaze dropped to her mouth, and he leaned in. Her soft breath shuddered past her lips and brushed against his own. He closed his eyes and—

"Lockhart!"

It was the harshness, the warning in Troy's tone as well as the fact that his old friend had addressed him by using his title instead of his first name that sent a cold shudder down Christopher's back. His eyes flew open, staring down into Juliet's, her own now wide and filled with alarm.

Still, more than anything, it was regret that surged through Christopher's body in that moment. Regret to have this perfect moment interrupted. "Curse your brother's timing," he muttered under his breath, his gaze locked upon Juliet's before it briefly darted to her lips. "Later," he told her with unmistakable meaning in his voice, delighting in the way her eyes fell from his for a brief moment before returning.

In the next moment, the door at Juliet's back opened, completely upending her balance.

CHAPTER FIVE

AN EVENTFUL DAY

If asked to choose one word to describe her life, Juliet would have said uneventful. Oddly enough, though, today was a marked exception. Everything seemed to be happening at once, allowing Juliet no time to make sense of it.

A moment ago, she had been staring past Christopher's shoulder at her brother's contorted face, outrage burning in his eyes as he glared at his oldest friend from across the entrance hall. And now, all of a sudden, the sturdy door at her back seemed to have disappeared in the blink of an eye, robbing her of every chance to keep her feet under her.

Juliet's balance shifted instantly, and she felt herself falling backward, her hands reaching out for something—anything!—to hold on to. Her stomach lurched, and her heart clenched into a tight ball as her lungs drew in a sharp breath. The world tilted, and she pinched her eyes shut, bracing for the pain and humiliation that would surely come.

And then, equally unexpectedly, the world slowed as strong arms enfolded her, slowing her descent and cushioning her fall.

Juliet's eyes blinked open, and she looked up into Christopher's face as he held her cradled in one arm while bracing the other upon the floor. How he had managed to catch her, Juliet did not know. However, he half-sat, half-kneeled upon the floor, his eyes wide and his breath coming fast. "Are you all right?" he asked as his gaze swept over her as though searching for injuries.

Juliet wanted to hug him, and without thinking, she reached out a tentative hand to touch his face. "Thank you," she gasped, trying to catch her breath. "I…Thank you."

"Well, well, well," came Harry's teasing voice in that moment, "what have we here?" Juliet's eyes snapped up and she was shocked to find her sisters—all her sisters as well as her cousin, her mother and her grandmother!—crowded around them, their eyes wide with curious interest. "This looks like fun," Harry remarked with a wicked grin. "Are we interrupting something?"

Amused chuckles echoed through the room, and Juliet felt her cheeks flush with heat for the…what?…tenth time that day.

Footsteps thundered closer, and Juliet turned her head to see her brother charging toward them, his face no longer contorted with outrage, but with concern instead. "Are you all right?" Troy demanded, all but shoving Christopher out of the way and pulling her back up onto her feet. His hands brushed tousled hair from her face before they grasped her by the shoulders. "Are you hurt?" Troy's pale blue eyes searched hers as the pulse in his neck thundered wildly.

"I'm all right," Juliet assured him, trying her best to smile. "Truly. I'm not hurt. Christopher caught me."

Her brother's jaw tensed, and he threw a dark glare over his shoulder at his friend before turning back to her. "I'm glad," he said then and pulled her into his arms.

Juliet leaned into him. As much as he tried to hide that fact from the world, Troy had always been a deeply caring brother. Still, in that moment, Juliet could not help but think that the reason his arm remained draped upon her shoulders was to keep her away from Christopher.

"Troy, would you help a pregnant lady up the stairs?" Louisa asked with an exhausted sigh that sounded a bit too theatrical to be genuine. "My husband seems to be conveniently absent, and I fear I need a little rest."

Reluctantly, Troy released Juliet and stepped toward Louisa. "Of course," he mumbled, taking her by the elbow. They slowly moved toward the staircase leading to the upper floor; however, he threw another warning glare over his shoulder at Christopher.

"I cannot help but wonder," Christina remarked, her right forefinger resting against her lips in thought, "why you fell?" Her eyes moved to Juliet. "Were you leaning against the door?"

All eyes turned to Juliet, and she wished the ground would open and swallow her whole. "I...was."

"Why?" Harriet asked, frowning; yet that wicked sparkle in her eyes remained. Was she enjoying this?

"Well, I was..." Juliet swallowed, unable to look at her family. This was truly embarrassing! What was she supposed to say? That Christopher had been about to...

Her gaze moved to him, and a corner of his lips curled upward into a lopsided smile. Then he turned to her family. "I suppose she was feeling a bit faint. Fortunately, the door was there to steady her, giving me time to cross the hall and reach her side."

"That was most fortunate," their mother exclaimed, brushing a comforting hand down Juliet's arm before giving her hand a gentle squeeze. "Do you feel better now? Or do you need to lie down?"

"I'm fine, Mother," Juliet assured her. "I...I don't know what brought on that dizzy spell." Still, her gaze moved past her mother's shoulder to Christopher, and she could barely keep an answering smile from her face as she saw him grinning at her with wicked delight.

Later.

That one word echoed in Juliet's mind, and she could not help but wonder if Christopher had meant it. Had he truly wanted to kiss her? He had been about to, had he not? Yet...why? Out of a sense of loyalty to their friendship years earlier?

"Now," Grandma Edie piped up as she hobbled a few steps forward, "I'm certain your husbands are already looking for you." She made a shooing motion with her left hand as though wishing to scatter a flock of birds. "Off you go. Give an old woman a moment to speak with our guest."

As Harry and Chris, and Leo and Anne strolled away arm in arm, laughing and chatting, Grandma Edie slipped her arm through Christopher's, tugging him back into the drawing room. "It is truly good to see you, young man," she told him with an affectionate chuckle. "You must promise me to spend at least a few weeks with us at Whickerton Grove."

Juliet's heart stilled in her chest as she looked after them, and she realized that the thought of Christopher leaving again made her feel utterly miserable.

"There is much to be said," Grandma Edie continued as Christopher moved to close the door on her behest, "before you return to distant shores." For a moment, his eyes looked into Juliet's, and she wished she knew why he had left all those years ago.

"Are you all right?" came her mother's voice, and Juliet flinched, having all but forgotten her presence.

Swallowing, she willed her features back under control. "I'm fine," she said with a smile she did not feel. "I'm only..." A deep sigh left her lips against her will.

A knowing smile came to her mother's lips. "You used to be good friends," she remarked, a watchful look in her eyes. "What happened?"

Juliet shrugged as her eyes filled with tears. "I wish I knew."

"Then ask him," her mother urged, wrapping an arm around her daughter. "Nothing is worse than not knowing."

Juliet nodded, then paused and looked at her mother. "Do you think he will leave again?" It was a foolish question. Of course, he would. For a reason Juliet could not even begin to suspect, Christopher no longer belonged in England. If only she knew why.

Cupping a hand to Juliet's cheek, her mother looked at her with imploring eyes. "Perhaps he is waiting for a reason to stay. Did you ever think of that?"

Juliet swallowed, uncertain how to interpret her mother's words. Long ago, Kit had been her friend, her dearest friend. Yet over the past few years, somewhere in the hidden recesses of her mind, Juliet had come to realize that friendship was not all she wanted from him. Indeed, as much as she had trembled with sudden nerves, she had wanted to kiss him today. Not because she finally wanted her first kiss but because it was him!

Later.

Promise had echoed in that word, and yet it had been no more than the promise of a kiss. Nothing more.

But if she kissed him and he left again? Perhaps it would have been easier if he had simply never returned. Before, she had been blissfully unaware of her affections toward him. Now, however, disappointment and loss lurked on the horizon.

What was she to do?

CHAPTER SIX

RETURNING HOME

Fartherington Hall, Autumn 1803
Two days later

The vast estate was Christopher's childhood home, the place where he had grown up with his parents as well as his elder brother Sebastian and his younger sister Nora. Now, his father and brother were gone, and he was the new earl.

Had been for six years.

It still felt wrong.

Just as it had six years ago.

Christopher did not feel like the Earl of Lockhart, and Fartherington Hall did not feel like home.

It was with a heavy heart that he alighted from the carriage, his gaze traveling upward over the majestic stone facade as he stood in the drive, unable to move.

"It looks exactly as I remember it," he murmured to himself as his mind tried to match the sight before his eyes to the memories of years past.

Slow steps carried him up to the front door and into the great hall, his footsteps echoing through the vaulted chamber, empty and still.

A trickle of laughter drifted through Christopher's memory, and he remembered how, to Nora's utter delight, Sebastian had once slid down this very banister—or rather how he had tried to. Halfway down, he had lost his hold on the smooth wood and fallen to the marble floor. Fortunately, he had only dislocated his shoulder. Still, his parents had been beside themselves with worry for their golden boy, their heir.

Christopher bent his head, that old yearning reawakening now that he had returned to the place of his childhood days. Why had they never deemed him good enough? To him, it had always seemed as though his parents viewed him as a threat to Sebastian when, in truth, Christopher had been only the second son, completely enamored with his elder brother. Never had he wanted the earldom. He would not hesitate to give up the title this very instant if it brought his brother back from the grave.

"Christopher?"

Lifting his head, Christopher's eyes fell not on his mother, as he had expected, but on his sister instead. Dressed in black as was befitting a grieving widow, she stood in the arched doorway to the drawing room, her mahogany tresses tied back into a bun and her face looking awfully pale, especially in contrast to her black skirts. "Nora," he whispered, and his eyes swept over his sister's beloved face as he strode toward her. "What are you doing here?"

A small smile curled up her lips. "Are you saying you don't want me here?"

Christopher grasped her hands. "Not at all," he assured her, his eyes still mesmerized to be looking at her again. "It's been too long."

Nora nodded. "It has." Tears came to her eyes. "I missed you, big brother." A sob tore from her throat, and a moment later, she was in his arms, her slender frame trembling as she held onto him with a strength that surprised him.

For a long time, brother and sister stood in a tight embrace, a bond still intact despite the years of separation. Christopher could feel it. With his father and brother gone, only his sister and mother remained of his family. Yet it was only Nora who made him feel at home. It was not in anything she said or did, but simply in the way she looked at him.

Nora loved him. It was as simple as that. She loved him as much as he loved her. Christopher had always known of her love. Yet she was the only one of his family to show him any affections; perhaps the only member of the family who possessed any.

"Why are you here?" Christopher asked as he pulled back and looked down into her eyes. "Why are you not at home? At Leighton?"

A bit of a chiding look came to Nora's brown eyes. "You know better than anyone that Leighton was never my home." She sighed, and a shuddering breath left her lips. "Now that my husband is dead, I have no place there any longer."

Christopher frowned. "Did his cousin turn you out?" he demanded, anger beginning to sizzle in his veins. "Because if—"

"No." Nora shook her head, a sad smile playing over her features. "In fact, his cousin was kinder to me than my husband ever was." Her lips thinned, and Christopher saw a deep sense of disillusionment in her eyes; eyes that had always sparkled with wonder and excitement.

But no longer.

"No, I simply wanted to come home." Nora's eyes held his, a silent plea in them; and in that moment, Christopher realized that his little sister felt even more alone in the world than he did.

Christopher smiled at her warmly. "You'll always be welcome here, and I am happy to see you."

"Thank you." Nora hugged him again, then strode away to the window. Sighing, she cast a quick look at him over her shoulder before turning back to the view outside. "And you? Why are you back in England?"

Christopher stepped into the room. "Grandma Edie sent me an invitation to Harriet's wedding." A chuckle drifted from his lips. "I suppose I was not brave enough to defy her."

Looking at him, Nora smiled, a smile that seemed almost genuine. "I think the word you're looking for is foolish. You were not foolish enough to defy her." She chuckled, then sighed, a wistful look coming into her eyes. "She still sends me the tea I like so much. It's a unique mixture I've never found anywhere else." She grinned. "Yet she refuses to reveal the ingredients to me, as though it is not merely tea but...a...a magical potion that might prolong one's youth." A soft chuckle drifted from her lips, and Christopher could not help but wonder how often his sister had reason to laugh these days.

"What about you?" Christopher asked as he came to stand beside her, the top of her head barely reaching his shoulder. "Why were you not there?"

Narrowed eyes met his. "I'm in mourning."

Christopher scoffed. "Are you? We both know you never cared for Hayward."

Nora bowed her head. "Whether I cared for him does not matter. He was my husband, and society would be outraged if I did not show the proper respect due—"

"You're finally free of him!" Christopher exclaimed, grasping his sister's hands. "Please, do as you wish. Be happy!"

Nora cast him a brave smile. "You speak as though I had no hand in my fate." She sighed. "I chose him. I *chose* to marry him."

"You did not know him," Christopher insisted. "You did not know the man he truly was."

Nora shrugged. "Perhaps not. But the choice was mine, nonetheless. I have no one to blame but myself for my regrets."

"Be that as it may," Christopher countered, hating that look of defeat in her eyes, as though her life were over, as though she had one foot in the grave already. "But please do not add more regrets to those you already have. This is your chance to start over. Please, take it."

A frown creased her forehead. "What would you have me do?" she asked, confusion marking her voice, as though she had not wasted a single thought on what to do with her future.

Christopher heaved an exhausted sigh. "Come with me to Whickerton Grove," he pleaded, and felt her hands tense within his own. "Please! Grandma Edie insists I visit. Come with me!"

Staring up at him, Nora slowly shook her head. "But I cannot. I'm still in mourning. I—"

"That is out of the question!" came their mother's harsh voice from the door, her familiar tone of disapproval like an ice-cold shudder snaking down Christopher's spine.

Reluctantly, he turned to greet her. His hands, however, remained wrapped around his sister's. "Hello, Mother."

Her eyes narrowed as her gaze briefly swept over him before settling on Nora. "You cannot attend any events while you're in mourning!"

Nora shook her head. "I know. I was just telling Chris—"

"I forbid it!"

"I—"

"Why would you even suggest such a thing?" Their mother's eyes narrowed further as she fixed them on Christopher. With her graying hair in a tight chignon—not unlike the one Nora wore, a fact, which Christopher found worrisome—and her chin raised in her usual haughty way, Elizabeth Hurst, Dowager Countess of Lockhart, was the epitome of a stiff, overbearing matron...a far cry from the devoted mother Lady Whickerton had always been.

Clearing his throat, Christopher met his mother's gaze, his own chin rising a fraction. "How wonderful to see you. How have you been?"

Her lips twisted into a snarl as she regarded him with displeasure. "Are you only here to cause trouble?"

Christopher sighed. For some reason, his parents had always accused him of causing trouble. Had he been such an awful child to put them on their guard in such a profound way? "I am here to see my sister," Christopher said pointedly, intentionally omitting his mother from his reason for returning to England. Indeed, the only reason for his presence here—aside from a meeting with his steward—was Nora.

Only Nora.

"Then do so," his mother replied with a huff, "but, please, refrain from any action that will harm the reputation of your father's title. Do you hear?" She shook her head. "You've already caused enough trouble. I forbid you from dragging your sister into it as well."

Christopher felt the urge to throw his mother's words back into her face; yet she was not wrong. He had acted foolishly and without thought for the earldom. It would seem she was determined not to let him forget that. "I did not suggest Nora attend a ball or similar event," Christopher sought to clarify. "I merely think that seeing old friends will do her good." He looked down into Nora's pale face. "She does not look well, and I am concerned."

His mother scoffed. "She looks precisely as a young widow ought to look during her year of mourning." Stepping forward, she once again fixed him with a pointed stare. "Do not lead her astray. Any wrongdoing on her part will severely harm her chances on the marriage mart once her year of mourn—"

"I will not marry again, Mother," came Nora's voice, stronger than Christopher would have expected.

Their mother blinked, then turned questioning eyes to her daughter. "Pardon? Why ever would you say that?"

Christopher watched as Nora pushed back her shoulders and met their mother's hard gaze. "Whether you like to hear it or not, Mother, no one would want me."

Their mother flinched, dark suspicions tensing her features. "Why? What have you done?"

Nora swallowed. "I failed to give my husband an heir." A muscle in her jaw twitched, and Christopher saw tears collecting in the corner of her eye. Yet it was not sadness or regret that swung in her voice as she spoke again, but...triumph? Satisfaction? "I was married five years, and yet I did not conceive once." She swallowed. "I'm barren, and everyone knows or at least suspects it." She shook her head, a defiant tilt to her head. "No one will want me, and...I am fine with that." And with that, she turned on her heel and walked out of the drawing room, her footsteps echoing on the marble floor.

Christopher was about to rush after her when his mother hissed, "That is your doing?"

Spinning back around, Christopher stared at her. "What? You blame me for this as well?" A dark chuckle left his lips as he shook his head, utter disbelief filling his heart. "I suppose I'm responsible for everything that went wrong in your life, am I not?"

His mother's lips thinned, and, for a brief moment, Christopher feared she might actually agree with him. Instead, she turned away and marched out of the room without another word.

Indeed, a most wonderful welcome!

Hanging his head, Christopher felt the overwhelming desire to leave...and never return. No, this place did not feel like home. Home was where...he was welcomed with open arms and joyous smiles. Home was...Whickerton Grove.

His heart paused for a moment or two as his thoughts drifted back to Juliet and how she had lain in his arms only two days prior. He had almost kissed her.

Almost.

A smile tickled the corners of his mouth at the memory of her moss-green eyes widening when he had whispered, *Later*.

Indeed, it was time he left...and headed home...to Whickerton Grove.

Thank you, Grandma Edie!

CHAPTER SEVEN
A KEEN-EYED HIGHLANDER

Whickerton Grove, Autumn 1803
Another day later

After their usual stroll through the gardens of Whickerton Grove, Juliet saw Grandma Edie settled in front of a warm fire in the drawing room with a cup of tea and a blanket wrapped around her legs. Then she sat down in the armchair opposite her and picked up the book her grandmother had chosen on their last visit to the library. With a smile, Juliet began to read and continued to do so until the old woman's soft snores could be heard drifting through the room.

Rising to her feet, Juliet stretched her legs, her gaze drawn to the window. Dark clouds now hung in the sky, and a strong wind tugged on the leaves still upon the trees.

"Oh! I beg yer pardon."

Turning around, Juliet found Keir standing in the doorway, his blue eyes moving from Grandma Edie's sleeping form to her, a bit of a sheepish grin coming to his face as he regarded her. "Would ye care for a stroll?" he asked in his Scottish brogue, his voice dropping to a whisper as he cast a sideways glance at Grandma Edie.

"In this weather?" Juliet chuckled with a questioning look at the sky. "I fear it might rain soon."

Keir moved into the room and came to stand beside her, his eyes turning toward the dark gray clouds. "Nay, rain is still a few hours off."

Juliet chuckled again. "How could you possibly know?" Still, she had to admit that the man looked rather like a woodsman with his long hair, a few strands braided here and there, pulled back and tied at his nape. His dark clothes were of a rougher fabric made for the outdoors, including a leather vest and heavy boots, and he always wore a small pouch attached to his belt. Juliet could easily imagine him with a quiver full of arrows on his back and a bow slung over his shoulder, sneaking through the woods, stalking a deer.

Keir laughed quietly; a deep, rich sound that made Juliet feel strangely at peace. "Ye learn a thing or two when ye spend yer days out of doors." He grinned at her, his deep blue eyes sweeping over her face as though she were an open book. "Come, lass." He held out his hand to her. "Let's try and catch the wind."

Before Juliet knew what was happening, she found herself dashing down the small slope leading into the gardens, a woolen cloak wrapped around her shoulders and her hand warm and safe in Keir's. Perhaps she ought not have allowed him to hold her hand; however, the moment the wind swept over her face, her legs rushing to keep up with Keir's large strides, Juliet felt...unburdened.

Her thoughts scattered, and her heart beat with purpose, strong and unafraid. Laughter spilled from her lips, and she stretched out her arms like a bird wanting to take flight.

"I dunna think I've ever heard ye laugh like that, lass," Keir remarked as he turned around to face her, sure steps carrying him backward, a wide smile upon his face.

"Careful! You'll fall," Juliet exclaimed, pulling on his hand to stop him.

"You're a kind lass," Keir told her, his blue eyes looking into hers, "but ye're sad, aren't ye?"

Juliet swallowed, unable to avert her eyes. An icy shiver snaked down her back, and suddenly, the day seemed as dark and gray as it was.

A soft expression came to Keir's face as he stepped closer. "'Tis yer heart, aye? Will ye not tell me who stole it from yer chest?"

Mortified, Juliet realized that tears were streaming down her face. "How do you know?" she sobbed, trying to turn away, but Keir's hand on her shoulder stopped her.

"Ye've got the look of it," he remarked, then pulled her arm through his. Together, they walked on, toward the far horizon until her tears had dried. "The one who sat beside ye at wee Harry's wedding?"

Bowing her head, Juliet closed her eyes, oddly unafraid to stumble and fall. With Keir beside her, she felt protected as she always had with Troy by her side. Only lately, he, too, seemed preoccupied, sadness clinging to his eyes. Perhaps she ought to speak to him.

"Have ye not spoken to him?" Keir asked as though echoing her thoughts. "The young lord? Yer grandmother told me about him."

Juliet stopped in her tracks and looked up at him. "What did she tell you?"

Keir ducked his head to look into her eyes. "That ye used to be friends. That ye still miss him." His brows rose in question.

Juliet swallowed. "I do," she whispered, then bowed her head, unable to bear Keir's inquisitive gaze any longer. "But he left... without a word, without..." Breathing in deeply, Juliet could smell the coming rain. "He only came back now because Grandmother invited him."

"Why do ye think she did so?"

Juliet shrugged. "He said he didn't know. Grandmother never even mentioned it to me."

"Did ye ask her?"

Shaking her head from side to side, Juliet dropped her gaze.

Keir's hand gently grasped her chin, and Juliet felt reminded of how Christopher had stood before her at Laurelwood Manor. "Perhaps," the tall Scot whispered, a gentle look in his warm eyes, "she did so for ye."

"For me?"

He nodded. "So ye could ask yer questions."

Juliet stared up into Keir's face as her heart thundered wildly in her chest. "What if...What if I don't like his answers? What if...?"

"At least, ye'll know," Keir replied calmly before a slight twitch tugged upon his lips. "But I dunna think ye need worry, lass. He cares for ye. He does."

For the second time that day, Juliet stared up at Keir MacKinnear, completely dumbfounded. "How could you possibly know?"

The Scot chuckled. "Because he's right over there," he gestured past her shoulder, "and the look upon his face screams bloody murder. Aye, he's jealous to find ye here with me."

Inhaling a shuddering breath, Juliet slowly turned around, grateful to feel Keir's strong arm beneath her trembling hand. Her knees went weak as her eyes found Christopher, a dark scowl upon his face as he approached, large, angry strides carrying him closer...and closer.

"Courage, lass," Keir whispered beside her ear, and Juliet could see Christopher's scowl deepen as he saw the Scot lean down to her. Was it possible that Keir was right? Could it be that Christopher...?

"Lady Juliet," Christopher greeted her in a bitter tone that sent an icy shiver down Juliet's back. Then his gaze moved from her to the man standing behind her shoulder. "Mr. MacKinnear."

While Juliet felt every inch of her body tense up, her tongue unable to form even a monosyllabic reply, Keir seemed utterly unimpressed by Christopher's hostile greeting. "A good day to ye as well, Lord Lockhart." Juliet found Keir glance down at her before his right hand moved to pat hers encouragingly, which still rested upon his left arm. "I shall leave ye to it then. I reckon ye have quite a lot of talking to do." A faint hint of amusement rumbled in his throat as he spoke.

Juliet swallowed, then lifted her gaze to Keir's. "Thank you," she managed to say before he nodded his head and then strode away.

With deepest unease, Juliet forced her gaze back to Christopher. She could not say what made her feel so apprehensive; yet she knew not what to say or do, afraid that he would still look at her with that icy expression in his eyes.

"You seem quite...close," Christopher remarked the moment her gaze dared to meet his. His brown eyes were slightly narrowed and questioning, looking at her in a way that made her feel as though she owed him an answer.

Oddly enough, Juliet felt a tiny spark of anger ignite. It burned perhaps for a moment or two, but it made her lift her head and straighten her shoulders. "Is something wrong?" she inquired, surprised to discover that her voice was not trembling, as though her heart were not beating wildly in her chest. "You seem to dislike Keir? Mr. MacKinnear, I mean? Is there some sort of problem?"

Instead of answering any of her questions, Christopher nodded, a knowing look coming to his eyes. "Keir." Again, his head bobbed up and down. "I see."

Juliet hesitated, understanding the dark suspicion in his eyes for what it was. Yet who was he to demand an explanation? On the other hand, he was not demanding one, was he?

After another few painful moments of silence, Juliet finally breathed in deeply and said, "He is a family friend, and, yes, I like him dearly. He is a good man, caring and kind and—"

"I see the two of you are quite well acquainted," Christopher snarled, his lips twisting into a grotesque imitation of a smile.

Juliet frowned. "He has been with us these past few weeks, and I have come to know him. Our grandmothers used to be the best of friends, and I cannot deny that he feels like family." Holding Christopher's gaze, Juliet took a step toward him. "Has anything happened that would make you dislike him? I cannot imagine what that could be."

Christopher's jaw seemed to clench as he stared down at her. "If he is such a good family friend as you say," he forced out through gritted teeth, "then why have you never met him before? Why is he here now? Do you not find that unusual?"

Juliet shrugged, remembering the explanation she had given Christopher at Harriet's wedding. "I do not know," she finally replied truthfully; after all, it was merely a suspicion and not even her own, but her sisters'. "He and his family live far away in the Highlands. I suppose travel is not that easy, and life has a way of keeping one busy, especially with a large family and a meddling grandmother." She cast him a careful smile. "Truth be told, neither one of our grandmothers has revealed why he is here. Perhaps, one day, we shall find out. Until then, all we can do is guess."

Casting Christopher a warm smile as a peace offering, Juliet hoped desperately that they could leave this behind and begin anew. There was so much to talk about, so much to ask and know that she did not wish to waste time with hostility. Who knew how long Christopher would stay? A fortnight? Or perhaps even less?

At the thought of watching him ride away, not knowing when or if he would return, Juliet's heart clenched painfully and her knees weakened once more, making her wish Keir was still by her side.

Making her wish that Christopher would hold her the way he often had in the past.

Making her wish that they could be Kit and Jules again.

Even if only for a few short days.

CHAPTER EIGHT

A LIFETIME IN A FEW WORDS

Christopher felt himself begin to relax at the sight of Juliet's soft smile. He knew she was not one to quarrel. He could not recall a moment when she had raised her voice in anger or even frustration. To someone who did not know her well, she might appear like one who did not experience powerful emotions, for she always seemed so calm and collected. Still, there were signs that whispered of an uproar deep inside.

Subtle signs.

The way she sometimes clenched her hands, the sinews standing out white, as though fighting for control, afraid to reveal anything to another.

The way her eyes darted around, never quite settling anywhere, as though afraid of what she might see or of what others might see in her if she did.

The way her teeth every so often sank into her bottom lip, a nervous glint in her eyes, before she reminded herself that she ought not.

"Truly, you do not need to worry," Juliet assured him, that soft, delicate and deeply alluring smile back upon her lips. "Keir is not a stranger. Even though I have not known him long, he is well known to my family, my grandmother." She took another step toward him, her right hand reaching out tentatively, as though she were uncertain about what to do. Then, however, she placed it gently upon his arm, her green eyes dark and bottomless as they looked up into his. "Please, do not worry. I am perfectly safe with him."

Christopher gritted his teeth even harder, inwardly laughing and cursing that she would think him merely concerned for her safety. Could she not see that every muscle in his body was tense at the thought of her heart belonging to another? Or did she simply not want to see it because...her heart had already chosen?

Christopher closed his eyes as he recalled the moment the dowager countess had ushered him into the drawing room at Laurelwood Manor. Three days had passed since, and yet Christopher remembered it as though it had only been five minutes. The shock of her words still reverberated in his bones, and whenever his thoughts drifted back, he once again felt sickened to his stomach.

"I am so glad to see you again, dear boy," the dowager had said with a wide smile that made Christopher feel warm and hopeful. "It has been too long, and Troy has missed you. You used to be such good friends, and I hope you shall be again."

"As do I," he had replied, his thoughts still reeling from the almost-kiss he had shared with Juliet only moments before.

"Would you object if I asked you for a favor?" The dowager had then asked abruptly, a thoughtful expression upon her face. Christopher had bid her to continue, and what she had said next had turned his world upside down. "Only recently, I have come to realize how much I monopolized my granddaughter's time. Juliet is almost thirty, and without intending to, it seems I've robbed her of every opportunity to find a match for herself." She had sighed deeply, regret in her pale eyes before she had seated herself in an armchair, another exhausted-sounding sigh drifting from her lips. "I wish to make amends," she had continued, looking up into his eyes. "It is the very reason I invited Mr. MacKinnear to visit us at Whickerton Grove. From what I know of him, I believe him to be the perfect match for our dear Juliet."

At her words, Christopher had almost rocked back on his heels. Unable to utter a single word, he could do nothing else besides nod.

"Would you tell me your opinion?" the dowager had asked, a hopeful expression in her eyes. "Will you come and join us at Whickerton Grove and tell me if you believe my hopes justified? You used to know her so well, and now with all her sisters married, I believe I could use some help." A soft chuckle had drifted from her lips. "Who knows? Perhaps we shall have another wedding in the family before the year is out."

Trapped in his thoughts, Christopher almost flinched when Juliet's hand touched his. He blinked, willing to focus his thoughts on the here and now once more. "Pardon me," he mumbled, seeing the questioning look in her eyes. "I suppose I..."

"Shall we have some tea?" Juliet asked and slowly removed her hand from his before glancing up at the sky. "It does look, as though it will rain soon."

Swallowing, Christopher nodded, and they turned to walk back towards the house, side by side, but not touching, not speaking. It felt odd, unnatural, as though he had all but forgotten how to speak to her, how to be around her.

Stepping over the threshold into the drawing room, Juliet paused, her head turning from side to side as her eyes swept over the interior. "I wonder where grandmother is," she mumbled to herself before turning to him. "I left her not long ago in that chair over there." Her gaze moved to the door. "I suppose I should see to her." She made to hasten away. "Will you excuse m—?"

Christopher stopped her with a hand on her arm. "Stay," he whispered, finding her green eyes wide as she looked back at him. "You know she's fine, and if she needs you, she will send for you."

Juliet's eyes darted to his hand upon her arm before she nodded. "Of course. You're right." A soft smile came to her features, and Christopher could see that she was not used to thinking of herself. Had she truly spent the last few years living for others? For her grandmother? The thought made him angry and sad at the same time. And yet—perhaps it was selfish of him—he did not want her to find her perfect match in Keir MacKinnear.

Or anyone else, for that matter.

After ringing for tea, they sat down near the fireplace, and once more, an uneasy silence fell over them. Christopher could see her wring her hands, her gaze darting around the room, moving to him every once in a while before dashing away. He could not help but smile as he noticed her teeth sink into her lower lip. Still, she seemed to chide herself inwardly only a moment later, forcing herself to relax. Then she finally looked up at him, a polite smile upon her face that made her seem like a stranger. "Did you enjoy visiting the continent?"

Christopher regarded her carefully, convinced that she was only asking him this to have something to say, something that would break this awful silence. It bothered him that she did not know the truth, that they spoke to each other as strangers, that she would ask him one of the many questions people tended to ask him and the thought that he would answer her as he always answered anyone else was almost unbearable. And so Christopher decided not to. "I never went to the continent."

As though ready to ask another question, Juliet's mouth opened, only to remain so when she paused, her eyes blinking before a slight frown came to her forehead. "You did not? But I thought..." Her frown deepened. "Did you not tell my grandmother all about your adventures on the continent? At Harriet's wedding?" She shook her head at him, confusion marking her features. "I know I was distracted at the time, but I could not have been so lost in thought as not to notice wh—"

Delighted to see her polite persona slip away, replaced by the honest and caring young woman he knew, Christopher smiled at her. "You were distracted? Are you saying you were not listening? Are my tales so boring?"

A faint blush came to her cheeks, and her mouth fell open once more, mortification in her green eyes. "I'm sorry," she replied, averting her gaze for a moment. "I suppose I...I had a lot on my mind that day."

Leaning forward, Christopher braced his elbows on his legs. "May I ask what distracted you?" He held her gaze and delighted in the flustered way she seemed to be groping for words. This was the Juliet he knew. The Juliet he had missed.

Incapable of lying.

Adoringly bashful.

Unique in every way.

Juliet bowed her head, and Christopher could see her breathing in deeply, her hands unclenching as she flattened them upon her legs. Then she looked up, and the flustered look in her eyes had disappeared. "Why did you not travel to the continent? And why do you tell people that you did, when…you didn't?"

Christopher laughed. "Does that mean you will not tell me what distracted you?" he teased, reveling in this moment of familiarity.

Juliet regarded him carefully, and her upper teeth once more brushed over her bottom lip before she stopped herself. "I might feel inclined to answer you if you were to answer my question." Her brows rose in challenge. "I believe I have much more of a right to an answer than you do."

Christopher exhaled a deep breath and leaned back in his chair. "Very well." He felt the lightheartedness of the moment slowly drift away as his thoughts turned to the past few years. "Frankly, I was never one who wished to see the world. I cannot imagine spending years traveling from one place to another, never finding—" He gritted his teeth as emotions welled up, he had long thought buried.

Juliet's eyes softened. "A home," she said, and it wasn't a question.

Christopher's heart relaxed. "Yes, a home." Always had she been able to tell what he was thinking, what he meant to say, and to have her do it now was the greatest gift he had received in a long time.

After tea was brought in, Juliet poured them both a cup, adding a little sugar to his and a dash of milk to hers. "Then…where have you been?" she asked, handing him his tea. "It's been five years, Christopher. Where did you go?"

After taking a sip from the hot amber liquid, Christopher set his cup down. "I went to Ireland."

Juliet's eyes grew round. "Ireland?" For a moment, she merely stared at him as though uncertain whether he truly had said what she had heard. "Why…? What…?"

Christopher shrugged, unwilling to tell her everything yet. Not after he had found her outside with Mr. MacKinnear, arm in arm, faces turned to one another in a way that had made him want to punch the

Scot in the face. "People speak English there," he said with a jesting tone before shrugging once more. "It is a beautiful place, remote and distant, and yet close to England."

"But why...why would you tell people you went to travel the continent?"

"Because it is what people want to hear," he replied, sickened by all the expectations put on him—put on everyone—for reasons that held no meaning at all. "A young Lord is to travel the continent, is he not? It is expected of him. He has to broaden his horizon, see the world, experience all manners of...adventures before returning to England to fulfill his societal obligations, marry and provide an heir, who in turn is expected to do these things as well." Gritting his teeth, Christopher shook his head. "My mother highly disapproves of my choice, but then again, she has never approved of anything I did."

Sadness rested in Juliet's eyes. "Is she the only one who knows?"

Christopher wondered if the sadness he saw was for him or for herself because he had not told her. "Nora knows as well. I invited her to come and stay with me more than once, but she refused." A harsh breath rushed from his lungs. "Societal expectations once again. Indeed, so long as all expectations are met, happiness or the lack thereof are of no consequence."

Juliet nodded knowingly. "When the two of you came to visit Whickerton Grove last year, she looked...so very sad. Not at all like herself, like I remembered her." Her hands tightened upon the teacup. "Her husband... Now that he has... Is she...?" Tentative green eyes looked up into his.

Christopher shook his head. "She is not heartbroken, far from it. I think she might even be relieved. After all, she never truly cared for him. Only now, she is without a purpose. My mother speaks of seeing her married again as soon as her mourning period has ended. However, Nora is determined not to."

Juliet nodded again. "Then what will she do?"

"I do not know. I believe neither does she. Perhaps all she needs is time."

Juliet's eyes glanced down at the cup in her hands before she brought it up to her lips, taking a tentative sip. "What about you?" she asked, finally releasing the cup and setting it down on the table. "Will you return to Ireland? Will you return...home?"

Christopher wondered why she would not ask for more details. He could see that she was curious, that there were questions. He had told her that he had gone to Ireland, that he had found a home there, but had not told her more. And she had not asked. She was not asking. Did she not care to know? Was she perhaps afraid of the answer?

Christopher nodded. "I will." The crestfallen look that came to her face made his heart soar.

"When?" The word fell from her lips in no more than a whisper, her eyes downcast, not daring to look at him.

"I have not decided yet." She looked up as he pushed to his feet and then stepped toward her. "Are we still friends?" he was surprised to hear himself asking.

Juliet swallowed, then rose as well, her green eyes blinking with tears. "I...I've always hoped so." She held his gaze. "Are we?"

Christopher inhaled a deep breath, then reached out and grasped her hands. "Friends until the world stops turning," he whispered, reciting the vow they had made up as children. "Friends until the end of time. Friends for now and always. I shall be yours—"

"And you shall be mine," Juliet finished for him, her smile widening in such a heartwarming way that Christopher was tempted to pull her into his arms then and there.

"You remember," Juliet whispered, tears glistening in her eyes as her hands grasped his more tightly. "I never thought you would. I..."

"Of course, I do," Christopher assured her, knowing he had recited their vow countless times in his head whenever his longing for her had nearly brought him to his knees.

And now she was right here. Her hands in his, and anything was possible.

Dimly, Christopher heard the soft drumming of rain upon the windowpanes, the soft whooshing of wind as it swirled around outside. "Do you remember," he whispered, "that night of All Hallows' Eve?"

Instantly, Juliet's eyes widened before they swept to the windows, taking in the downpour outside with a look of utter disbelief. "No, you cannot possibly..." Her voice trailed off, and she stared at him. "Christopher, we were children then. We cannot—"

Clasping her hands within his own, Christopher tugged her after him as he rushed to the terrace doors and threw them open. Instantly, the rushing sound of wind and rain filled his ears and the fresh smell of wet ground drifted to his nose. The sky was dark as though night had already fallen, and he blinked out into a dim world.

"Christopher, we cannot. We—"

With a swift tug, he pulled Juliet over the threshold and out into the pouring rain. He felt the small droplets like pinpricks upon his skin, his clothes soaked through within moments. Yet he kept going, a wide grin upon his face as he looked back at Juliet, her steps slower, but no longer hesitant.

A wide smile stood upon her face as she closed her eyes and lifted her face to the sky. Never had she looked more beautiful.

CHAPTER NINE
TIMES LONG GONE

If there was one word in the English language that did not describe Juliet, it was reckless. Indeed, she knew her place, her responsibility to her family, the expectations put on her by society. She had learned to comport herself with grace and decorum and had never strayed from the path set before her. Except in one regard: she had failed to make a suitable match.

Nevertheless, in Juliet's childhood, there had been moments when she had acted recklessly. Not on her own behest.

Not even on her own.

But with Kit.

As much as he had tried to please his parents, he, too, had experienced moments of defeat, of hopelessness, realizing that no matter what he did, he would never be good enough in their eyes. In these moments, Kit had often been tempted to act without thinking. To be impulsive and do whatever caught his fancy.

And Juliet had always gone along.

After all, he was her friend, and friends stood together, did they not? Especially in the darkest of times.

Faster and faster, they raced onward through the gardens. The rain pelted down on them, and the dark clouds above almost blocked out every bit of light. Juliet felt her clothes clinging to her skin, goosebumps racing each other up and down her arms and legs. She was cold. She was shivering, and for the life of her, she could not stop smiling.

Neither, as it seemed, could Christopher.

Together, hand in hand, they darted across the soaked lawn, tiptoeing around deeper puddles and laughing whenever they could not, splashing through instead. Juliet knew her clothes would be ruined, but she did not care. She felt reminded of that night years ago, All Hallows' Eve. She had been only ten years of age, and Christopher had dared her to step outside and risk meeting ghosts and goblins on the spookiest night of the year. Then, too, it had rained, or rather it had begun to rain by the time they had been halfway down the slope. Juliet had wanted to turn back, but Christopher had not allowed her.

The mere thought of that night brought a wide smile to Juliet's face. She had been frightened at first, but then she had loved their mad dash through the rain, shrieking and laughing as though demons were lapping at their heels. She had felt truly alive in that moment, something that was not a familiar sentiment for Juliet.

While her sisters seemed to find their own adventures with ease, she had somehow always stayed behind, her life a series of uneventful moments, pouring endlessly from one into the next. Only when Christopher had been by her side had life been different.

She had been different. Had dared to be different.

"You are mad!" Juliet laughed, trying to be heard over the rushing sound of the wind and the rain. "I cannot believe it! We're soaked through!"

Christopher spun around to look into her face, his brown eyes sparkling wickedly. "Do you truly mind? Or do you simply believe you should?" He cocked one eyebrow at her in the way he had always done in their youth, and Julie had always thought it made him look devilish.

Feeling the rain run down her face, her neck and then slip under her garments and trail a path down her back, Juliet stared at her old friend in disbelief. "What will my parents think when they see us?" Her hands flew up to cover her mouth in shock. "My grandmother!" Her gaze darted from him to herself, taking in the way the fabric of her soaked gown clung to her limbs.

Christopher laughed loudly. "Oh, dearest Jules, you look positively scandalous!" he remarked with utter delight in his voice. "Any regrets?" He stepped toward her and then his hand once more reached out to grasp hers. "Any regrets?" he asked once again, his voice now possessed by a more serious note as he looked into her eyes.

Juliet swallowed, returning the soft pressure upon her hand. "None," she whispered, surprised to find that she spoke the truth.

A wide grin came to Christopher's face, and in the next moment, he tugged her onward again. "Come!"

Together, they chased down the length of the garden, rounding a hedge here and there, jumping over a well-tended flower bed, before Juliet saw the small pavilion come into view.

Instantly, her heart tensed in her chest, for this place was now forever tied to the moment before Christopher had vanished from her life. She remembered how they had met here the morning after learning of his brother's passing., Her feet faltered, hesitant and reluctant, as Christopher pulled her up the few steps of the pavilion and out of the rain.

The rain drummed down mercilessly on the wooden roof, coming down in sheets all around them, wrapping them in a world all their own. A small world outside of time and place where nothing and no one existed but them.

Juliet stared across the small expanse of no more than a few feet that separated them. Suddenly, all laughter had stopped, and she could feel unspoken things hanging in the air between them as they stared into each other's eyes. Another shiver snaked down her back when the chilled autumn air brushed over her. "You always used to drag me along on your adventures." Juliet tried to speak lightly, unable to bear this tense silence any longer. "Some were more foolish than others." She chuckled, well aware that Christopher was watching her intently. "Once, I caught such an awful cold that I was certain I would—" Her voice broke off as he suddenly stepped toward her.

"You're shivering," Christopher remarked as his gaze swept over her.

Instantly, Juliet wrapped her arms around herself and gritted her teeth to keep them from chattering. "I'm f-fine," she stammered, trying to smile at him. "T-Truly. I-I'm f-fine."

"I'm sorry," he murmured, then reached out to place his hands upon her shoulders. Slowly, he slid them down her back and then up again, the movement sending swirls of warmth through her. And all the while, his gaze never left hers, something unspoken there that Juliet wished she could understand. "I often thought of this," Christopher whispered, his breath warm against her chilled skin. "Of us. The way we used to be." A small smile tugged on his lips as he continued to rub warmth into her. "I missed you." He swallowed. "I missed who I was with you, who we were together."

Juliet's breath came fast as she stared up into Christopher's eyes. For so long, he had been nothing more than a memory that a part of her had trouble believing that he was truly here with her. "I missed you as well," she whispered in reply, knowing there was more to say—much more!—but unable to find the words or the courage to speak them.

"Did he kiss you?" Christopher asked abruptly, his jaw suddenly tense as he stared at her with an intensity that made Juliet retreat a step.

The cold returned as his hands fell away, and her arms wrapped themselves more tightly around her body. "What? What do you speak of?" she asked, her mind confused by this abrupt change of topic.

"Mr. MacKinnear," Christopher growled, his hands balling into fists at his sides. "Keir. Did he kiss you?"

Taken aback by his sudden anger, Juliet shook her head. "No." She took another step back until the wooden railing stopped her, wondering why he would ask her such a thing.

For a moment, she thought to see relief flash over his face before the muscles in his jaw tightened again. "Did you want him to?"

His gaze all but burned into hers, and Juliet felt her shivers lessened as heat suddenly swept through her. "Why would you—?"

Christopher took an abrupt step toward her. "Did you?"

Juliet flinched, confused to see him thus. "No." She shook her head. "Christopher, why would you—?" Again, she stared at him. "You're not acting like yourself. What has gotten into you?"

His brown eyes darkened as he seemed to weigh his words. Then he bridged the small distance still separating them, and his hands grasped her arms. "Three days ago, at Laurelwood Manor," Christopher began, and Juliet felt her heart skip a beat, knowing precisely which moment he spoke of, "did you truly want me to kiss you?"

And there it was, the moment of truth. What was she to say? Generally, honesty was considered the right path, but what if its consequences shattered her? Had Keir been right when he had said that Christopher cared for her? Had he meant as a friend?

Of course, Juliet knew Christopher cared for her as a friend. They had been friends for years before he had suddenly left without a word. Were they still? Was this friendship?

The look on his face screams bloody murder. Aye, he's jealous to find ye here with me.

Those had been Keir's words, had they not? Was it possible that Christopher had truly come to care for her...beyond the friendship that had once connected them? Did she dare believe it? Would that be wise? Or would it destroy her because it was nothing more than wishful thinking?

When Christopher had left all those years ago, it had...it had broken Juliet's heart. Weeks and months had passed, in which she had replayed their last moments together in her mind, desperately searching for something that would explain what had happened. She had never found it, though, and eventually been forced to accept that she would simply never know.

What if Christopher kissed her? What if she told him that her heart was his? Would it make matters worse once he left again? Or would her heart break just the same?

If only she knew.

CHAPTER TEN

FRIENDS ONCE MORE

Waiting was torture, and Christopher had a hard time remaining still. He wanted to shake her, demand she answer him. Yet he did not. Instead, he watched a range of emotions play over her lovely face, her green eyes guarded as though she did not dare allow him even a glimpse of what went through her mind.

"Did you?" Christopher whispered again when the silence became too weighty.

Juliet swallowed, her gaze once more focusing on his, the look in her eyes telling him all he needed to know.

Christopher's heart sank.

"I don't think it would be wise," Juliet said as she stepped back, her hands touching his arms, urging him to release her. "We're friends." A hitch in her voice gave him pause, and he frowned when he saw a smile come to her face.

A smile that looked forced, as though it were a shield she was holding up in front of her as a defense.

"Are you certain?"

Instantly, Juliet nodded, two quick steps carrying her to the edge of the pavilion. "Race you back to the house?" Her voice was trembling, and Christopher could see how she rapidly blinked her eyes to discourage the tears that were collecting there. Still, that smile—the defensive smile—continued to linger.

Christopher knew she was lying. She was putting on a brave face when truly she was close to breaking down. But why? He wanted nothing more but to push her for the truth, but he did not dare.

Not now.

Never had he seen Juliet like this. She seemed to be hanging on by a thread, dangling over a deep abyss, terrified of plunging down into the dark at any moment. Something frightened her. If only he knew what it was.

"Very well," Christopher finally said with a quick nod. Still, he knew this was not the last time they would speak of this. He would have the truth from her, even if it was not today. Perhaps this day could simply be about getting to know one another again, about reminiscing, about rediscovering all those little things they used to know.

Tomorrow would come.

Christopher would make certain of that.

"On the count of three?" Juliet asked, relief upon her face as she looked at him.

Christopher nodded, moving to stand beside her. "On the count of three," he agreed, fighting the urge to reach out and pull her into his arms. "One." Her hands grasped a fistful of her skirts. "Two." Leaning forward, she raised her skirts a little to keep herself from tripping over them. "Three!"

In a dash, they both shot from the pavilion back out into the rain. Christopher blinked as water ran over his face, blurring his vision. His breath quickened, and his legs felt heavy.

Beside him, Juliet seemed like a water sprite, her brown hair flying in the wind behind her, its strands soaked and darker than he remembered. It had come undone, and Christopher tried to remember the last time he had seen her with her hair flowing freely down her shoulders. It made her seem younger, unburdened, and he loved the sparks that lit up her eyes.

Once, Juliet almost stumbled and fell, her legs entangled in her wet skirts. But she caught herself in the last moment, doubling her efforts as she raced ahead.

Christopher laughed, knowing he ought to do his best, that she would be furious with him if he did not. Still, he only pushed on enough to pull even with her, reveling in the sight of her flushed face.

Together, they reached the terrace, darted across, and then burst through the double doors and into the drawing room, panting and out of breath.

"You could have won easily," Juliet accused as he had known she would. "Why didn't you?" Her cheeks burned a deep red, and her chest rose and fell quickly with each rapid breath as her enchanting green eyes stared into his chidingly.

Christopher wiped the rain from his face, grinning from ear to ear as he looked at her. "I take no pleasure in winning," he told her, laughing, mesmerized by the sight of her.

Juliet frowned. "What do you take pleasure in?"

Christopher's grin broadened, and he loved the flustered look that came to her face when she grasped his meaning. He moved toward her, his breath still coming as fast as hers. Her eyes were wide; yet she did not retreat. "I enjoy seeing you like this," he whispered, then chuckled when he saw her teeth once more brush over her bottom lip. "Red-faced, panting for breath—"

Juliet rolled her eyes at him. "What a nuisance you are. A gentleman would not speak like this."

Christopher chuckled. "Well, perhaps I am simply not a gentleman."

"Then what are you?"

Inhaling a deep breath, Christopher swallowed. "I'm your friend, am I not?"

Holding his gaze, Juliet nodded, her eyes luminous. "Friends, yes." She smiled at him; a smile more genuine than the one before, but still one that held sadness.

Christopher took a step closer. "Only friends?" he asked before his gaze darted to her lips, temptation urging him closer still.

Juliet's eyes widened once again, her mouth opening and closing as she no doubt searched for something to say. Yet before she could make up her mind, they were interrupted by the sound of someone clearing their throat in a highly disapproving way.

Christopher closed his eyes, for he knew before even turning toward the door who it was.

Troy.

"Your brother truly has impeccable timing," Christopher murmured under his breath before moving a step away and facing his friend's dark scowl.

"Troy!" Juliet exclaimed, a slight tremor in her voice as she moved toward him. "Oh, I better not step any closer." She laughed nervously, then looked down at her soaked skirts. "I suppose we got a little wet." Grinning, she looked over her shoulder at Christopher.

Christopher laughed. "The understatement of the year, my lady." He bowed to her formally, and she shook her head at him.

"You'd better go change," Troy said in a tight voice, his pale blue eyes narrowed into slits, "before you catch cold."

Juliet nodded, then strode past him. Yet before she vanished, her green eyes once more returned to look into Christopher's and he could feel the effect of that brief moment all the way to his toes.

As his sister's footsteps receded down the hall, Troy stepped into the drawing room and closed the door behind him. "What are you doing?" His voice was hard, and a warning burned in his eyes.

Christopher swallowed. Indeed, what was he doing? He could not deny that thus far he had lived in the moment, ignoring all that lay ahead, decisions he would be forced to make and consequences he could not escape.

Running a hand through his wet hair, Christopher shrugged. "I don't know," he said quietly before stepping forward and meeting his friend's gaze. "I assure you nothing happened." But was that the truth? Indeed, Christopher could not deny that ever since returning to England, ever since seeing Juliet again—speaking to her, looking into her eyes, simply being near her—he felt like a changed man.

Troy regarded him carefully, doubt in his eyes as he considered what to say. "When you left, it broke her heart." His voice was a dark growl as he stalked toward Christopher, rage radiating off him. "I will not see her hurt again; do you hear? Not again."

Christopher blinked, surprised not only by his friend's words but also by the dark expression on his face. "I assure you I would never—"

"Be certain," Troy snapped, his jaw set and a finger raised in warning. "Be absolutely certain of what you want." He drew in a slow breath and then spun around and stalked back toward the door.

It was the pain in Troy's gaze that gave Christopher pause. He had seen it before. Years ago, when he had been uncertain what it meant. Now, he knew.

"Perhaps," Christopher spoke up the moment Troy's hand settled upon the door handle, "we should not speak of your sister," he paused as did his friend, "but of mine."

For a long moment, Troy remained immobile, his back to Christopher and his hand on the door handle. His shoulders slowly moved with each breath he took, and Christopher wondered if the day would ever come that they could speak about what had happened five years ago.

Christopher knew he had failed his friend. He had not known it then. But he did now. Would he ever get a chance to make amends? Was this it?

Without another word, Troy opened the door and left, leaving Christopher behind with nothing but regrets. He had made mistakes. More than one. He knew that. Only he did not know what to do about them. How to fix them...if indeed they could be fixed.

Some mistakes once committed could never be undone, could they?

CHAPTER ELEVEN

OBSERVATIONS

"It'll no doubt be a cold winter," Grandma Edie remarked with a shiver over breakfast the next morning. "I can feel it in my bones."

"Do you want more tea?" Juliet asked, concerned as always with her grandmother's well-being. "It'll warm you. Or perhaps we should stoke the fire and—"

With a warm smile, Grandma Edie patted her hand. "You're a darling girl. But you don't need to worry about me. I enjoy complaining about the weather." Her eyes twinkled. "It's good fun."

Her parents as well as Troy and even Christopher laughed, exchanging meaningful glances as they reached for their own cups. "Perhaps this weather is the perfect excuse," Christopher chuckled, wiggling his brows at her, "to drink more tea."

While the others continued their conversation, Juliet paused. Frowning at Christopher across the table, she could not shake the feeling that his words held a hidden meaning. But what could it be?

"How is your sister, dear boy?" Grandma Edie asked, her gaze shifting to Christopher as she wrapped both her hands around her teacup.

Out of the corner of her eye, Juliet saw her brother tense. His gaze fell to his plate, and he barely moved as he listened to his friend's reply.

"She is still in mourning, of course," Christopher explained as his gaze darted to Troy before returning to Grandma Edie.

"Her husband's passing was quite...unexpected," Juliet's father remarked with a disapproving note. She did not know how Lord Hayward had found his grave, but from the bits and pieces she had overheard, it had been a rather scandalous affair.

Christopher nodded. "I believe it came as quite the shock to her. She never expected to find herself a widow so soon."

Juliet watched as her brother's hand tensed upon the teacup and feared the delicate porcelain cup would not survive such pressure for long.

Only too well did Juliet remember the day of Nora's wedding. Excitement had been in the air, and she recalled her sisters' flushed faces as they had hurried to ready themselves for the special event. Only Troy had been absent, nowhere to be found. She had thought it odd but had been too preoccupied to dwell upon it. Only later that night, after he had failed to appear at Nora's wedding, had she found him in the library, slumped in a chair by the fire, an empty bottle of brandy on the floor beside him.

Troy had never known that she had seen him that night. Neither did he know she suspected that Nora had broken his heart that day by marrying another.

Sighing, Juliet reached for her tea and took a sip, only to flinch when the sickeningly sweet liquid ran over her tongue. It tasted as though the entire sugar pot had been dumped in—

Her eyes flew up and met Christopher's, barely contained glee written all over his face. Again, he wiggled his brows at her, a wide grin upon his face.

Closing her eyes, Juliet could not help the smile that came to her own. Of course, she ought to have known. How often had he played this trick on her when they had been younger? She ought to consider herself lucky that he had used sugar instead of salt this time.

"Juliet, would you care to go riding with me after breakfast?" Christopher asked across the table, drawing all eyes to them.

Juliet's mouth fell open, uncomfortable with the sudden attention. More so, she wondered if the others could see how she felt about Christopher. Had Troy said anything to their parents about the day before? She had wanted to speak to him but had been unable to muster the courage.

"I'm afraid I cannot," Juliet replied, unsettled by the slight tremor in her voice. "Grandmother and I always take a stroll through the gardens this time of day." She smiled at the old woman. "But perhaps you would like to accompany us." Perhaps it would be wiser not to meet Christopher alone. After what had almost happened the day before, Juliet felt rather uncertain at the thought of being alone with him.

"Honestly, my dear," Grandma Edie said with a tired smile, "I don't feel quite up to it today. I think I'll stay here and rest a little if you don't mind."

Juliet turned concerned eyes to her grandmother. "Are you well? Do you feel ill?"

"Oh, I am perfectly fine, my dear. Only tired." She chuckled impishly. "One of the downsides of advanced age. I do not recommend it." She looked across the table at Christopher. "You go riding with our dear boy. I assure you, you will have much more fun with Christopher than sitting by my bedside, worrying as you are wont to do." Grinning, she patted Juliet's hand. "Truly, I insist."

Juliet nodded, then cast a careful look across the table at Christopher. The look in his eyes made her inhale a shuddering breath. Why, she could not say. He simply did not remind her of Kit, her childhood friend, at that moment. No, here and now, he was Christopher, a man she hardly knew. "Very well," she agreed reluctantly, surprised as well as a bit annoyed by her grandmother's sudden decision to remain indoors. In fact, Juliet could not recall her grandmother ever having felt too tired for a stroll. As frail and weak as she often seemed, Juliet knew what hidden strength remained in the old woman. Did she have to choose today of all days to be tired?

Swallowing hard, Juliet forced her gaze from Christopher and looked toward her brother. "Troy, would you like to accompany us? It is such a beautiful day." Her voice trembled, and when she cast another glance at Christopher, she could see by the look on his face that he knew precisely what she was doing.

Heat surged to her face, and Juliet fixed her eyes upon her brother.

Troy cleared his throat, finally lifting his eyes from the plate before him. "As much as I would like to," he said, his voice hard and strangely controlled, "there are things regarding the autumn ball that I need to see to."

Disappointed, Juliet nodded. Then her eyes swept around the table once more and, rather belatedly, she realized that someone was missing. "What about Keir?" she asked, not daring to look at Christopher. "Has he not risen yet? Perhaps he would like to accompany us?"

Beside her, her grandmother chuckled. "Oh, he has risen. At the crack of dawn, in fact. I sent him on a little errand, but don't worry he shall be back shortly."

Everyone at the table frowned. "An errand?" Juliet's father asked, a somewhat suspicious expression coming to his face. "Mother, what are you planning now?"

With a rather innocent look upon her face, Grandma Edie shook her head. "I do not know what you're talking about." Then she rose from the table, waving every offer of assistance away, and headed out of the breakfast parlor. "Do not worry about me. I shall do what old ladies do these days."

Again, Juliet saw her father roll his eyes. "I wonder what that is," he remarked, exchanging a meaningful look with her mother. "I doubt she was referring to the rest she proclaimed she needed."

With a smile, Juliet's mother grasped her husband's hand. "You know how she is. There is no use in worrying about it."

Her father sighed. "I suppose you're right."

As though Grandma Edie's departure had given them all leave to return to their own activities, the breakfast table emptied, and one by one all the Whickertons disappeared until only Juliet and Christopher remained.

With her eyes downcast, Juliet slowly rose to her feet, well aware that Christopher was slowly rounding the table toward her. "If I did not know any better," he said quietly, a tense note mingling with the humor in his voice, "I would think you were afraid to be alone with me."

Tense laughter fell from Juliet's lips as she forced her eyes up. "Oh, don't be silly. I was simply thinking that…" She faltered for a moment, for her heart seemed to trip in her chest as Christopher's dark eyes looked down into hers. "That…That they would like to join us." She swallowed. "Troy spends too much time locked away, always busy with one thing or another. It's been a long time since I last saw him smile."

A knowing expression came to Christopher's face, and he nodded. "He seems…burdened," he remarked with a deep sigh.

"You see it as well?"

Christopher nodded.

"I wish I knew what to do for him," Juliet replied, relieved to have something to say. Indeed, with each word that was spoken, she felt herself begin to relax, reminded of the ease that had once existed between them.

An odd expression came to Christopher's face, and for a moment, she could not help but think that he believed Troy's subdued state of mind to be his fault. But how could that be possible? Christopher had not even been on English soil these past few years.

"Shall we be on our way then?" he asked abruptly, willing a smile onto his face that seemed tense. "Only if you wish, of course."

Juliet nodded, her thoughts now directed toward cheering Christopher up. Something was clearly on his mind, a burden he appeared to have been carrying around with him for some time. Would he confide in her? she wondered. Was that not what friends did?

CHAPTER TWELVE
A HEART'S DESIRE

"It is quite odd," Christopher remarked as they guided their horses down into the field bordering the gardens, "to be here at Whickerton Grove without your sisters milling around somewhere." He chuckled, allowing his gaze to sweep over this beloved place of his childhood once more.

Beside him, Juliet sighed, a touch of sadness in her green eyes. "I know what you mean. Within the span of a year, all my sisters have married and moved away. Nothing is as it once was. Everything has changed." Another heavy sigh drifted from her lips, her gaze distant. "Except for me, I suppose."

Regret lingered in her voice, and Christopher urged his mount closer to hers. He tried to look into her eyes to better understand what was going through her mind. "Do you wish to marry?"

Juliet's head snapped around, and her eyes were wide as they met his.

Christopher chuckled. "The question surprises you?"

"No, I simply..." She shook her head. "No."

"Well?" Christopher pressed once her silence stretched from one moment to the next and then the next.

Juliet inhaled deeply before she turned to look at him again, an oddly bright smile upon her face. "Frankly, I am quite content remaining precisely where I am. I have never been one to venture out into the unknown, as you well know. I like...being here, taking care of my grandmother and ensuring that my family is well."

Christopher frowned. "That does not answer my question." He urged his mount into a quick trot, then pulled around, forcing Juliet's mare to a halt. He pushed closer until his knee almost touched hers, her eyes wide as she looked at him in surprise. "Do you wish to marry?"

Juliet swallowed. "I...I've never thought about it much." Another forced little smile appeared on her face. "Life keeps me so busy. I—"

"Are you only lying to me," Christopher asked, anger igniting in his heart at the look of sadness upon her face, "or also to yourself?"

Juliet's jaw dropped, and she stared at him in a way that made his heart clench painfully. "Why would you...? Not everyone wishes for the same thing. Not everyone dreams of marriage and children. Not everyone—"

"I know," Christopher cut her off, and his hand reached out to grasp hers. "All I ask is if you do?"

Juliet's mouth opened and closed a few times before her eyes fluttered shut and her teeth sank into her lower lip. "It doesn't matter."

"Of course, it does!"

Her eyes were hard when they met his again. "No, it does not. It does not matter what I wish for. It does not matter whether I wish to be married if there is no one who wishes to marry me." Tears shimmered in her eyes, and yet her jaw remained stubbornly set. "I would appreciate it if you did not ask me such questions." Then she pulled on her reins and kicked her horse's flanks, galloping down the field and away from him.

Cursing himself, Christopher rushed after her. He had seen the hurt in her eyes and knew that her words had been true. Or at least that she believed them to be true. But how was that possible? He wondered once again, remembering his relief to find her unwed when he had returned to England last year.

Together, they charged across the field, not unlike the way they had raced each other back to the house only the night before. The sun shone brightly overhead, and a mild breeze stirred the changing leaves.

Up ahead, a grove of trees barred their way and Christopher was relieved to see Juliet slowing down. Her cheeks were flushed, and yet he could not help but notice her shoulders slumping forward as her mare slowed to a walk. Indeed, she seemed more than merely tired or even exasperated. She had a look about her that made him think she was on the brink of finally letting go of a dream that had always been precious to her.

And it broke her heart.

Jumping out of the saddle, Christopher hastened to her side. He held out his hands to her, and although she hesitated for a moment, he was relieved when she accepted his assistance. Her hands settled upon his shoulders, and she allowed herself to slide out of the saddle.

Christopher caught her, held her close, savoring the moment as she stood in his arms. A deep sigh left her lips, and yet he smiled when she laid her head against his shoulder. It felt right to be here with her, and he dreaded the moment he would have to bid her farewell. But what was he to do?

For a long while, they stood like this as the wind brushed over them, rustling the small leaves overhead. Quite a few danced down, swirling through the air before settling upon the ground.

Christopher picked one such leaf from Juliet's brown tresses, then he brushed a hand down her back. "Do not deny yourself happiness," he whispered to the top of her head, wishing he could see her face. "If there is something your heart desires, then march out and secure it for yourself." He looked down at her and gently grasped her chin, tilting up her head. "Don't be afraid."

A sad smile played over her lips. "Your words sound wonderful," Juliet said almost mournfully. "Yet they do not hold up against the world that is."

Frowning at her, Christopher shook his head. "How is that possible?" His gaze swept over her lovely face as he brushed a curl back behind her ear. "How can the world deny you anything?"

Anger rang in the scoff that left her lips as she stepped back, slipping out of his embrace. "I know you mean well, but you know nothing of what you speak." Her jaw clenched and, for a moment, she looked down at the ground before her head rose once more, her eyes hard as she looked at him. "I'm almost thirty years of age, and I can count on one hand the times I've been asked to dance. I've never received flowers or been invited to a drive through the park." With a dark laugh, she shook her head. "No, it does not matter what I want, for I shall never have it. Instead, I have chosen to be happy with what I do have. I am, indeed, fortunate. My family does not pressure me to seek a husband at all cost. They do not force me into a match I would not want, allowing me to remain here with them in a place that is home where I can see to my grandmother and someday soon be an aunt to my nephews and nieces." Inhaling a deep sigh, she nodded. "It will be a good life. I know it will."

Despite her words, deep sadness rested in her eyes, mixed with a longing that Christopher understood.

Her green eyes looked into his. "Why are you here?" Juliet whispered, yet her voice held no small measure of determination. "Why did you come?"

Christopher swallowed. "Your grandmother invit—"

"No," Juliet interrupted him. "Here? Now? Why are you not at Fartherington Hall? Why are you here?"

Gritting his teeth, Christopher stared at her. "For the same reason," he replied, knowing that although it was the truth, it was not the complete truth.

Nodding, Juliet dropped her gaze and then turned away. Soft steps carried her closer to a thick trunk, the tree's leaves drifting down to settle in her hair. She reached out her hands and touched the rough bark almost lovingly.

"Why did you ask about Mr. MacKinnear?" The moment the words left his lips, Christopher could have kicked himself. "Why did you want him to join us?"

A slight frown creased her forehead as Juliet turned to look at him over her shoulder. "Because I thought he would enjoy it. As I've told you, he's a friend."

Christopher raked a hand through his hair, dislodging the leaves that had settled there. "Do you care for him?" he asked, dimly aware that he had done so before. Yet she had not answered his question to his satisfaction.

Juliet chuckled, her gaze still sweeping over the tree's bark as though it held something deeply fascinating. "Why do you keep asking me that? Is it about what my sisters suspected? It was nothing more than a silly idea. I can assure you it is not true."

"But it is!"

Slowly, Juliet turned to face him, a deep frown upon her face as she regarded him. "What? No, you're wrong. Why would you think that?"

Moving toward her, Christopher felt his insides twist and turn, urging him to take back his words. What if they gave her hope? What if she realized that marriage to Mr. MacKinnear would allow her to hold on to her dreams?

"It cannot be true! It is not!" Juliet insisted stubbornly, her gaze fixed upon him as he approached. "Why would you—?"

"Because your grandmother told me so." The words rushed from his lips in a deep breath.

Juliet stared at him in shock.

"She said she felt guilty for hindering your chances all those years," Christopher told her, needing her to understand that there had been other reasons she had never received an offer of marriage. "She wants to make it up to you, and she believes that Mr. MacKinnear is...your perfect match." Those last words he gritted out through clenched teeth, his pulse thundering in his veins.

Still staring at him, Juliet shook her head. "It cannot be," she mumbled. "Why...Why would she tell you that? You and no one else?"

Christopher sighed. "Because she asked for my opinion. Since we used to be close friends, she thought I would be able to see if you...felt something for him."

Her teeth sank into her lower lip, not releasing it as she nodded her head in understanding. "Is that why you keep asking me if I care for him?"

Christopher did not dare answer her. "You are not without choices," he told her instead, wondering if she ever—even if only for a moment—contemplated marrying him, Christopher.

"Are you saying I ought to marry him?" Juliet asked unexpectedly, the look in her eyes twisting his insides painfully.

"No!" His answer came like a bullet fired from a pistol, making her flinch. Gritting his teeth, Christopher cast her an apologetic look. "I'm sorry. I mean, you should carefully consider...what it is you want." *Who you want*, he added silently.

Holding his gaze, Juliet nodded, the look in her eyes distant. "Of course," she mumbled under her breath. "Of course." Then she strode past him and pulled herself back into the saddle. "I think I'll return home. I feel a bit...overwhelmed."

Nodding in agreement, Christopher followed her, once again cursing himself for not being honest, for allowing her to believe that it did not matter to him whom she married so long as she was happy.

Indeed, he was too selfish to simply step back. He wanted her but worried that she would never have him once she knew about the mistakes he had made. That she would not even be his friend any longer. Yet if he kept silent, he would lose her to another. Christopher had no doubt. Perhaps it was time to tell her everything and pray that she would still look at him with affection in her heart.

CHAPTER THIRTEEN
IN THE PAVILION

Confusion seemed to be Juliet's constant companion as of late. Ever since Christopher told her of her grandmother's reason for inviting Keir to Whickerton Grove, Juliet had been unable to think of him and not think of it.

"Is something amiss, lass?" Keir asked promptly as he returned from her grandmother's mysterious errand a few days later.

Juliet was about to step down into the garden when he spotted her and immediately changed direction, heading toward her. "N-Nothing," Juliet stuttered in reply as her cheeks blazed with heat.

A warm chuckle rumbled in his throat as he moved closer, his blue eyes narrowing as though he could all but see the thoughts that coursed through her head. "Why so nervous?" Frown lines appeared on his forehead. "Why, ye can barely meet my eyes? What's happened?"

Juliet wanted to sink into a hole in the ground; unfortunately, none was available. "I'm glad to...see you've returned," she said, pulling her cloak tighter around her shoulders. "My grandmother said she sent you on an errand."

Keir laughed, then shook his head. "I'll not let ye distract me, lass. Out with it. What happened?"

Closing her eyes, Juliet shook her head. "I cannot tell you. I already feel like a fool." His hand settled on her shoulder, and reluctantly, she opened her eyes to look at him.

"Is it yer Lord Lockhart?" Keir asked gently. "Have ye spoken to him?"

Juliet's heart slammed against her ribcage as she remembered the many contradicting moments she and Christopher had shared over the past sennight. Sometimes, he had looked at her in a way that melted her heart, and then at other times, he seemed distant, almost angry, as though she had done something wrong. "I'm afraid you were wrong," Juliet finally admitted, relieved to have something else to say. "He is my friend and nothing more."

Doubt sparked in Keir's blue eyes. "Are ye certain? Did he say so?"

Juliet shook her head. "He did not have to. He is merely here to..." she swallowed, "to speak to my brother. Troy has been rather taciturn as of late, as though something is bothering him." Oh, was it wrong of her to drag her brother into this?

Keir nodded. "Aye, I've noticed that, too." Juliet wondered how he could have. After all, he had not known Troy before. "Still..." Keir's voice trailed off; yet the look in his eyes told Juliet that he did not believe her...at least not completely.

"I'll see you later," Juliet said as a way to steal from his presence and stepped away, her feet directed her down into the gardens.

"Going for a stroll?" Keir asked, and when she nodded, he added, "Care for some company?"

Juliet bit her lip. "That is kind of you; however, I'd rather..."

"Be alone?" Keir asked smiling, then nodded. "Aye, lass, and think about whether ye'd like to tell me the truth later." His brows rose teasingly before he turned and strode away.

Juliet closed her eyes, then spun around and all but fled. Her mind was in an uproar, and yet warmth lingered in her heart. Indeed, Keir was a kind and thoughtful man. He would make any woman a fine husband. Perhaps her grandmother was right, and Juliet truly ought to consider marrying him—if he would have her, of course.

The only problem was: he was not Christopher.

Perhaps listing that as the only problem was not quite right. Of course, there were others. Clearly, Christopher only saw her as a friend and soon he would leave once more and return to Ireland.

His home. Was there someone he loved there? Someone waiting for him?

Juliet breathed in deeply as she walked along the rose bushes, tears springing to her eyes. How long would he be gone this time? For good?

Brushing a stray tear from her cheek, Juliet headed along the tall-growing hedge and then turned down the soft slope. Her eyes fell on the pavilion before she had even realized where she was headed. Although her heart clenched at the sight of it, she could not bring herself to turn back.

With a heavy heart, Juliet climbed the few stairs, her gaze swinging around to look back the way she had come. More tears gathered, welling up despite her determination to keep them away. Indeed, she was a fool. After all, the truth was that Kit had left her life years ago and she would do well to make her peace with it. She had cried over him once. Only a fool would do so again.

Closing her eyes, Juliet leaned her forehead against a wooden pillar, her teeth digging into her lower lip as she fought the sobs that rose in her throat. What was she to do? If only Christopher had never returned! She had been fine before. She had made her peace with the past, had she not? She had been looking forward to being an aunt, to spend the rest of her life surrounded by a large and loud and loving family. She could have been happy.

Now, that future seemed to slip farther away with every day that passed. Now, Juliet's heart had begun to ache for something more. Now she was no longer content.

"Curse you, Kit," Juliet growled, pounding her fist halfheartedly against the pillar.

"Why?"

At the sound of Christopher's voice, Juliet spun around, that awful heat once more shooting up into her cheeks. Why was it he always found her in such a desolate state?

At the sight of her tears, the look on his face changed. "What happened?" he asked, large strides carrying him to her. "Are you all right? Are you hurt?"

Juliet shook her head and moved back. "I'm fine." She wiped the tears from her face. "Why are you here?"

A muscle in Christopher's jaw twitched angrily. "Mr. MacKinnear told me to go and find you," he said with a questioning tone in his voice. "He said you wished to talk to me."

Juliet flinched, completely caught off guard by these sudden and intense emotions that boiled beneath her skin. She could not recall ever having felt quite so overwhelmed, so ill-equipped to deal with her own state of mind.

Again, Christopher moved toward her, something deeply unsettling in his eyes. "What is it?" he all but growled. "What do you wish to tell me?"

"Nothing," Juliet said quickly, wishing he would simply leave. "He was wrong. I—"

"Have you chosen him?" Christopher snapped all of a sudden before his hands surged forward and grasped her arms.

Breathing heavily, Juliet stared up into his face. His eyes flashed dangerously, and his hands clamped tightly around her arms. His breath came as rapidly as her own, and she could not shake the feeling that one word from her would send him away. Was that not what she wanted? For Christopher to leave so that she could return to her old life?

Perhaps it was still possible. He had come back into her life less than a fortnight ago. Surely, after such a short time...

Juliet swallowed and raised her chin. "Yes," she told him, willing the tears that pricked her eyes to remain hidden, to wait until he would leave and not see them. "Yes, I've chosen him." A shiver surged through her, and she gritted her teeth to hold it at bay. "Grandma was right. He is my...perfect match."

At her words, Christopher's face fell. It fell in a way that brought physical pain to Juliet's heart, reminding her of the day he had come to her six years ago...after losing his brother. Disbelief stood in his eyes, mixed with such sorrow and anguish that Juliet felt the need to comfort him. It was a need as natural as drawing breath, and to refuse him her comfort sent a jolt of pain through her. It felt wrong and cruel and...

Juliet tried to swallow the lump in her throat. "Please, release me," she whispered breathlessly, afraid of what she might do if he did not. She was beginning to feel dizzy, bright spots dancing before her eyes as she blinked them open and closed.

A deep breath rushed from Christopher's lips as his hands slowly fell away. Then, he staggered backward, still staring at her in utter shock. "It cannot be true," he mumbled, shaking his head, a determined set coming to his jaw as his gaze slowly turned to steel. "It cannot be true." His voice grew harder.

Juliet straightened her shoulders, grateful for the pillar at her back as the world began to sway around her. "But it is." She swallowed. "You should leave and return to Ireland." Pain speared her heart, and she gritted her teeth against the sobs that rose in her throat.

Raking a hand through his hair, Christopher glared at her, his teeth grinding together as he grappled with her news. Had she truly hurt him? Juliet wondered, shaken by the look of him. Indeed, he seemed as heartbroken as she felt. Had she made a mistake? Was there a chance that...? "You always intended to return, did you not?" she asked quickly, before her courage failed. What she ought to have asked, however, was if there was someone waiting for him in Ireland?

Something unknown flashed over Christopher's face before he nodded. "I must." He nodded again. "I want to."

"I see," Juliet mumbled as the world turned upon its axis, her hands reaching behind her to grasp the pillar at her back. "Pleasant journey, then."

Christopher nodded as though in agreement, and for a moment, Juliet thought he would simply turn and leave. Then, however, he paused, and his gaze returned to her, looking at her as though he had never truly seen her before this very moment. "I came here to kiss you."

Juliet's eyes flew open. "What?"

An odd smile curled up the corners of his mouth, speaking of a stubborn determination but also of a deep longing. "You asked me to kiss you," Christopher reminded her as he stalked closer, his brown eyes fixed upon hers. "And as you might recall, I said yes." His hands reached for her, gently this time, slipping around her waist with a feather-light touch. "If we had not been interrupted, I would have kissed you then."

Staring up at him, Juliet felt the breath rush from her lungs. "You cannot," she insisted stubbornly; her voice, however, sounded weak and uncertain.

"Why not?" Christopher whispered as he lowered his head to hers, his breath tickling her lips. "Give me one good reason, and I shall walk away."

That ought to be simple, ought it not? Juliet thought dimly as she fought against the dizziness that swirled in her mind. After all, there were so many good reasons why she should not allow him.

Because he had already broken her heart once.

Because he would leave again.

Because even now he was keeping something from her.

Because...she was so very afraid of what would happen if she did not stop him.

"Because..." Her voice was only a breathy whisper. "Because...I'm betrothed to another." She had meant it to be discouraging, but it seemed to have the opposite effect.

A hair's breadth from her lips, Christopher stilled. Juliet could feel him grow rigid, his hands tensing upon her waist as his eyes snapped up to meet hers. A menacing growl rose from his throat, and something dangerous sparked in his eyes.

In the next second, his gaze fell to her lips and Juliet knew what he intended.

Drawing in a sharp breath, Juliet felt her heart dance in anticipation, nevertheless. Again, bright spots appeared before her eyes. She felt her knees grow weak and her breath come fast as up and down became utterly unfamiliar concepts. Her hands clamped onto his arms as her eyes closed.

The moment Juliet felt the soft brush of Christopher's lips against hers, everything went dark.

CHAPTER FOURTEEN
THE LAST NAIL IN THE COFFIN

Whatever Christopher had expected to happen, it was definitely not this. One moment, he was leaning down to kiss her, and in the next, Juliet slumped down as her legs gave out and her head rolled back.

Moving quickly, Christopher caught her before she hit the floor of the pavilion and pulled her into his arms, carefully cradling her head against his shoulder. His breath came fast as he stared down into her face, her eyes closed and a slight flush darkening her cheeks. "Jules?" he whispered, still unable to believe that she had...fainted.

Never had he known her to be faint-hearted. Although quiet and hesitant, Juliet had always possessed a strong heart. Never had she shied away from anything...not even when it frightened her.

Bowing his head, Christopher closed his eyes as shame washed over him. What had he done? He had tried to force a kiss on her, one she had clearly not wanted, and it had frightened her to such an extent that her body had collapsed.

Perhaps Juliet had been wise to choose Mr. MacKinnear. Perhaps she had seen something in him, Christopher, that he had not even been aware of. At least, married to Mr. MacKinnear, she would be safe, would she not?

Brushing a stray curl from Juliet's forehead, Christopher gently traced a finger over her eyebrow and then down her temple. She looked so peaceful, as though she were merely sleeping, the sight of her achingly beautiful. A deep longing pulsed in his heart, and he wished life had led them down a different path. If only...

Christopher shook his head. There was no point in lamenting what was or what would never be. It was time for him to accept that.

Carefully gathering Juliet into his arms, he slowly pushed to his feet. Then, he inhaled a deep breath and stepped out of the pavilion. It was as though each step closer to the house was a step farther away from her. He knew he needed to bid her farewell. Had she not just asked him to leave? To return to Ireland?

Less than a fortnight had passed since Juliet had come back into his life, and yet nothing felt as it had before. Christopher had not expected this. He had been certain that seeing her again would bring back old memories, old longings. Yet what he felt here, now, in this moment was much more than that. He could not explain it. He could not put into words what she meant to him, what he felt, knowing there would never be a future for the two of them.

As he drew closer to the house, the sound of a myriad voices drifted to his ears, interrupting his thoughts and drawing his attention to the French doors leading into the drawing room. Christopher moved closer and saw that, apparently, Juliet's sisters and their husbands had arrived, no doubt for the autumn ball that was to take place soon. Christopher had hoped to stay until then. Now, he was uncertain if that was a good idea. Perhaps he should simply pack his things and leave.

Abruptly, the double doors opened, and the Whickertons poured out onto the terrace, their eyes wide and full of concern as they saw Juliet cradled in his arms. "What happened?" Lady Whickerton exclaimed as she rushed forward, gently brushing her hands over her daughter's face. "Is she all right?"

"Did she fall?" Harriet inquired, eyes quickly darting to her husband, who stood behind her shoulder. "She doesn't look hurt. What happened?"

More questions flew from their lips. Everyone was speaking at once, and Christopher felt his head begin to buzz with the sound. Then a few loud raps on the terrace floor cut off their questions, and all eyes turned to the dowager countess.

"You sound like a beehive," the old lady remarked as she waved her walking cane dangerously close to those grouped around Christopher and Juliet. "Give the man a moment to catch his breath." Stern eyes looked around, from one to the next and then the next. "Now, dear boy, tell us what happened?"

Christopher drew in a deep breath, well aware that all eyes were trained on him. "She...fainted," he said lamely, equally well aware that one look would suffice for all of them to know that those two words were not the complete story. Indeed, he saw Troy's gaze narrow in dark suspicion and Mr. MacKinnear's do the same. Only the look in his eyes held neither jealousy nor outrage but confusion and perhaps a hint of amusement.

Stepping forward, Lord Whickerton took his daughter from Christopher's arms, his wife by his side. "Take her upstairs," she spoke softly, her eyes trained upon Juliet's unconscious face, deep concern in them. "Have someone bring us a bowl of water and some linens," she added over her shoulder as she followed her husband back inside.

Instantly, the sisters dashed away, and Christopher knew they would not even dream to think of alerting a maid but instead would see to their sister themselves. It was who they were. Christopher had always liked that about them.

Left behind among the sisters' husbands, Christopher looked up when Troy stepped toward him, a tense expression upon his face. "In the study," he hissed under his breath. "Now." Then he turned on his heel and marched back into the house.

While Harriet's and Leonora's husbands, Jack and Drake, regarded Christopher with rather questioning and somewhat disapproving looks, Louisa's and Christina's, Phineas and Thorne, appeared more amused than concerned. Ignoring them all, including Mr. MacKinnear, Christopher stepped into the house and followed in his friend's wake.

When he reached the end of the corridor, Christopher saw that the door to the study stood open and so he walked inside without bothering to knock. Troy stood by the window; his hands linked behind his back as he gazed out at the gardens. The moment Christopher stepped across the threshold, he spoke, his voice vibrating with restrained anger, "I warned you, did I not?" Slowly, he turned around, his gaze hard and accusing. "What happened? Why did she faint? What did you do?"

Exhaling slowly, Christopher closed his eyes. "I...I overstepped." He felt his hands ball into fists at the memory of what he had done. "She told me she had...chosen another, and I did not want to hear it so–"

"She did?" Troy stared at him with a deeply confused expression upon his face. He took a step forward, regarding Christopher closely. "Are you saying she is to be...married?" Incredulity rang in his voice.

Gritting his teeth, Christopher nodded.

"Who?"

Christopher swallowed hard, trying his best not to spit the man's name. "Mr. MacKinnear."

Troy's eyes widened. "That...is a surprise."

Christopher nodded, still reeling from the shock of hearing Juliet speak those words to him.

"She told you that?" Troy inquired, that look of disbelief still in his eyes.

Again, Christopher nodded.

"And she fainted because...?" Troy pressed; brows lifted in warning as he glared at Christopher.

Inhaling deeply, Christopher closed his eyes. "I tried to kiss her."

"You did what?" Troy snapped, thunderous footsteps carrying him toward Christopher. "Without her consent?"

Despite all the mistakes he had made in his life, Christopher had never felt...smaller, less worthy to be in this house, among this family... by Juliet's side. "There is no excuse," he mumbled, meeting his friend's accusing eyes. "I will apologize to her, and then I shall leave." He swallowed hard at the thought of leaving these shores, knowing that the next time he returned, Juliet would be married.

For a long moment, Troy simply looked at him, something indecisive in his eyes, as though he did not know whether to agree or rather convince Christopher to stay. "I believe that would be wise."

Hearing his friend's words, Christopher hung his head, for they felt like the final nail to his coffin. The last shred of hope that had remained died on the spot, and he knew that there was no turning back.

He had to leave.

CHAPTER FIFTEEN

AMONG SISTERS

The moment Juliet came to, she knew that something awful had happened. At first, what precisely that was remained a blur. Then, however, as the seconds ticked by, the fog in her mind began to clear and she remembered being out at the pavilion with Christopher. She remembered her lie. She remembered a heart-breakingly painful expression coming to Christopher's face. She remembered...that he had leaned in to kiss her. And what had she done?

An agonizing groan left her lips as Juliet turned to bury her face in her pillows.

"Look! She's waking up," came Louisa's voice from across the room.

Instantly, more voices erupted around her, and she felt the mattress dip here and there as her sisters surged forward and sat down on the sides of her bed.

"Juliet, dear?" It was her mother's soft voice, concern mingling with relief as she spoke. "Are you all right?" A gentle hand brushed over the back of her head and then down her arm.

Juliet wished she could remain where she was, her face buried in the pillows, and not return to the world outside. It was too mortifying! And yet she knew she had no choice.

Slowly, Juliet turned to face her family, offering them a tentative smile as they helped her to sit up, stuffing pillows behind her back to make her more comfortable. "You're all here," she remarked, looking from one sister to the next, remembering that they had not been at Whickerton Grove this morning. Indeed, she had missed quite a lot.

"We are here for the autumn ball, remember?" Christina reminded her with a gentle pat on her hand. "What happened? Did you fall and hit your head?"

Juliet felt her cheeks heat up as she found herself the center of attention, seven pairs of eyes staring curiously at her. Not only were her sisters and mother present, but she also spotted Anne, her beloved cousin, as well as Grandma Edie, sitting in an armchair by the window. It seemed all the women of Whickerton Grove were assembled in her small chamber, making it look crowded.

"Do you not remember?" Harriet inquired before she paused and looked at her mother. "Is it possible that she truly does not remember?"

Their mother shrugged, her kind eyes sweeping over Juliet's face as she reached out her hands to touch her cheeks. "Darling girl, do you remember where you were?"

Juliet continued to stare, unable to utter a single word. She felt completely and utterly overwhelmed, somehow removed from the goings-on in her chamber, as though she were a mere observer not meant to take part. Her eyelids felt heavy again, and when they closed, she wished for them to remain so.

"Perhaps we should send for a doctor," Anne remarked, a questioning tone in her voice. "She looks pale, does she not?"

"Are you unwell, dear?" her mother asked, feeling her forehead. "Feverish or dizzy or—"

"Tired," Juliet mumbled, and her eyes closed again as her head settled deeper into the pillow. "Very tired." Indeed, closing her eyes felt wonderful. It somehow shut out the world around her and all those in it. She did not want their questions. She could not bear them. She could not even bear to think of what had happened.

Of Christopher.

At the thought of him, another groan almost slipped from her lips, but she managed to grit her teeth and force it back down. She did not want anyone to know what had happened. Had Christopher already left? How much time had passed? How long had she been unconscious?

"Then sleep, dear," her mother whispered gently as her hands continued to brush over Juliet's head, easing her curls away from her face. Her touch felt soothing, and Juliet sighed deeply, listening to the faint sounds of her sisters moving back to the other side of her chamber.

For a long while, the world around her remained quiet. A distant part of Juliet's mind wondered about her sisters not speaking for a prolonged time. It felt unusual, odd, suspicious somehow. Yet it also felt wonderful, allowing Juliet to relax. She closed her eyes more tightly, determined to escape reality for as long as she could. However, as exhaustion tugged upon her mind and she felt herself drift off, their voices drifted to her ears once more.

"I've had another letter from Sarah," Christina said under her breath, deep concern in her voice as she spoke. "It seems her parents are once more determined to find her a match." An angry growl rose from her lips. "Any match that is profitable."

Instantly, the others voiced their outrage in whispered tones. "As much as I hate to say this," Harriet grumbled, "we need to see her married. It is the only way to keep her safe permanently."

"That is easier said than done," Anne remarked with sadness in her voice. "By now, everyone everywhere knows of her parents' circumstances. Finding her a decent match now will be almost impossible."

"I agree," Louisa chimed in. "Young men of good character and fortune can have their pick of young ladies. They will be unlikely to tie themselves to her parents. Unless one of them happens to fall hopelessly in love with Sarah, they will choose differently."

"Perhaps she simply needs to widen her circle," Leonora suggested with a hopeful tone in her voice. "There certainly is a perfect match for her out there. She simply has to find him, and sometimes it can take time."

"But she doesn't have time," Christina huffed out with impatience. "You know her parents, Leo. They care very little for her happiness. All they want is an advantageous match that solves their problems. They did so with her sister, and they will do the same with Sarah."

"So, we need to be quick about this," Harriet concluded, her usual eagerness in her voice, as though she wished to rush out the door at this very moment and see things settled. "We need to find her a match, and we need to find one now. Rather today than tomorrow."

"May I ask who you would suggest?" Leonora inquired in a calm and rational voice. "Can you truly think of someone we have not yet considered these past few months?"

A painful silence settled over the room, and Juliet felt her heart go out to Sarah, a young woman just like she and her sisters, a former neighbor, a good friend faced with an unbearable future. Indeed, Juliet had always considered herself fortunate that, unlike Sarah's parents, her own always put her well-being, her happiness first. They would never dream of forcing Juliet into a match she did not desire.

"What about Christopher?" Harriet suggested, with barely concealed excitement in her voice.

As much as her family's mumbled voices had soothed Juliet's mind and helped her drift off into a rather drowsy state, her youngest sister's suggestion instantly jerked her back from the edge of slumber. Her heart clenched painfully in her chest, and she barely dared to draw breath.

"Do you believe they would be a good match?" Leonora inquired thoughtfully. "I don't think they've ever spoken to one another, do you? It is unlikely with him gone these past few years."

"Then perhaps we should introduce them, don't you think?" Christina inquired, her voice no longer subdued but suddenly hopeful. "Christopher is a kind and decent man. We have known him all our lives, and I am certain that he would treat Sarah kindly."

"But could he love her?" Anne put in, and the doubt in her voice eased the tension that now lingered in Juliet's body.

Christina heaved a deep sigh. "Of course, I would want her to have a love match, the same as all of us found. She deserves no less; however, under the circumstances, I'm not certain she has the luxury to wait for one. Her parents do not care what she wants, and they will make the decision without her. We've seen it before. More than once, it was only due to a last-minute interference that she did not end up married to the wrong man. Can we truly risk that again?"

"Perhaps this is not the right place to discuss this," their mother said gently, and Juliet could all but feel her gaze upon her as she slowly rose from the mattress. "Juliet needs rest. If you wish to discuss this further, then perhaps you should go downstairs." Juliet all but held her breath as she heard the sound of rustling skirts and soft footsteps, then that of the door opening.

"Go and see to things, Mother," Leonora said softly. "I know with the autumn ball just around the corner, there are a lot of matters that require your attention. I will stay with Juliet."

"Thank you, dear. Please send for me the moment she awakens."

When the door closed behind Juliet's family, she could hear their soft footfall as well as the sound of Grandma Edie's walking cane disappearing down the hall. As exhausted as she had felt before, now Juliet's senses were on high alert. She wished Leonora had gone downstairs with the others, for she needed time to...think. Did her sisters truly intend to match Christopher with Sarah?

The thought sent a pain through Juliet's heart she had never experienced before. It was a sense of utter hopelessness, of loss, and she could barely keep the tears at bay that pricked the backs of her eyes. Oh, if only Leonora would leave!

"I know you are awake," came Leonora's gentle voice a moment before she sat down on the bedside.

Drawing in a sharp breath, Juliet blinked her eyes open, her hands clenching around the blanket. Slowly, Leonora's face came into focus, soft dark curls framing her lovely face. Her blue eyes shone with kindness and understanding, able to see into Juliet's heart as others could not. Always had it been Leonora's talent to do so.

With a gentle smile, Leonora reached for Juliet's hand, carefully loosened its tight grip upon the blanket before holding it safely within her own. "What happened that frightened you so?"

Knowing she could not hide from Leonora, Juliet closed her eyes and heaved a deep sigh. "He tried to kiss me," she whispered, holding her eyes pinched shut.

"And you did not want him to?"

"I don't know." Indeed, why had she fainted? It had never happened to her before; why now? "You're not laughing at me?" she tried to say lightly.

"Of course not. None of us would." A small chuckle fell from Leonora's lips. "Harriet and Louisa might tease you about it, but you know how they are. They don't mean anything by it."

Slowly opening her eyes, Juliet looked at her sister. "What am I to do?"

Leonora squeezed her hand. "What do you want to do?"

"I don't know."

Leonora's eyes looked deep into hers. "You better find out before it's too late."

CHAPTER SIXTEEN

FAREWELL

Christopher felt as though he was going mad. Two days had passed since the moment in the pavilion, and Juliet had still not left her chamber. According to her family, she was quite well but preferred to remain in her chamber as she felt exhausted and needed rest. But was that the truth? Or was she simply avoiding seeing him?

With the autumn ball only a few days off, all of Whickerton Grove was abuzz. It was as Christopher remembered it, a house full of people, loud and chaotic and...joyful. These were people who enjoyed being with one another, who could not keep away from one another for more than a few days. Indeed, all the Whickerton sisters had come with their husbands, and he smiled when he saw Christina's adopted little daughter dance from one room to the next, the same wide-eyed expression upon her face that Christopher had felt many times before on his own face when he had been young.

"Will you come to the ball as well?" young Samantha asked, her eyes sparkling with excitement. "I've never been to a ball. Will you dance with me?"

Christopher could not recall ever having been invited to one of his parents' balls when he had been young. However, the Whickertons were different, and they did things differently. "It will be my great honor," he told her with a formal bow.

Grinning from ear to ear, Samantha performed an almost perfect curtesy, especially considering that she was only six years old. "You are too kind, my lord." She giggled and then continued twirling around and around, from one room to the next, as she watched all the preparations being done around her.

Impatience sent Christopher outdoors, and over the course of two days, he managed to explore the gardens of Whickerton Grove quite thoroughly. Yet his mind remained absent, fixed upon one single moment, as his feet moved. Again and again, he relived the moment in the pavilion. It tortured him. Reminded him that he had been the one to hurt Juliet. He had overstepped and, unable to make herself understood, Juliet's mind had taken the only way out that had remained to her.

As Whickerton Grove prepared for the coming ball, Christopher wracked his mind about what to do, how to proceed. He needed to leave, but he could not without at least bidding Juliet farewell.

Or was he lying to himself? As frustrated as he was with her for hiding in her chamber, Christopher could not deny that her actions kept him at Whickerton Grove.

Kept him here.

By her side.

The trouble was that he knew what he wanted—he had always known what he wanted!—but had not known how to see his dreams realized. After all, he had made grave mistakes. He had lied. He had hidden the truth. He was hiding the truth.

And now, it was too late. Juliet was promised to another. He had missed his chance—if he had ever had one. He ought to have spoken to her the moment of his return. He ought to have insisted. He...

The tall clock in the corner struck midnight, and Christopher flinched. He had all but forgotten the world around him, shocked to see that darkness had fallen and that the house lay silent. Had he even sat down to supper with the others? Had Juliet been there? Had they sat across from one another without him realizing it?

Christopher shook his head. No, that was not possible. It was more likely that he had simply forgotten the time, ignorant of everything around him, his mind dwelling on this one obsession.

Again, he began to pace, his hands linked behind his back as he contemplated what to do. How much longer did Juliet intend to stay in her chamber? She was avoiding him, was she not? And there was nothing he could do about it. After all, he couldn't simply—

Christopher pulled to a halt. Why ever not?

Not daring to dwell any longer upon this outrageous thought that had suddenly entered his mind, he strode from the drawing room and out into the foyer. Quick strides carried him up the stairs and then down the corridor. He moved silently through the dark hallways, his ears listening for sounds that might alert him to another's approach. Yet there were none.

The house seemed fast asleep; he the only one plagued by insomnia.

And then he stood outside Juliet's door, his hand lifted to knock. He hesitated for only a moment, then gave the smooth wood two quick raps. Reasoning with himself that she was probably already asleep, completely unaware of the fact that someone was standing outside her door, Christopher drew in a sharp breath when he suddenly heard someone moving around inside.

The sounds were soft, almost inaudible, yet they spoke to him loud and clear. Was he perhaps not the only one plagued by insomnia after all? Had she been pacing the length of her chamber as he had downstairs in the drawing room?

And then the door opened, and his eyes fell upon Juliet, her hair undone and a robe tied over her nightgown. A candle burned somewhere in the room behind her, illuminating her and casting soft shadows over her face. Wide eyes met his, and for a long moment, neither one of them spoke.

Then Christopher took a step toward her, and instead of closing the door or insisting he leave, Juliet moved back, allowing him inside. Her wide eyes remained upon his as he closed the door behind him, words—any words!—still stuck in his throat.

"Why are you here?" she asked as the silence stretched between them. A timid smile played over her face as she pulled her robe tighter around her. "If Troy finds you here..."

Christopher nodded. "I know," he croaked, then cleared his throat. "I needed to see you." He looked into her eyes. "You've been avoiding me."

Even in the dim light, he could see a soft rosy glow come to her cheeks. "I suppose I have." She turned away, crossing to the other side of the chamber.

"Why?" He knew why, did he not? Yet he needed her to say it.

"I was embarrassed," Juliet said in a small voice before she tentatively lifted her eyes to his.

In the dim light, Christopher could barely make out her features, and so he moved closer. "There is nothing for you to be embarrassed about," he told her in a tight voice. "I, however, must apologize. I should never have—" The words would not make it past his lips.

Juliet regarded him carefully, her teeth digging into her lower lip. "Do you regret what happened?"

Christopher was about to say yes when he paused, wondering what she was asking. He did regret being too forward, but he did not regret trying to steal a kiss.

Her kiss.

Their kiss.

For the third time, it had ended before it had even begun. Another almost kiss. Perhaps the next time would...

No! He could not think like this! He needed to leave...but first...

"Are we still friends?" Christopher asked instead of answering her.

A surprised look came to her face. "Of course, we are." Then she stilled. "Or do you not wish to be?"

The bashful expression on her face made Christopher smile despite the sadness that lingered in his heart. "I cannot imagine ever having a better friend, Jules. All my life, you've been my heart and soul, my conscience, my strength and my solace." Tears glistened in her eyes. "These past six years, I've missed you terribly, only truly realizing how much when I saw you again at your sister's wedding. Will you...?" He swallowed, coming to stand in front of her. "Will you call me Kit again? I've always been Kit to you, and I want to be Kit again. I want—"

I want you to love me, was what Christopher wanted to say. He did not though. He had no right to. She had made her choice, and he would respect it. Now, all he could hope for was her friendship.

"Of course, I will," Juliet breathed, tears glistening in her eyes as she smiled at him. It was the same smile he had seen and cherished all his life. It was the kind of smile that made him feel treasured and loved. "Kit." Her smile deepened, whispered of longing, as though she had only waited for him to ask this of her. "You'll always be Kit to me. The boy who pulled me out into the rain. The boy who climbed up to my chamber when I was ill. The boy who snatched a spider from my hair even though he hated them as well." A warm chuckle left her lips, and she sighed. "You'll always be Kit to me. Nothing can change that."

Not even marriage to another man? Christopher wondered, feeling his insides tense at the thought of Juliet with Mr. MacKinnear.

"Thank you," Christopher told her, realizing that there was nothing else left to say. He had apologized, had he not? He was not quite certain. Looking into her glistening green eyes, he felt the world drift away. All that was and would be no longer important.

"Kit?"

"Mmh?" Christopher blinked, then shook his head. Had he been staring at her? "I need to go. I—" He sighed, smiling at her. "I wish I could stay," he said despite his better judgement. "But..."

Juliet nodded as she bowed her head, her eyes falling from his. "I know. It is for the best." She inhaled a shaky breath, then looked up at him once more. "Does someone await your return in Ireland?"

Christopher swallowed. "Yes," he replied before he could stop himself, knowing that he did not wish to lie to her. If only he could explain. If only she could know and still look at him with that smile upon her lips.

"I see," Juliet mumbled, then turned away and stepped up to the window. "I wish you a safe journey." She spoke without looking at him, and Christopher knew that there was nothing he could say to bring that smile back to her lips.

"Goodbye, Jules," he whispered and then stepped from the room, his heart breaking in two as he did so.

CHAPTER SEVENTEEN

THE HIGHLANDER SPEAKS AGAIN

He was gone!

The next morning, Juliet finally left her chamber after two days of solitude, of retreat, of...loneliness. She dreaded every step, and yet she needed to know. Had Christopher truly left? Was he gone?

"Are you saying he left in the night?" came her mother's voice as Juliet approached the breakfast parlor, her eyes sweeping over her assembled family as she pulled to a halt just outside the doorway. "That is most unusual."

Troy nodded. "I spoke to him," Juliet stilled and listened, her hands trembling as she clamped them tightly together, "and he asked me to bid you all farewell on his behalf."

"Why did he leave so abruptly?" her father inquired, a deep frown upon his face. Then his eyes moved and found Juliet's. His features softened, and a sad smile tugged at the corners of his mouth. Could her father see the sadness that threatened to crush her heart?

Unable to bear the thought of her family's questions, Juliet slowly and quietly retreated, one step at a time, until she reached the end of the corridor. Then she spun around and rushed outside.

An almost icy wind met her as she hastened across the terrace. Fool that she was, she had not even bothered to don a cloak, let alone gloves or appropriate footwear for the outdoors. Wetness seeped through her delicate slippers, and within moments, her hem was soaked.

"Juliet!"

For a moment, Juliet thought it was Christopher calling her name and her heart soared to the heavens. She spun around, hoping against hope, and the moment her eyes fell on Keir, it died a quick death, wiping the smile from her face in the blink of an eye.

"I can tell ye're overjoyed to see me," Keir chuckled, sympathy in his gaze as he moved toward her. His eyes swept over her inappropriate attire, and concern darkened his friendly features. "Come back inside, lass. Ye'll catch yer death if ye stay out here much longer."

Thick tears blurred Juliet's vision. "I cannot meet them! I cannot! They'll ask, and I…I…"

Shrugging out of his coat, Keir placed it upon her shivering shoulders, then gently steered her back to the house. "I know, lass. I'll smuggle ye inside with no one the wiser. I promise."

Leaning into him, Juliet placed one step in front of the other, allowing Keir to steer her along, her own eyes unseeing. Her heart ached with longing and regret and…anger.

At herself.

Oh, why had she lied to Christopher? Why had she fainted? She had seen the distraught look upon his face. He thought she had passed out from shock because she had not wanted his kiss. He had tried to be her friend and answer her request, and what had she done?

She had made him feel guilty for overstepping a line that had not even been there.

"Sit," Keir ordered beside her ear, then gave her shoulders a slight push.

Blinking, Juliet dropped into a chair. She was back in her bedchamber, and the door was closed, keeping her misery safely concealed from anyone who might walk by. Yet Keir was still here, and at this very moment, he kneeled down to remove her soaked slippers.

Juliet knew she ought to stop him. More than that, she ought to send him from her chamber. This was far from appropriate; however, in this moment, Juliet could not bring herself to care.

Always—always!—had she played by the rules; and what had that gotten her?

A broken heart.

A lonely future.

And regrets.

"Ye need to change, lass," Keir remarked as he reached for the blanket draped over the foot of her bed. "Shall I send for yer mother? Or—?"

"No." Shaking her head, Juliet pushed to her feet. "I'm fine. I..." Looking up into his blue eyes, Juliet sighed, once more overcome by regrets, regrets about things she had let slip through her fingers.

"I'll leave then." Keir stepped toward the door. "But if ye wish to speak about what—"

"Would you kiss me?" Juliet did not know where that question had come from, but it slipped past her lips with more ease than she would have expected.

Keir turned to look at her over his shoulder, a deep frown marking his face. Then he moved toward her, his blue eyes sweeping her face. "Why would ye ask me that, lass?"

Desperation blazed in Juliet's veins, and she barely felt the tremble in her hands or heard the slight stutter in her voice. "I've never been kissed, and I wish to know what it feels like."

Watching her with an odd expression in his eyes, Keir moved closer. "Why do ye ask me? Why not yer Lord Lockhart?"

At the mention of Christopher, something sharp and painful speared her heart and Juliet's courage faltered. Her gaze fell from Keir's, and she felt tears gather in her eyes. "Do not speak of him."

Juliet heard Keir breathe in deeply before his right hand reached out and his fingers grasped her chin. "Look at me, lass."

Reluctantly, Juliet did as he said, mortification over her request already burning through her veins. What was wrong with her? Lately, she seemed to stumble from one foolish mistake into another. "I'm sorry," she stammered as he lifted her head, her eyes darting around the room, afraid to meet his. "I shouldn't have asked this of you. If you do not wish—"

Keir laughed. "Oh, lass, I'd kiss ye in a heartbeat," he grinned at her when her eyes finally settled upon his, "but I dunna believe it is me ye wish to kiss. Is that not so?"

Juliet's eyes closed at his words as resignation fell over her heart. "I couldn't let him," she whispered, more to herself than to Keir.

"Why not?"

Blinking her eyes open, Juliet looked up into his face. For a reason she could not name, she felt she could be honest with Keir. He had become a friend, and yet he had not shared in her life until a few weeks ago. Perhaps Keir was the perfect blend between confidante and stranger. "I always knew he wanted to leave again. I couldn't let myself feel..." She swallowed the lump that settled in her throat. "This way, it's easier to let go."

A doubtful frown creased Keir's forehead as he released her chin and took a step back. "Is it, lass?"

Fresh tears pooled in Juliet's eyes, but instead of sorrow, she felt anger well up in her heart. "Yes!" she almost growled, her hands balling into fists as she shook them with vehemence. "It must be! It has to be! It..." Gritting her teeth, she shook her head, then stared at him. "I deserve to not have my heart broken again, do I not?"

An indulgent smile came to Keir's face. "That is not how life works, lass, and ye know it." His blue gaze narrowed. "Did ye tell him?"

Instantly, Juliet's eyes fell from his and she turned away, shivering as her bare feet moved over the parquet floor. She knew what he was asking but refused to answer.

"I see," Keir mumbled behind her, a hint of reproach in his face.

"It would not have mattered," Juliet defended herself as she stared out the window. "It wouldn't have made a difference. I know so."

For a long moment, silence lingered upon the room before she heard Keir move closer, his footsteps barely audible. Then his large hands grasped her shoulders, warm and comforting, but also insistent. "Ye assume, lass," he said in that deep, slightly raspy voice of his. "Ye dunna know. Ye assume." He inhaled slowly, and she felt his hands give her shoulders a slight squeeze. "People assume a great deal, thinking 'tis the truth they see when truly 'tis nothing more than what they wish for...or fear."

Juliet closed her eyes, unwilling to hear what he was saying, but knowing in her heart that he spoke the truth.

"Ye assume that he doesna care for ye. Ye assume that—"

Juliet whirled around. "He said there was someone waiting for him in Ireland," she blurted out, brandishing her last available shield as she fought to hang on to her composure. "He said someone was awaiting his return."

Keir's gaze did not waver. "Who?"

Juliet swallowed as an odd cold seized her limbs.

"Ye didna ask him, did ye, lass?" An understanding smile touched his lips. "Ye merely assumed."

Juliet stared up at him. "But...But it has to be..." Her voice broke off. "Who else could possibly be waiting for his return?"

Keir shrugged. "I dunna know, but neither do ye."

Dumbfounded, Juliet stared at the man standing no more than an arm's length in front of her. His blue eyes shone almost crystal clear, reflecting his direct nature. He never said what he did not mean and spoke his mind at all times. "What...What should I do?"

Keir smiled at her. "Ask him?"

"Ask him what?"

"Whether he loves ye, lass? 'Tis what ye wish to know, is it not?"

His words almost knocked Juliet off her feet. "I cannot!" she exclaimed, shaking her head for emphasis. "What if he...? I would die of mortification. I—"

"Ye wouldna," Keir objected. "People dunna die of mortification, but they do wither away with regret." His brows rose meaningfully. "Ask him, lass."

Still staring up at Keir, Juliet felt her head begin to spin. It was a similar sensation to the one she had experienced in the pavilion right before she had passed out. "I cannot. I—"

Keir's hands grasped her shoulders. "Ye're stronger than ye give yerself credit for, lass." His blue eyes looked deep into hers, and slowly, they came back into focus. "Stand tall and take a deep breath."

Holding his gaze as though it were an anchor, Juliet did as he instructed. Slowly, she breathed in and out, grateful when the world settled back into place and the dizziness retreated.

"Good. Now, go and ask him."

Juliet stilled, yet her heart skipped a beat, sending a deep longing into every fiber of her being. "I…I cannot. He…He left."

"Aye, no more than a few hours past." Again, Keir's brows rose meaningfully. "What will ye do, lass? Will ye stay here and wallow in self-pity? Or will ye go after the man and ask him what ye wish to know?"

Shocked out of her wits, Juliet stared at the tall Scot. As unorthodox as her family was, no one had ever spoken to her quite this way. "I…I cannot go…by myself. I—"

"I'll take ye," Keir offered without hesitation, the look in his eyes daring her to bring forth another reason why she could not go after Christopher, ready to present a solution for each and every one.

"But…the ball is in a matter of days. My family…they…"

He smiled at her. "They'll understand. Ye know this to be true."

Juliet did. Yet…"I c-can't," she stammered, overwhelmed by this choice suddenly looming in front of her. Although she had been daring upon occasion, Juliet had never been so on her own. Christopher had always been by her side. "I can't. Grandmother needs me."

"Does she?" Keir asked, a doubtful tone in his voice. "Ever since Lord Lockhart arrived, she hasna needed ye a great deal, has she?"

"What are you saying?"

"I'm saying that I'm not the only one who sees what's between the two of ye."

As she looked into Keir's patient eyes, Juliet realized that he spoke the truth. While her grandmother had always monopolized her time, she had not done so these past few weeks, often finding excuses for retiring to her chamber, allowing Juliet time to spend with…Christopher. "She…She told Christopher that…" She swallowed. "She told him she asked you here to Whickerton Grove because she thought you and I would…suit."

Keir laughed. "Did she now?" Then his hands once more settled upon Juliet's shoulders, and he leaned closer, his gaze holding hers.

"Well, to tell ye the truth, lass, she gave me an entirely different reason."

"Why then?"

"I'm not at liberty to say," Keir chuckled, "but it has nothing to do with ye."

Juliet frowned, annoyed with all the secrets surrounding her. Had life always been like this and she had simply never taken note of it? "Why then would she say so to Christopher?"

Keir shrugged. "Perhaps to motivate him."

"Motivate him?" Juliet frowned. "What—?"

"To make him realize what he wants," Keir explained, that rather indulgent smile once more teasing his lips. "Men are simple creatures, lass. Sometimes a bit of competition helps us realize what we want." He paused, and a thoughtful expression came to his face. "What did ye say to the man to make him leave?"

Heat surged to Juliet's face.

"Out with it!"

Swallowing, Juliet glanced up at him. "I told him I...I'd chosen you, that...that we were...betrothed."

Instead of laugh or scowl at her, Keir asked, "And how did he react to that?"

Juliet frowned, trying to recall all that had happened in the pavilion. "He...He became angry, and then he...he tried to kiss me."

Now Keir did laugh. "And ye still doubt the man's feelings for ye?" He shook his head at her. "Go and speak to him, lass. Ask him if he loves ye, and ye'll see." He stepped back, his blue eyes holding hers. "What will it be, lass? Ye're at a crossroad, and the choice is yers. Will ye stay? Or will ye go after him?"

CHAPTER EIGHTEEN

HIS GREATEST FEAR

After procuring passage from the Port of Liverpool to Ireland, Christopher sought the nearest inn and asked for a room. The ship would not leave for another two days, and he was weary from a night spent on the road. His limbs ached, and his heart felt as though it might break out of his chest at any moment. He had ridden like a madman, determined to leave Whickerton Grove well behind him. The sooner the better. An image of Juliet with Mr. MacKinnear haunting him like nothing ever had.

Still, at the same time, he had felt something tugging him back, like an invisible bond that urged him to turn around.

Now, after a hearty meal, Christopher felt exhausted. Lead lingered in his limbs, and his eyes closed repeatedly. Still, his heart continued to ache, torn in two different directions. Half of it belonged in Ireland while the other wished it could remain in Whickerton Grove forever.

Yet the choice was not his, was it? Juliet had made hers, effectively taking it out of his hands. Still, a part of Christopher knew that it was not that simple. He could not place all responsibility on her. She had chosen, yes, but he had failed to make his intentions known. If he had told her the truth, not only about his feelings but also about his past, would she have turned from him the way his mother had? Or...?

Rolling over in his bed, Christopher pummeled his pillow with tired fists. He knew he was running away rather than confronting what could be, for the simple truth was that he was afraid.

Afraid to be disappointed yet again.

Afraid to be a disappointment yet again.

Afraid to see his memory of Juliet tainted.

It was all he had left. He could not risk losing it. He could not. And yet...

Surging out of bed, Christopher began to pace, his mind replaying every word they had spoken over the course of the last few weeks. It had felt wonderful to be around Juliet again. He had felt like...himself again. He had not simply missed her, but he had also missed the man he was with her by his side. Years ago, they had told each other everything, and now?

Now, he was keeping essential parts of his life from her.

After leaving Juliet's bedchamber, Christopher had felt restless. A part of him had wanted to depart immediately while another argued that he ought to wait so he could bid everyone farewell. Once again, he had found his way downstairs into the drawing room. And then, when the clock had struck one in the morning, hobbled footsteps had echoed to his ears from down the hall.

Christopher had paused, torn from his thoughts, and then turned to see the dowager countess step over the threshold, her pale eyes coming to land upon him without even the slightest hint of surprise, as though she had expected to find him there. "Restless, my boy?"

Christopher nodded. "I...I need to return home," he said, reminding himself that Juliet was the only one who knew of Ireland. "My sister needs me now."

Seating herself near the dying embers of the fire, the dowager had nodded. Still, the look on her face made him think she did not quite believe him. "Have you met little Sam?" she asked abruptly, her gaze moving to him.

Christopher frowned, confused by her question. Indeed, he had expected her to comment upon his desolate state or inquire as to its origin. "I have," he replied slowly, unable to understand her reasons for asking; and he was certain she had her reasons. After all, Grandma Edie never did anything without an agenda, did she?

Or rarely.

The old woman sighed, a warm smile upon her face as she leaned back into the chair. "She is a darling girl." She set aside her walking stick before her gaze rose to meet his. "My first great-grandchild!"

"You have my congratulations," Christopher replied, still at odds with this strange conversation.

"We are blessed to have her in our lives," the dowager continued, her voice calm and relaxed as though she did not have a care in the world. "Christina could not possibly love her more if the girl were her own flesh and blood." She chuckled. "Yet, I admit, she was a bit...overwhelmed at first, but that had more to do with the fact that her husband had failed to inform her of the child before they were married." The moment the last word left her lips, her gaze moved to settle upon his in a way that sent an icy chill down Christopher's back.

He blinked, completely taken aback, when understanding finally dawned. "You...know?" he gasped, feeling the blood drain from his face as he stared at the dowager. Why he was surprised that she knew his secret he could not say? After all, Grandma Edie always knew.

A warm smile came over the dowager's face. "It is written all over your face, dear boy. You're torn." She reached for her walking cane and then slowly pushed to her feet. "And you're afraid."

Christopher swallowed as the dowager moved toward him. She was not his grandmother, and yet it felt as though she was. Always had he called her Grandma Edie, and always had she called him dear boy. She had seen him grow up, and he had always heeded her counsel. "What shall I do?" Christopher asked, wishing she would simply tell him and take this decision out of his hands.

Placing a weathered hand upon his arm, Grandma Edie smiled at him. "Speak to her," she urged gently. "Tell her how you feel. You never have, have you?"

Christopher hung his head. "What good will it do now? She has made her choice."

The hint of a frown came to the dowager's face. "She has?"

Christopher nodded, gritting his teeth against another wave of jealousy that rolled through him. "She is to marry...Mr. MacKinnear."

For a brief moment, the dowager's frown deepened ever so slightly before it just as quickly disappeared, as though it had never been.

"She is betrothed," Christopher said with vehemence, his eyes fixed upon the dowager, wishing she would contradict him.

When her eyes glanced at him once more, Grandma Edie simply shrugged. "Perhaps. But she's not married yet, is she?"

Running his hands through his hair, Christopher turned away, his gaze directed out the window into the dark of night. Behind him, he heard Grandma Edie shuffling upon her feet as she retreated to the door, the soft tap of her walking stick upon the parquet echoing to his ears. Then she paused, and he heard her sigh deeply. "We all make mistakes. We all have moments of weakness. However, nothing is harder to forgive than lies." Again, she sighed before Christopher heard her walk away down the hall.

Truer words had never been spoken. Christopher had been dishonest. He had told lies...or at least half-truths, and he had omitted the most important part of his life when he had told Juliet about his home in Ireland.

Now, however, standing at the inn's window and looking down at the darkened street, Christopher paused. Yes, he had left Whickerton Grove the night before—surprised to stumble upon Troy on his way out—because of what Grandma Edie had said. He had lied and lies could not be forgiven. Yet, standing here now and hearing her words echo in his mind anew, Christopher wondered if perhaps the dowager had meant to tell him something entirely different.

His gaze moved down the street and toward the harbor. Indeed, if he left now, he would remain a liar. He would waste his chance to speak the truth and ask for forgiveness. Yes, Juliet might not grant it, but would that truly be worse than this? Then leaving without a word of explanation? Would he not forever wonder what she would have said if only he had told her? Would this not torment him until the end of his days?

Christopher hung his head, realizing rather belatedly that he could not leave like this. Juliet needed to know the truth—even if it came far too late. She needed to know why he had left all those years ago, and she needed to know how he felt about her.

After dressing quickly, Christopher gathered his belongings and then rushed down to the stables. He saddled his horse and was on the road back toward Whickerton Grove before he could think better of it.

Doubts still remained. That, however, was nothing unusual. Christopher's life had always been full of doubts, beginning in his early childhood. Even then, he had doubted his parents' love for him. He had been aware that they did not look at him with the same pride and joy that had shone in their eyes whenever they had gazed upon his brother and sister.

And these doubts had continued throughout his life. This early experience had taught Christopher to be wary, to doubt affection and disregard alike. What was true? And what was not? He had come to doubt everything and everyone...except for Juliet.

Always had she had a way about her that had called to him. Those soft green eyes shining with utter honesty, as though she had never even heard of the existence of lies, as though she did not even know their meaning. Was that why he had been so quick to believe her when she had told him of her betrothal?

Remembering the moment now, Christopher realized she had been unable to hold his gaze. Perhaps it had been simply because she had not wished to hurt him. It was an explanation, certainly. But was it the correct one?

Again, doubts coursed through his mind, and Christopher gritted his teeth as he urged his mount onward. The sun was beginning to rise upon the horizon, and no matter how deeply unsettled he felt by the doubts that still lived in his heart, he could not turn back now.

He had run away before, and it had broken his heart. He had been a fool for most of his life, and it had brought him regret above all.

No, he would not run again and he would not be a fool any longer. He would face his greatest fear and—if need be—learn to live with the consequences.

CHAPTER NINETEEN
UPON THE OPEN ROAD

Juliet felt as though some unseen hand had plucked her from her own familiar life and then dropped her in a stranger's, for her heart beat in a rather unfamiliar rhythm as she followed Keir away from the inn and down the road toward Liverpool.

As they had set off from Whickerton Grove the day before, Juliet had assumed—there was that word again!—that they would take a carriage. Keir, however, had insisted that they would be faster on horseback. "Ye do want to reach him before he sets sail, do ye not, lass?"

Juliet had felt herself nod, her eyes seeing and her limbs moving as though on their own, as though she was not the one in control. It was an odd feeling!

Fortunately, after speaking to her grandmother, Keir had managed to sneak them out of the house with no one else the wiser. More than anything, Juliet had dreaded meeting her family's curious gazes, their eager questions assaulting her like a thousand needle pricks. She would not have known what to answer. Her thoughts were a jumbled mess, doubts warring with hope, eagerness in an open battle with caution. One moment Juliet felt a surge of energy at the prospect of confronting Christopher, of finally receiving answers, and in the next, utter terror seized her, sending a chill through her that made her shiver uncontrollably.

After one day on the road, they had stopped at an inn; yet Juliet had barely slept that night and so they had set out early the next morning. Would they make it in time? It was the one question that kept repeating in Juliet's mind. What if she had waited too long? What if Christopher was already gone?

"Ireland is not at the other end of the world," Keir remarked with a bit of a grin as he urged his mount closer to hers. "Even if he's already left..." He lifted his brows meaningfully and his grin broadened.

Juliet could not help but laugh, and it loosened a knot deep inside. She breathed in deeply. "Are you saying I should go to Ireland?"

Keir shrugged. "If need be."

Juliet smiled at him. "Life is simple to you, is it not?" she asked him, bewildered by the certainty she always saw in his gaze. Oh, if only she could call a sliver of his certainty her own!

He offered her a regretful grin. "I find people tend to make it more complicated than it needs to be." He sighed, then looked at her. "Dunna waste this chance, lass. Be bold."

Juliet chuckled nervously. "I've never been bold. I...I'm not the bold one. Harriet and Louisa are. Even Christina and, yes, Leonora, especially after everything she has been through, everything she has faced so bravely. But me?" She scoffed, shaking her head. "I've never done anything...bold in my life."

Grinning, Keir leaned closer, his blue eyes sparkling with mischief. "Then 'tis about time, lass." Good-naturedly, he bumped her knee with his own, then spurred on his horse, urging her to follow.

Laughing, Juliet did, and all of a sudden, the odd thumping in her chest no longer felt all that...odd.

Coming around a bend in the road, Christopher pulled his mount to a halt when he saw two riders approaching from up ahead. At first, they were no more than blurred shapes in the distance, illuminated by the midday sun. Then, however, as he moved closer, he could tell that it was a man and a woman.

Christopher could not say what it was, but from the first, he could feel a nervous tingle chase itself up and down his arms and legs, as though they were connected to him.

And then he recognized Juliet.

Perhaps it was something in the way she sat atop the horse, or the way she tilted her head or...

Christopher did not know, but he was certain it was her. Instantly, his heart skipped a beat...and his gaze wandered to her companion.

It was none other than Keir MacKinnear...her betrothed!

His insides turned and twisted painfully as he kicked his horse's flanks. What were they doing here? Had something happened? To his sister, perhaps? But then, why would Juliet and Mr. MacKinnear be the ones to go after him? It did not make any sense.

As the three riders drew closer to one another, Christopher's gaze remained locked on Juliet. Her cheeks were flushed, and loose tendrils danced down her temples. Her green eyes shone vibrantly, and yet something hesitant rested in them as they met his. What could be the meaning of this?

Christopher was about to ask for an explanation when the Scot spoke first. "Ah, Lord Lockhart, how fortunate for us to meet ye here." Then he turned and grinned at Juliet, something...meaningful in his gaze.

Tensing, Christopher huffed out an irritated breath. Were they already able to converse without words? This was not what he had had in mind when he had decided to turn back and speak to Juliet. At the very least, he would have expected to have some priva—

"Off the horse with ye, lass," the Scot instructed, "and speak to the man. I'll be," he looked around, "over there." He gestured to a grove of trees near the bend that had first obstructed Christopher's view.

Juliet nodded, her face suddenly pale before she inhaled a deep breath and dismounted.

After watching Mr. MacKinnear ride away, Christopher turned back to Juliet with wide eyes. If he did not know any better, he would think that Mr. MacKinnear was...somehow...on his—Christopher's—

side, leaving them alone together so they could talk. This did not make any sense, either! He dropped to the ground and then led his horse over to her. "What are you doing here?" he asked, once more glancing over his shoulder at Mr. MacKinnear's receding back. This was truly odd! Was the man not supposed to stay at his fiancée's side?

A hesitant smile slowly claimed Juliet's face. "I came to speak with you."

Christopher stilled, for not only her words but also something in her gaze echoed within him. Was she here for the same reason as he? Had she come to—?

Swallowing hard, Christopher nodded. "Shall we...?" He looked around until his gaze fell on a lonely tree off to the side, its softly swaying leaves painted in warm colors of brown, red, orange and gold. "Over there?"

Juliet nodded, and together, they left the road and walked across the meadow toward the tree. Neither one of them said a word, and Christopher could feel his heart almost beat out of his chest. He carefully lifted his gaze and looked over at her, only to feel as though struck by lightning the moment his eyes met hers.

After tying their horses' reins to a low-hanging branch, they finally stood before one another, nothing left to distract them from the weighty moment that had found them both so unexpectedly.

Christopher was about to ask what she was doing here when he saw Juliet straighten and then draw in a deep breath, as though she were a soldier readying herself for battle. A moment later, she blurted out, "Do you love me?"

Christopher almost rocked back on his heels.

CHAPTER TWENTY

A QUESTION OF LOVE

Heat shot up Juliet's neck and rose into her cheeks, but she ignored it. She had come this far; she would not falter now. Yet the look on Christopher's face made her want to hide somewhere. He looked thoroughly shocked by her question, his eyes going wide as he stared at her.

"No," Juliet heard herself murmuring all of a sudden, "that's wrong. That's not what I meant. Of course, you love me. We've always loved each other, have we not?" She prattled on, then stopped herself and straightened. "What I meant to ask was, are...are you in love with me?" Her head felt as though it was about to explode.

For a long, agonizing moment, Christopher remained quiet, still, almost immobile. He stared at her in shock, his brown eyes open wide and fixed upon her face, as though he could not believe what she had just asked him.

Then he blinked. "Yes," was all he said before the blank expression on his face shattered and a smile curled up the corners of his mouth.

At his answer, a deep breath rushed from Juliet's lungs, and she almost dropped to the ground with relief. "Good," she exclaimed as tears shot to her eyes, her head bobbing up and down foolishly. "That's good." Tears snaked down cheeks turned up into a tentative smile. "That's truly good."

A wide smile transformed Christopher's face as he stepped toward her. "You came to ask me this?" he inquired; his brows slightly drawn as he reached for her hands.

Juliet nodded, and a shuddering breath left her lips as his large hands wrapped warmly around hers.

Christopher breathed in deeply. "You didn't know?"

Eyes flying open, Juliet slapped him on the shoulder. "How could I?" She stared up at him, shaking her head. "You never said anything. You never... You..."

Smiling, Christopher reached for her hands once again, then pulled her closer. "Neither did you," he remarked with a teasing grin. Then he paused, and Juliet saw a flicker of uncertainty light up his eyes. "Are you...Are you in love with me as well?"

Juliet fought to blink back tears. "Would I be here if I wasn't?" She frowned. "What are you doing here? I thought you wanted to return to Ireland."

Christopher sighed. "I realized I couldn't leave without telling you that...I love you." A disbelieving chuckle left his lips as his hands wrapped more tightly around hers. "I've always loved you...for as long as I can remember. I..." Words seemed to fail him as he looked into her eyes, such joy upon his face that Juliet wanted to weep helplessly. Oh, she had been such a fool to not have reached for this sooner!

Suddenly, Christopher's face darkened. "Are you...Are you betrothed to Mr. MacKinnear?"

Juliet swallowed, trying to dislodge the sudden lump in her throat as fresh heat shot to her cheeks. Oh, what had she done?

Christopher felt every muscle in his body tense painfully. He could not help it. Despite everything that had been said these past few moments, he could not forget the moment Juliet had told him she had chosen another. But if that were so, what was she doing here? Why had she just told him...that she was in love with him? Had he imagined it? Was this moment even real?

Casting a careful glance around himself, Christopher saw a soft autumn breeze stir the golden leaves overhead. They swayed gently, the warm colors in stark contrast to the pale blue sky. He could smell rain upon the air with a distant tinge of salt from the sea nearby. He could hear birds trilling and saw their horses grazing only a few paces beside them. Yes, the world seemed...real. Everything in it seemed real, except for Juliet. To him, in that moment, she felt like she had stepped straight out of a dream. But was this dream about to turn into a nightmare?

The moment the thought crossed his mind, Juliet spoke. "No, I am not." For a moment, her gaze dropped from his, mortification darkening her cheeks before she looked up at him once more, a sheepish expression upon her face. "I'm so sorry for what I said. I did not mean it. I assure you. It is not true, and it never was."

Exhaling deeply, Christopher shook his head in confusion. "Then why did you say it?" Although he heard her words, part of him did not yet dare believe them. "Why did you tell me you were betrothed to him?"

Juliet sighed deeply. "Because...Because I hoped it would make you leave."

Her words felt like a stab to his heart.

"Please, let me explain," Juliet pleaded as she stepped forward, her hands slipping from his and reaching to cup his face, her deep green eyes looking up into his own. "I wanted you to leave because I was afraid that with every day you stayed, my heart would break a little more." More tears came to her eyes, and yet she did not look away. "I've always loved you. I suppose, at first, I did not know. However, when you left all those years ago, it broke my heart. And I knew you were going to leave again, so..." She shrugged helplessly. "I did not know what to do. I wanted you to stay, and I wanted you to leave. So, when you told me what Grandmother had said about her reasons for bringing Mr. MacKinnear here, I reached for it. It was...a spur of the moment thought. I simply did not want you to—"

Christopher swallowed, and his gaze dropped to her lips for a heartbeat or two. "You didn't want me to kiss you, did you?" He gritted his teeth. "You...You fainted." The question burned in Christopher's heart, yet he did not have the words to ask it.

Juliet nodded. "I thought if I...I thought it would make it worse. I thought if you kissed me, I would never be able to let you go. I thought—"

"When you asked me to kiss you after your sister's wedding," Christopher asked abruptly, the need to know burning in every fiber of his being, "did you truly mean it? Did you want me to kiss you? Or was I simply the first one to cross your path? Would you have asked another—Mr. MacKinnear—if he had been the one to find you in that moment?"

A deep sigh left Juliet's lips. "For a long time, I tried to convince myself that I only wanted to know what a kiss felt like, that it had nothing to do with you because I knew it would not be wise to allow myself to think of you in that way." She stepped closer, and Christopher could feel her hand sliding down his face until only the tips of her fingers brushed against his skin. Then her hands came to rest upon his chest, right above his wildly beating heart.

Christopher began to feel lightheaded as the meaning of her words sank in. His gaze locked onto hers, and his hands reached out to grasp her tiny waist and pulled her closer. "You're not betrothed?" he asked, needing to sort through the confusion in his head.

A shy smile came to Juliet's face before she shook her head no. "I am not."

Christopher's hands on her tightened, and his gaze fell to her lips. "You asked me to kiss you," Christopher said, inching closer until his forehead leaned against hers, their breaths mingling, "did you mean it?"

"I did," came Juliet's breathless reply.

Christopher's heart did another somersault. "Would you...object," he began, his voice strained as his pulse hammered in his veins, "if I kissed you now?"

Juliet chuckled shyly. "Are you asking if I'll faint again?"

Smiling, Christopher reached out to slip a hand up along the line of her neck and then to the back of her head, urging her closer still. He heard her draw in a sharp breath and felt her pulse skip a beat...not unlike his own. "I'm asking," he whispered against her lips, "if you want me to kiss you."

"Do...Do you want to kiss me?" Juliet asked in return, her voice tentative, but oddly daring at the same time.

Lifting his head a fraction, Christopher looked down into her wide green eyes, the same green eyes that had looked at him all his life. "Yes," was all he said, and he hoped she could hear the longing and desire that swung in that one word.

Joy flickered across her face for a split second before Juliet raised her chin a fraction, bringing her lips closer to his. "I do as well," she whispered, her warm breath teasing his lips.

As his heart threatened to beat out of his chest, Christopher stared down at the woman he had loved all his life. He watched her face as the distance between them slowly shrank into nothing. "I've dreamed of this," he whispered against her lips.

"So have I," Juliet whispered back, and it was more than Christopher had ever hoped for. Of course, more needed to be said, but that could wait. It had to wait. Right here and now, all he wanted was this kiss.

Finally.

After six years of waiting...and hoping...and...

Closing his eyes, Christopher dipped his head and kissed her.

Juliet.

Jules.

His Jules.

Oh, he ought to have done this years ago!

CHAPTER TWENTY-ONE

LADY JULIET'S FIRST KISS

Oh, no, she would not faint again! Yet Juliet's head seemed to be spinning, her heart beating so wildly that she could barely draw breath. And then Christopher's lips touched hers, soft and gentle, and the world suddenly righted itself.

Juliet was unsure what she had expected a kiss to feel like. It certainly felt odd to be this close to another, to feel Christopher's body pressed to hers, one of his hands upon the small of her back while the other cupped the back of her head, holding her to him. It was not merely a touch of his lips to hers, but much more. She felt his heart beat against her own; she felt the slight tremor that rocked him as she kissed him back.

A kiss seemed a thousand times more complicated than Juliet had ever imagined it to be, and yet it was the simplest thing in the world, was it not?

Slowly, Christopher pushed closer, his hands reaching to cup her face as he brushed his mouth against hers. Juliet felt herself shiver, her hands curling into his lapels, seeking his warmth. She knew theirs was not a passionate kiss, but one that whispered of two souls exploring a new facet of who they knew each other to be. She felt his pulse beat against the tip of her fingers and knew that he felt hers as well as he held her face cradled in his hands.

Juliet leaned closer, the soft pressure of her lips against his tentative. Yet she was curious, wishing she knew how to communicate how much she wanted this.

Gently, Christopher deepened their kiss, and Juliet almost smiled, touched that somehow he had understood her. He held her heart in his hands. He always had but now he finally knew. He was in love with her! Had he not said so?

A part of Juliet was still considering the possibility that she had strayed into a dream, that she was at home in bed or out strolling the grounds, her head lost in this achingly beautiful moment.

A moment that only existed in her mind.

Yet Christopher felt so real. His heart beat strong beneath her hands, and when his arms came around her and he touched the tip of his tongue to hers, every last bit of doubt about whether this was truly happening went out the window. Never could Juliet have imagined a kiss like this.

Never.

Yet it was not enough. It would never be enough. She wanted more than a few stolen kisses. More than friendship. More than passion. More than...love even. She wanted him in her life for all the days to come. Always had he been her friend; only now she also wanted him to be her husband.

Somewhere deep down, Juliet had always known that she wanted him, but she was afraid to admit to herself what it was she wanted. Perhaps Grandma Edie's dependence upon her had not truly hindered Juliet's chances of making a match. Perhaps, after all, it had been her own doing, knowing full-well that no other man would ever do.

Indeed, the thought of losing Christopher even now was devastating. Yet it was not a thought she could easily push aside. Yes, he loved her but...secrets remained.

Was this moment the beginning of a wonderful life? Or only a heartbreaking farewell?

Knowing they could not remain locked in this moment forever, Juliet pulled back, breaking their kiss. She looked up into his eyes and felt tears gathering in her own. "Will you still leave? Or will you come back with me?"

A shadow crossed over Christopher's face, proving without a doubt that there were things in his life he had yet to share with her. But would he?

Juliet awaited his answer with bated breath when the sudden sound of hoofbeats made her flinch. Christopher's head, too, snapped up, and they both turned toward the sound.

"I'm verra sorry to interrupt ye," Keir said before he cast a cautious look over his shoulder at the horizon, "but the sky has grown dark, and I think we should return to the inn." He met her eyes, a teasing spark lighting up their pale blue. "Ye'll not want to be soaked to the skin."

Juliet nodded, and she heard Christopher clear his throat. "Right," he mumbled, a faraway look in his eyes, as though he needed a moment to remember the world around them.

Assisting her onto her horse, Christopher then mounted his own. He urged the animal closer to Keir, and for a moment, the two men looked at one another, something silent passing between them that Juliet could not quite grasp. Then Christopher gave a quick nod. "Thank you."

Keir returned the sentiment before guiding his mount back toward the road. "Quickly," he called back to them. "Before the heavens break open and drench us all." A chuckle flew from his lips as Juliet and Christopher hurried to catch up with him.

Fortunately, the inn was not too far away, and they reached its stables just as the first heavy drops began to fall from the sky. Large clouds lingered above, darkening the sky, as though it were not midday but rather moments before nightfall. "Hand me the reins and head inside," Keir instructed in his usual manner. "See yerselves settled." His blue eyes met Juliet's meaningfully before he led their horses away.

Christopher grasped her arm and pulled her along. "Come! Quick!" He held her close, guiding her to the entrance and holding the door open so she could slip inside the warm taproom.

A warm fire burned in the hearth, and delicious smells tickled Juliet's nose and made her stomach rumble. Christopher quickly procured rooms and then led her upstairs. "Do you wish for a bath?"

Juliet shook her head as he stood in the hall and held open the door to her chamber. "I admit I'm hungry," she told him with a hesitant look, "but what I want most of all is to speak with you." She stepped inside, hoping he would follow.

Christopher merely nodded, yet Juliet breathed a sigh of relief when she saw that the look in his eyes spoke of the same need. "I ordered food to be brought to your room, but perhaps we should eat downstairs...so we can talk."

Juliet hesitated, but then she gestured for him to come in. "We can talk here, can we not? Alone."

A reluctant expression came to his face as he stood outside her chamber, unwilling to step inside. "I'm not certain we should—"

"I don't care about my reputation," Juliet interrupted, feeling oddly reminded of her youngest sister's fiery temperament. Indeed, Harry had never cared a fig about what other people thought of her choices. And the world had yet to end! Besides, Juliet had already risked ruination when she had set out after Christopher with only Keir as her companion.

"But your parents—"

"My parents trust me," Juliet objected, not the slightest doubt in her mind. "As they trust you." She smiled at him. "That's all that matters."

Christopher gritted his teeth. "Are you certain?" When Juliet nodded, he finally stepped over the threshold and then slowly, hesitantly, closed the door.

For a long moment, they simply looked at one another, uncertain how to begin again. Then Christopher stepped forward, gallantly lifted her cloak off her shoulders and hung it by the fire to dry off. He shrugged out of his own coat and draped it over the backrest of a chair. "Are you cold?"

Juliet shook her head. "No, I'm fine." She looked at him with expectant eyes. This was it! The moment she had been waiting for for six years. She could only hope it would not break her heart anew.

Holding out a chair for her, Christopher cleared his throat, his face tense.

"Thank you," Juliet mumbled, seating herself, her eyes following him as he moved to sit across from her. His gaze darted to hers and then away before he closed his eyes and inhaled a deep breath.

Juliet could all but feel the tension in the room. It was as though she could reach out her hand and touch it. What was Christopher so afraid of? What had happened six years ago? Why had he disappeared? Why...Why had he never come back...at least, not truly...until now?

Reaching across the table, Christopher gently took her hands within his own, his brown eyes finally meeting hers. Rain drummed down on the roof above their heads, and darkness began to fall over the land, wrapping them in a cocoon all their own. "There is...something I need to tell you. Something I've been meaning to tell you...for so long." He sighed, his jaw rigid, and Juliet realized how deeply he feared her reaction. He truly loved her, did he not?

"Tell me," Juliet urged, and she felt as though her heart was about to jump out of her chest as she once more found herself on the precipice between joy and dread.

He loved her! Christopher loved her! And yet...

"Please," she said gently, their hands clasped together tightly as though they both feared that something might rip them apart. "Is it about Ireland?" He swallowed hard. "About...why you left?"

Slowly, Christopher nodded. "It is a long story, and I should have told it to you long ago."

Juliet nodded, giving his hands an encouraging squeeze. "Then tell me now."

CHAPTER TWENTY-TWO

A LONG STORY

A knock on the door ripped through the heavy blanket that hung over the moment, and Christopher felt Juliet flinch at the sound. He smiled at her reassuringly and then rose to open the door. Two serving maids bustled into the chamber, quickly setting the table with steaming dishes and then equally quickly excused themselves.

"Eat," Christopher urged her gently as he took his seat once more, holding out the breadbasket to her. "Even from here, I can hear your stomach growling like a ferocious beast." He grinned at her.

A fetching blush came to Juliet's cheeks, and she averted her gaze before fixing him with a chiding look. "And here I thought you were a gentleman, Lord Lockhart."

The smile died on Christopher's face and hers followed just as swiftly as she saw his expression. For a long moment, silence reigned before Juliet reached across the table and took his hand once more. "Tell me, Christopher, and I swear I will not think less of you."

Dumbfounded, Christopher stared at her, wondering how she knew. Could she truly look into his heart and know where it hurt? Where fear lingered? "Very well," Christopher mumbled, nodding his head up and down. "I..." He inhaled a deep breath and willed himself not to look away. "I have a child."

Christopher flinched when he saw Juliet's jaw drop and her eyes go round. "A...A child?" she stammered, staring at him in incomprehension. "A child? You have a child?" Her forehead furrowed as she leaned closer, her green eyes searching his face, seeking something that would help her understand the words he had spoken.

Sighing, Christopher nodded. Of course, he had expected her to be...shocked. How could she not be? Yet it was not what he feared. What he feared was that her green eyes would no longer look at him the way they always had. "A son," he said, taken aback by the sudden surge of pride that welled up in his heart and swung in his voice as he thought of him. "He...He is five years old."

Juliet's eyes closed. "He is the reason you left," she whispered, and her hands tightened on his.

Christopher was relieved that she did not shy away from him but instead held on tighter. "Yes."

Her eyes opened and looked into his once more. "And he is the one who awaits your return in Ireland."

"Yes. I...I don't like leaving him alone for too long. The only reason I ever leave Ireland is because of Mrs. O'Brien. She is his nurse, but she feels almost like family. She has been with us from the beginning and dotes on him as any grandmother would." Belatedly, he realized that he was smiling, and a deep longing to return home and see his son welled up in his chest.

"What about his mother?" Juliet asked tentatively, her voice unsteady and the look in her eyes marked with fear. "Is she in Ireland as well? Are you...Are you married?" Her hands slackened within his.

As though on instinct, Christopher held on to Juliet tighter. "No!" he exclaimed, his eyes fixed upon hers, and then again, "No, I'm not married. I never was."

Juliet's eyes closed in relief, and Christopher's heart rejoiced at the very sight. Part of him had feared that she would leave the moment she learned of his son. Despite everything he knew about her, her kindness, her understanding heart, this fear had lingered in the back of his head all these years, keeping his lips sealed and the truth hidden.

Yet she was still here.

After exhaling a slow breath, Juliet's eyes opened to look into his once more. He saw hope there, restrained but visible, as well as curiosity and the need to understand. "Will you tell me what happened? How...How do you have a son? Who's his mother? And why...why do you now live in Ireland?" Her brows drew down. "Is his mother Irish? How did you meet her? Where is she now?"

The questions flew from her lips, and Christopher realized that his leaving home, England even, had to have been on Juliet's mind a lot. Deep down, Christopher had always hoped so, had wondered whether she ever thought of him, whether she had ever stopped thinking of him. They had been close friends, but then years had passed without words exchanged between them.

Christopher sighed. "It is a long story," he repeated, a tentative smile coming to his face, "but I will tell you everything you wish to know. I promise."

Juliet nodded, a grateful smile tickling the corners of her mouth. "Thank you. I've been wondering for so long. I truly wish to know." Yet tension continued to linger in her hands. Christopher could feel it as he could feel his own.

Urging Juliet to eat, Christopher sat across from her, his own plate untouched except for the crust of bread he was picking apart with his fingers, crumbs falling onto the tabletop. "It all began the night my brother died," he said slowly, his gaze distant, but his mind well aware that she was watching him, hanging on every word. "It is a night I am not proud of, but one I also cannot regret." He cast her a sad smile.

Juliet's green eyes held his as she reached out and placed her hand upon his. Even though he could feel her trembling, there was something kind and strong in the way she reached out to soothe his fears, and Christopher loved her all the more for it.

"You know that my parents were never all that...fond of me," Christopher began, his jaw clenched as he remembered one of the darkest nights of his life. "We were all heartbroken to learn of Sebastian's death, but..." He closed his eyes, recalling only too vividly the way his parents had looked at him that night. "Father and Mother grieved, yes, but fear soon came to their eyes, fear when they realized Sebastian was truly gone and that now…I was the heir." Rising to his feet, Christopher paced to the door and then back, anger humming in his veins at the memory. "I remember the exact moment they realized that I would now be the future of the earldom and…to put it mildly, they didn't like it."

Compassion rested in Juliet's eyes as she rose to her feet and moved toward him, her hands reaching out as they always had. Always had she been the counterweight to his parents' callous dismissal. "They were wrong to treat you thus," she whispered, dipping her head a little to look into his downcast eyes. "I shall never understand why they favored your brother. You were both their children, and you are such a good man. You always have been. In the end, it does not matter why. What matters is that it was their choice and not your fault. You did nothing wrong." She shrugged helplessly. "Who knows why they were unable to see how wonderful you are." She smiled up at him, gently reaching out to touch his face. "It is their loss. Do you hear me, Kit? Do not try to find fault within yourself."

Impulsively, Christopher drew her tightly into his arms and held her close. He rested his chin on the top of her head and closed his eyes. This was precisely who she had always been to him, the one who knew him best, the one who always managed to see his good side, who held his hand and told him what his heart longed to hear. "I missed you so much," he murmured, his arms tightening upon her. "From the very first, you were the one I loved most, the one I needed most. Every decision I made, I made based on your moral guidance, not my parents'. You've always been my conscience, and what I feared most of my life was to disappoint you, to lose your respect." He breathed in slowly and then took a step back, looking down at her eyes. "It is why I left," he finally said. "Because I could not bear the thought of you turning away from me the way they always did. I did something that night…" He closed his eyes and shook his head. "It was foolish and thoughtless, but I felt…"

Her hand rose to cup his cheek. "Why did you not come to me? Of course, I would've been there for you. Your brother had just died and—"

"I wanted to," Christopher interrupted, remembering the

desperate need he had felt in that moment. "You were the first thing on my mind, and I knew that I needed you. I was almost out the door when my father called me back. He warned me not to embarrass him, to not embarrass the family. He told me I was now the heir." Christopher gritted his teeth. "He all but spat the word. He said I finally had to grow up, that I could no longer run around and do as I pleased. He said I now had a responsibility to the earldom and that I could not simply ride over to Whickerton Grove in the middle of the night and climb up to your window."

The expression on Juliet's face hardened in a way Christopher had never seen before. Anger flashed in her green eyes, and the hand that cupped his cheek held him with more vehemence. "He was wrong," she snapped, something protective resonating in her voice. "Your brother had just passed, and you were heartbroken; of course, he was wrong. I never would've sent you away or been disappointed in you."

Brushing a stray curl from her face, Christopher smiled down at her. "I never thought you would. Yet..." He sighed. "Everything changed in that moment, and I did not know what to do. I felt overwhelmed, and when my father told me I could not see you, I simply rushed out of the house and rode away. I did not know where I was going, but eventually I found myself in the village, facing the tavern, the very one from which I often had to drag my inebriated brother home." He huffed out a deep breath, shrugging his shoulders. "I loved him dearly, but we both know that he liked to drink and gamble and... who knows what else? He was not the responsible type, and yet somehow he could do no wrong." Christopher did not want to dislike his brother for his behavior; yet the way their parents had always favored him despite his shortcomings did not make it easy. Perhaps if this feeling had not stood between them, they could have been closer.

Now, it was too late. His brother was gone, and there would be no do-over.

"What happened then?" Juliet asked carefully, and the look in her eyes revealed how torn she was. On the one hand, she clearly wished to know, to understand while, on the other, a part of her feared what he might say.

Christopher swallowed hard. "I went inside, and for the first time in my life, I got drunk. Of course, I'm not proud of it, but that night..." He shook his head. "It felt as though nothing mattered any longer." He met Juliet's gaze reluctantly, wondering how to put into words what had happened next. Even now, he could hear his late father's voice, demanding he show decorum and not speak of such matters in the presence of a lady. Of course, his father would surely have suffered an apoplexy if he could see his son now.

At an inn.

With Lady Juliet.

Alone.

"I do not remember much of that night," Christopher finally said, holding Juliet's gaze instead of averting his eyes like a coward. "What I do remember is waking the next morning in a bed that was not mine." He tried to swallow the lump in his throat. "With...a woman whose name I could not recall." He felt her tense in his arms, her eyes wide and unblinking. "I'm so sorry," he whispered, seeing his worst fears realized. "I never wanted to hurt you. I'm so very sorry. I wish I could undo it, and yet..." He shrugged helplessly, thinking of his son's sweet, innocent face and his wide blue eyes. "I do not."

CHAPTER TWENTY-THREE

ONCE UPON A TIME

Juliet felt her hands begin to tremble as she stepped back. At least for a moment, she needed a bit of distance to wrap her mind around Christopher's confession. She was not angry with him. Of course not. They had been friends then: nothing more. Yet the thought of another in his arms made her heart ache painfully.

"I'm so very sorry," Christopher said again, anguish in his voice. His warm brown eyes held such pain that Juliet could not help but feel for him. "I never meant for it to happen." He hung his head, exhaled a deep breath, and then said, "A few weeks later, she sought me out and told me she was with child." Shaking his head, he raked a hand through his already tousled hair. "My parents were furious. Finally, they had unerring proof that I was as flawed as they had always known me to be." He scoffed, a dark sound full of regret and anger. Then his eyes dimmed. "My father suffered a heart attack the next day." Tears clung to his eyes. "My mother never forgave me for..." He shrugged.

Thunderstruck, Juliet stared at Christopher. "Your father's death was not your fault, Kit! Do you hear me?" She shot forward and grasped his hands, looking up into his face. "How dare she place that upon your shoulders? I will...talk to her. Yes, I will talk to her and—"

Christopher chuckled, a warm glow suddenly upon his face. "Are you my knight in shining armor then, trying to save me?"

Rolling her eyes, Juliet slapped him on the shoulder. "Don't act as though they did nothing wrong, Kit! As though you have no right to be angry? They are your parents. It is their job to love you, to—" Christopher could not help his grin from widening. "Don't laugh at me!"

Shaking his head, he pulled her back into his arms. "I'm not. Truly, I'm not. You're simply so...so adorable. I...I missed you so much. I'd forgotten what it felt like to have you in my corner."

Juliet swallowed, feeling the full weight of those dark brown eyes looking into hers. "What does it feel like?"

Christopher's shoulders rose and fell with a deep sigh. "When you're with me," he whispered, leaning his forehead against hers, "I feel whole." His warm breath tickled her lips, and Juliet closed her eyes, allowing herself to savor the moment.

It had been too long.

"Are you not upset with me?" Christopher asked then, and his head rose, his eyes seeking hers.

Juliet frowned, momentarily at a loss. Her heart beat fast and forcefully, welcoming the emotions Christopher's embrace roused within her. "Upset with you?"

He nodded. "I betrayed you. That night, I..."

"We were friends," Juliet said quickly, loathe to speak of him in the arms of another. "There was no understanding between us that..." She dropped her gaze.

"I loved you even then."

Juliet's head snapped up, and she stared into his eyes. "You did?"

His head bobbed up and down slowly as his brown eyes looked deep into hers. "That night made me realize what I wanted. It made me realize you were the one I wanted all along. It made me realize I wanted more than your friendship." His eyes closed, and a dark scoff left his lips. "The very moment I lost you, I finally realized how much I wanted you." His hands tightened on hers, anguish in his eyes. "It nearly killed me. I wanted to tell you everything, but after everything that I'd already lost—my brother, my father, my mother's respect—

what little of it she had for me—I could not bear the thought of seeing you turn from me as well."

Juliet flinched. "I never would have, you fool!" she exclaimed, shocking herself. How long had it been since she had responded to another with such vehemence? Christopher had always been the one to bring it out in her. With him, she was someone she did not dare be on her own. "I loved you as well," she whispered with a sigh, "and it was only when you left that I realized it. Far too late."

Shaking his head, Christopher chuckled. "We are a pair, are we not? Our timing could not have been worse."

"Why did you leave without a word?" Juliet finally asked after six long years. "Why did you not tell me...something? Anything? That is what I'm upset about. You do not know how long I tortured myself with questions, wondering if it had been something I'd done or said." Glaring at him, she shook her head. "You should have told me! You should have said something! You should have—" Her voice broke off as she ran out of words, anger over the pain she had suffered still burning in her veins. "Damn it, Kit, you hurt me!"

Christopher stared at her, and Juliet wondered if it had been her admission, or rather her unfortunate choice of words. She had not meant to swear; yet it seemed appropriate. She hoped it made him listen, made him truly hear her and understand how deeply his actions had shaken her.

Contrition came to Christopher's face. "I'm so sorry. I know I should have spoken to you, explained at least..." He hung his head. "I realized I loved you, and yet I had just fathered a child with another. How could I face you? I was afraid if I told you, you'd turn from me and then I'd lose more than your friendship. I'd also lose the memory of who we used to be together, unable to forget the way disappointment chased away all tender feelings you might have had for me once." His eyes were pleading, and Juliet realized that he was still afraid.

Even now.

Inhaling deeply, she stepped toward him, her hands grasping his. "I might be disappointed, Kit, but that doesn't mean I no longer love you. Yes, you were a fool. Such a fool!" She squeezed his hands so hard, he yelped. "How could you think I'd ever leave your side?"

Something soft and tender came to his eyes at her words, and Juliet felt her insides soften in turn. Yet more needed to be said. "What happened then?" she asked, holding his gaze. "When...she—?"

"Alice," Christopher supplied with a contrite look. "Her name is Alice."

Juliet nodded, her jaw tense. "What happened when...Alice told you she was with child?"

Christopher inhaled a deep breath. "I...I told my parents because... because at least a part of me wanted to punish them. They'd always expected the worst of me, and I suppose I wanted them to suffer for once." He shrugged. "So, I told them, and the next day, my father was dead."

"And then?" Juliet pressed, wanting to hear it all now, without delay.

"My mother said no one could ever know," Christopher remembered, a grave look upon his face. "She sent Alice away, promised her anything if she were to keep that secret and, thus, shame away from our family." His teeth gritted together. "Alice was more than happy to comply."

Juliet frowned. "Then how did your son end up with you?"

Christopher rolled his shoulders, then stretched his neck from side to side. "At first, I too complied with my mother's wishes. She lectured me for hours, and I came to realize that whether I liked it or not, a lot of people suddenly depended on me. So, I played along as best as I could until I happened upon a letter addressed to my mother. It was the day of my sister's wedding, and the entire house was in an uproar. I suppose my mother must have set it down and forgotten it." He shrugged.

"What did it say?"

A small smile came to Christopher's face, both sad and joyful. "It informed her of my son's birth. She hadn't even bothered to tell me." His hands suddenly gestured wildly, and Juliet could see raw emotions on his face. "The moment I read it, I knew I needed to see him, and so I left the second my sister was wed. Unlike our mother, she understood and told me to go."

Tears stood in Christopher's eyes. "I knew I was to forget about him, but the moment I saw him, held him, I knew I couldn't." He closed his eyes. "Alice had no interest in him. What she wanted was the monthly stipend my mother sent, and I realized if I did nothing, my son would grow up thinking no one wanted him, loved him, no doubt wondering what he had done wrong."

"So, you took him away to Ireland?" Christopher nodded. "He's been there with you all this time?" Again, Christopher nodded. "Why Ireland?"

With a tense jaw, Christopher shrugged. "I knew that in England he would forever be branded a bastard. He is my son, but he will never be my heir." Anger flashed in his eyes. "I...I wanted something untainted for him. A place for us to begin again and pretend the rest of the world did not exist. I wanted him to grow up feeling loved and wanted." He looked into her eyes, and Juliet could see how deeply he needed her to understand. "To my mother, he was nothing more than a mistake, and I knew that the rest of society would look at him the same way. I did not want that for him, and so I took him away."

A deep, heartfelt smile came to Juliet's face as she looked up at Christopher. The words he had just spoken touched her deeply and made her proud of the man he had become. He had found himself in an impossible situation, and yet where others would have turned a blind eye, he had faced up to his responsibility, had gone beyond even that and followed his heart. He had not seen the mistake but an innocent child who deserved a home, a family.

Holding Christopher's hands tightly within her own, Juliet looked up into his eyes. "What is your son's name?"

At her question, his features relaxed, and a tentative smile came to his face. "Sebastian," he murmured, pride and love and longing resonating in his voice as he spoke of his son. "His name is Sebastian."

"After your brother."

Heaving a deep sigh, Christopher nodded. "Yes, after my brother."

CHAPTER TWENTY-FOUR
RETURNING TO WHICKERTON GROVE

Despite the threatening look of dark, heavy clouds looming in the sky, rain did not fall when they set off the next morning. Although Christopher still felt torn, one part of him wishing to return to Ireland while the other wanted nothing more than to retrace his steps to Whickerton Grove. Much had been said the night before, and his chest felt lighter than it ever had since that day six years ago. Finally, Juliet knew the truth. She knew why he had left, and she knew about his son. Indeed, it felt as though a heavy burden had been lifted off his shoulders, allowing him to breathe more easily.

Yet...where did they stand now? Christopher could not say. As they rode down the road, his gaze occasionally moved to Mr. MacKinnear. By now, he knew nothing had ever been between him and Juliet. Still, for her to tell such a lie, she truly had to have wanted him to leave. He had hurt her, and Christopher knew he would never forgive himself for it. He had been terrified of telling the truth. Now, he was terrified of what his lies might have done. Where would they go from here?

Countless times throughout the day, Christopher felt Juliet's gaze turn to him. Sometimes, their eyes met, and she would smile at him.

Other times, she quickly glanced away, as though not wanting him to know whatever was on her mind.

Christopher was dying to talk to her, to find out how she felt. He had finally confessed his love, and so had she. But...?

Unfortunately, Mr. MacKinnear's presence made that impossible. Even when the Scotsman rode ahead or fell behind, Christopher could not bring himself to ask the questions that burned in his soul. He forced himself to wait, knowing that the moment needed to be theirs.

Theirs alone.

And so, when Whickerton Grove finally came into view, everything was still as unresolved as before. Christopher's heart beat wildly in his chest, and impatience began to flood his blood as he dismounted and then quickly moved to assist Juliet. It was no more than an excuse to be close to her again, to feel her hands upon his arms as he helped her down. The look in her eyes was tentative as well as yearning, matching the slow but meaningful smile that teased her lips. Christopher was mesmerized, and all but forgot the world around him until a loud commotion erupted from the door.

Not surprisingly, Juliet's absence had been noted, and now, the rest of the Whickerton clan came pouring out of the front hall, their faces eager and their eyes curious. Instantly, their voices rose to the heavens, as they all seemed to be speaking at once.

"Juliet, what has happened?"

"You left without a word. We were so worried."

"Did you elope with Keir?" Although knowing better now, Christopher flinched at that one.

"We were afraid you'd miss the ball."

While Grandma Edie remained in the background, a most amused smile upon her lips, it was Troy who stepped forward, his pale blue eyes going back and forth between his sister and Christopher. Yet he did not say a word, did not ask a question. His jaw tightened, and his shoulders drew back.

Christopher could not help but think that Troy disapproved, that he had not wanted Christopher to return. It was time they talked about everything, with nothing held back.

Although more questions kept coming, Lord Whickerton quickly ushered everyone inside and out of the cold. Moments later, they were all seated in the drawing room near a roaring fire and with a hot cup of tea in their hands. Expectant eyes moved from Juliet to Mr. MacKinnear and then to Christopher. Perhaps it would have been wise to talk on the road after all. Now, here, Christopher had no clue what to say or how to explain where they had been and what had happened. From the look on her face, neither did Juliet.

Fortunately, Mr. MacKinnear came to their rescue. "As much as we would like to tell ye all that's happened," he said, looking around the room at all of them, "we're afraid we canna." His gaze moved to the dowager countess seated nearest to the fireplace, a rather conspiratorial look passing between them. "'Tis not our secret to tell as we were sent on an errand by another."

Instantly, all eyes turned to the dowager. "Mother, what have you done now?" Lord Whickerton asked with a slightly exasperated huff.

"Another errand?" Phineas, Louisa's husband, asked with a smirk, clearly amused by the level of secret-keeping currently abounding within the Whickerton clan.

Indeed, even Christopher had taken note of the fact that no one yet knew why the dowager had invited Mr. MacKinnear to visit them at Whickerton Grove. Yet everyone was certain that a most serious reason lay at its root. Like the others, Christopher, too, had noted that the Scotsman had come and gone several times over the past few weeks, tending to rather mysterious errands. As it was the dowager's secret, of course, no one knew anything about it and would not until she decided the time had come to make it known.

However, for the Scotsman to pretend another such errand had been the reason for their disappearance when Christopher knew that to be wrong made him wonder. Was it wrong? Or had he and Juliet merely acted out another one of Grandma Edie's plans without them even being aware of it?

Shaking his head, Christopher chuckled. He would not put it past the old woman.

"I do not have the slightest inkling what you're talking about," Grandma Edie intoned rather solemnly; yet mischief sparkled in her eyes, and she did not even bother trying to hide it. "All I do know is that there is a ball here tomorrow night and a lot still needs to be done." Her gaze moved to her granddaughters.

Christopher frowned, noting the way the sisters all but jumped to their feet, their heads nodding in agreement. Then they quickly grabbed hold of Juliet's hands and pulled her out the door. Indeed, if he was not at all mistaken, it looked very much as though another plan was afoot.

A shadow fell over Christopher, and as he turned away from the door, he found Troy standing in front of him. "We need to talk," his friend said meaningfully, his voice tense, not unlike the muscles in his jaw and neck.

Christopher nodded and then rose to his feet. "Of course." He had seen this coming, and yet he could not help but wonder at the deep emotions he had seen on his friend's face. Did Troy truly disapprove of him? Would he rather his sister marry another?

Following his friend down the hall, Christopher almost tripped over his own feet at the thought. Yes, he had dreamed of marrying Juliet for years, and yet had never quite allowed that thought to voice itself clearly, afraid that if he admitted to himself what it was he truly wanted, it would only hurt more to know it could never be. But things had changed now, had they not? What would happen if he asked Juliet to marry him? Would she agree? Or could there be reasons which would cause her to carefully consider his offer?

After holding the door open for Christopher, Troy closed it behind them. His eyes were narrowed, and Christopher could feel his friend's calculating gaze upon him. "You left," Troy finally said. It was a statement, and yet also question.

Christopher nodded. "I did."

Troy's shoulders rose and fell with a deep breath. Then he turned away and strode over to the fireplace, resting one elbow upon its mantle as he looked at Christopher over his shoulder. "And yet you are here." Another statement. Another question.

Approaching his friend, Christopher made up his mind. Enough lies had been told. Enough secrets had been kept. "What is it you wish to know? Ask it, and I shall answer you honestly. I promise."

At his words, the expression on Troy's face softened. It was as though a mask slid off, revealing a man exhausted and in need of a reprieve. "I am not your enemy, nor do I wish to be." Troy's eyes looked into Christopher's. "I need you to believe that."

Christopher nodded. "I never thought so. Not for a moment." He stepped toward his friend. "Neither do you believe that I hold any ill intentions toward your sister."

Slowly, Troy nodded. "You are correct; yet I have been wrong before." He stepped away from the mantle and faced Christopher directly. "Tell me here and now what it is you want. Why did you come back? Why did you not leave? What," he took a step closer, a warning in his eyes, "are your intentions?"

"I love her," Christopher blurted out, surprised at the little dance his heart did just then. "I've always loved her, yet I never knew how much until I thought her lost to me."

Troy nodded. "And?"

"I wish to marry her," Christopher said honestly. "Yet more needs to be said. We—"

"Does she know of your son?"

Christopher froze. "You... You know?" For a second, he wondered if perhaps the dowager countess had shared this information with her grandson. "Who told you?"

Troy scoffed. "Am I correct to assume that my grandmother also knows?" He shook his head. "No, she did not tell me. When you left without a word," Troy's gaze narrowed accusingly, "I watched my sister torture herself for weeks, months, wondering what she had done to drive you away, to lose your friendship." His lips pressed into a thin line. "So, I made some inquiries."

Christopher nodded in acknowledgment. "I never meant to keep this from you, from her. I simply did not know what to do. It was a mistake, and yet the thought that my son had never been born is pure torture. I cannot look at him and see a mistake. I cannot say I'm sorry for what happened because a part of me simply is not. It cannot be." He threw up his hands, realizing how much he had wanted to talk to his friend about this, how much he had wanted his counsel. "It was one moment, one single moment, and it changed everything. I did not plan it. I did not see it coming. It simply happened, and afterward, I felt like such a fool." He looked up and met Troy's gaze. "Do you know what that's like?"

To his surprise, his friend nodded slowly, the look in his eyes distant.

Frowning, Christopher took another step toward his friend. "Nora?" he asked carefully.

Troy almost flinched at the sound of her name. His face paled, and a look of deep anguish came to his eyes. Then, however, he shook himself, chasing away whatever thoughts her name had conjured. He met Christopher's eyes with a hard stare. "Speak to Juliet and do it quickly." He moved closer, his gaze dark and threatening. "You are my friend, but if you hurt her again, I will end you. Is that understood?"

Slowly nodding his head up and down, Christopher could barely help the smile that threatened to claim his face. Indeed, he had always loved the Whickertons for their fierce protectiveness, wishing he could be one of them. "Of course." He placed a hand on Troy's shoulder. "You have my word."

CHAPTER TWENTY-FIVE
IN PREPARATION FOR THE BALL

"Do you like it?" Christina asked as Juliet stood upon a small pedestal surrounded not only by her sisters and cousin but also by a rather intimidating number of mirrors. She was entranced—a bit shocked, too—by her own appearance, seeing her own eyes staring back at her, as she moved from one foot onto the other, her skirts swishing around her legs.

"Oh, I think it looks perfect on you!" Louisa exclaimed, seated in a comfortable armchair. Anne and their sisters nodded in agreement.

"Truly?" Juliet asked, her gaze sweeping not only over the exquisite gown, shining in a rare green but also over the elaborate hairstyle and the sparkling emeralds adorning her neck.

Harriet nodded eagerly. "You look beautiful, dearest Jules. I have no doubt that you'll catch the eye of every man at tomorrow's ball."

I only wish to catch the eye of one man, Juliet thought, still frowning at her own appearance. Although she could not deny that her sisters were right—the gown looked beautiful—she felt...odd wearing it.

Juliet had never minded not being the center of attention. She rather preferred standing on the edge of the ballroom, able to observe others while remaining in the shadows herself. She did not need praise and admiration, and she despised compliments made out of politeness or duty alone. The only thing Juliet ever wanted was to be seen by those who mattered to her.

By Christopher.

And now he had seen her, had he not? Even without fancy dresses and emeralds glittering around her neck. He had seen her. The real her. And he had kissed her.

Standing in front of all these mirrors, surrounded by her sisters and her cousin, Juliet experienced a moment of disbelief, wondering if the past few days had truly happened. Had she truly set out with Keir in pursuit of Christopher? Had she truly asked him if he was in love with her? Had he truly confessed his love? Had he truly...kissed her?

So much had happened since they had come upon Christopher on the road. So much had been said and asked that their kiss had almost slipped her mind, pushed aside by more pressing matters. And yet it had happened, had it not?

"Whatever you're thinking of right now," Harriet remarked with a big grin upon her face, jarring Juliet from her thoughts, "hold on to it because it puts the most fetching blush on your face!"

It took a moment for Juliet to comprehend her sister's words; however, when she did, she felt herself blush even more deeply with mortification, wondering if Harriet could truly guess what was going through her mind. Harriet could not possibly know what had happened between Juliet and Christopher, could she? No one knew... except for Keir...and most likely their grandmother.

"Why are you blushing?" Christina asked gently before casting a look over her shoulder at their sisters. "Are you so excited for tomorrow's ball?"

Juliet shrugged, relieved to drop her gaze and let it sweep downward over her gown. "I cannot help but feel that this is wrong. I don't feel well dressing up like this. It's not...me."

"You look beautiful," Anne remarked, a glowing smile upon her face. "Everyone will be looking at you."

"I don't want everyone looking at me," Juliet exclaimed, possibly with a bit too much vehemence.

Her sisters eyed her curiously, consternation marking their

features. "You don't?" Louisa remarked from her spot by the fireplace. "And here I thought it was only Grandma Edie's interference that kept you from mingling all these years."

While Leonora refrained from saying a single word—her wide blue eyes meeting Juliet's every so often—Christina, Harriet and Anne wholeheartedly agreed. "Now that we're all here," Christina exclaimed, "we thought we could find a way to pry her from your side."

Harriet nodded eagerly. "Yes." She grinned at the others. "Strength in numbers."

Juliet's sisters laughed. "Do you not wish to marry?" Anne inquired thoughtfully, one hand on her slightly rounded belly. "And have children? I always assumed you did."

Juliet sighed. What was she to say? Before she could even attempt to explain anything to her sisters, she needed to speak to Christopher. She needed to—

"Or have you already lost your heart?" Louisa asked with a shrewd expression upon her face. "Do you not wish for us to doll you up because you've already caught the eye of a gentleman?"

As unease spread through Juliet, eagerness spread over her sisters' faces. "Is it true?" Christina exclaimed, her eyes wide, before she exchanged a meaningful look with Harriet. "Who is it? You must tell us!"

Juliet felt like a gazelle cornered by a pride of hungry lions.

"Keir!" Harriet exclaimed, a triumphant look upon her face. "It has to be him!" She turned to look at her sisters. "That is why Grandma Edie invited him here!" She turned back to Juliet. "Isn't it? We are right, aren't we? We have been all along!"

"Do you truly think so?" Anne inquired, saving Juliet from having to conjure an answer out of nowhere. "Why then does she send him on so many errands? Whatever they are."

"But who else could it be?" Harriet threw in, her gaze narrowed as she watched Juliet try not to squirm where she stood. "Or we're wrong and—?" She broke off and frowned. "Why can't you tell us where you went these past few days and why?"

Juliet heaved a deep sigh as she found herself the focus of five sets of eyes. "I'm sorry I cannot," she mumbled, worried the pulse hammering in her neck might give her away. Her sisters knew her well. Was it even possible that they would believe her?

As a collective, all their shoulders slumped. "I never knew you to be one who kept secrets," Louisa grumbled, shaking her head disappointedly. Still, Juliet could not shake the feeling that her sister seemed oddly pleased with Juliet's answer.

Once again, Juliet felt as though she did not see something that was right in front of her. As though there was a secret, and she was the only one unaware of it.

"Let's change the topic," Anne suggested with a compassionate smile at Juliet.

Juliet inclined her head to her gratefully as she carefully stepped down from the pedestal, uncertain if she truly ought to wear this gown to the ball the next day.

"Is Sarah coming tomorrow?" Anne asked, seating herself next to Christina on Juliet's bed.

Christina's face darkened. "I wrote to invite her, of course, but—"

"Only her?" Leonora interrupted with a raised brow.

"Of course not," Christina replied with a huff. "I asked Mother to address the invitation to her parents, but I suppose it did not make a difference. They will not let her come here, believing us responsible for their failed marriage plans."

"I'm sorry," Harriet said with a sigh. "I—"

"Don't be sorry," Christina interjected, placing a hand upon her sister's. "You kept Sarah from being sold into a marriage to a most awful man, a man who belonged behind bars if indeed English law saw fit to punish his kind."

Leonora's face fell at the mention of her attacker, and the sisters quickly moved on. "If only she could attend," Christina murmured. "It would have been the perfect opportunity to introduce her to Christopher."

Juliet's heart stumbled, and as she looked up, she found herself looking into Leonora's eyes. Her sister had not moved and did not say a word. Yet the look in her eyes spoke volumes.

"Then we must find some other way to have them meet," Louisa remarked in a tone that suggested that solution should have been obvious to everyone. "The next Season is—"

"We cannot wait that long," Christina interjected vehemently, fear for her friend tinging her voice. "Who knows whom her parents will choose next?"

"Should we simply speak to Christopher?" Harriet suggested with a shrug. "Perhaps he'd be willing to meet her. It would be much easier if we didn't have to maneuver both to a certain place. Perhaps with his cooperation, we—"

"No!" Juliet exclaimed without thinking, shock slamming into her with an overwhelming force as her sisters turned to stare at her with wide eyes. "I…I mean…" She swallowed, trying her best to ignore the contemplative looks on her sisters' and cousin's faces. "I feel quite fatigued. Would you mind if we continued this conversation tomorrow?"

Or never.

Although Juliet could have sworn she saw suspicion and perhaps even a spark of triumph light up her sisters' eyes, they complied without another question, once again looking oddly pleased.

Perhaps she was imagining things. After all, the last few days had been rather eventful, and she did feel exhausted.

In more ways than one.

After the others had filed out of Juliet's bedchamber, their voices still echoing to her ears as they moved down the corridor, Leonora paused on the threshold, her blue eyes returning to meet Juliet's. "I believe you finally know what you want," Leonora whispered with a gentle smile on her face.

Juliet sighed. "If only I knew what he wanted."

"Then ask him," Leonora advised, squeezing Juliet's hand encouragingly before following the others.

Closing the door behind herself, Juliet closed her eyes, resting her head against the smooth wood. Did she know? So much had happened, and Juliet had not had the time to process it all. Had Christopher's confession changed anything about how she felt about him? Could she accept his son in her life? Christopher loved him; that much she was absolutely certain of.

Little Sebastian.

Juliet smiled despite the tension that held her in its talons. What did he look like? Did he have Christopher's kind brown eyes? Perhaps even his namesake's unruly hair? Or did he look like his mother?

Alice was her name.

Moving over to the window, Juliet looked out at the horizon and watched as darkness slowly fell over the world. Could she be a mother to another woman's child? The thought instantly conjured an image of little Samantha as the girl flung herself into Christina's arms.

Yes, perhaps she could. Perhaps she ought to speak to her sister and ask her counsel. If anyone could understand, it would be Christina. Yet...if she did, what was she to say without revealing all that had happened?

Juliet sighed and rested her heated forehead against the cool windowpane. Never had she kept secrets from her family. Yet she had never breathed a word to anyone about how she felt about Christopher. Admittedly, it had not felt like a lie or even an omission at the time, for she had not even admitted her true feelings to herself, afraid of the consequences.

Only now, everything was different. Christopher loved her, and she loved him. Should life not be simple now? Did love mean that he wished to marry her? Did love mean that she could also love his child?

His, but not hers.

Every child deserved love, and Juliet knew she could not be selfish if it brought heartache to an innocent little soul. Too well did she remember Christopher's suffering because of his parents' neglect, their disapproval, as though their hearts had never opened to him. Was it possible that hers would never open to little Sebastian? How was she to know?

Heaving a deep sigh, Juliet rang for her maid to assist her out of this monstrosity of a gown. As beautiful as it was, she did not feel like herself in it.

CHAPTER TWENTY-SIX
A LETTER

"What kind of a husband do you hope for, Jules?"

At the sound of Harriet's voice, Christopher pulled to a sudden halt outside the drawing room. Another step, and he would stand in its doorway. As it was, no one inside was currently aware of his presence just around the corner.

"H-Husband?" Juliet stuttered, and Christopher felt his heart constrict painfully, the pain over thinking her betrothed to Mr. MacKinnear still too fresh.

"Yes, husband," Christina laughed, and Christopher heard footsteps as someone moved through the room. "We promise—all of us—that we will do what we can to give you the same chance we had. I know Grandmother can be a bit...challenging, but together, we shall break her hold on you."

"But...But...," came Juliet's breathless stammer.

"Don't worry about Grandmother," their cousin counseled, a soft note in her voice. "I know you always worry and think it your responsibility to see to her. But you're not alone. We're all here to see to her. It falls not only on you. She is our grandmother as well, and we love her just the same."

"You see?" Louisa inquired with a hint of triumph in her voice, like someone on the brink of winning an argument. "There is nothing holding you back. At tonight's ball, we shall do all that we can to see you dance with each and every eligible gentleman so that you can take your pick."

Ice and fire swept through Christopher at the thought, shock and anger. He was close to charging into the room and claim Juliet for his own. Yet at the last moment, he held himself back.

This was a decision Juliet needed to make. After all, if she accepted him, she would not only gain a husband, but a child as well. Never would Christopher do to Sebastian what his parents had done to him with their disinterest. No, he needed Juliet to love his son. But would she be able to? It was not something to be decided on a whim. She needed time to think this through and figure out how she truly felt about the future he wanted them to have.

"Perhaps...Perhaps," came Juliet's shaky voice again, "I do not wish to marry. Did you never think of that?"

Christopher breathed out a sigh of relief, hoping that her answer meant what he hoped it did.

Harriet laughed. "I'm afraid you might not have a say in this. The Whickertons are destined to have great loves, and not even I could escape that fate." Again, she laughed, happiness and affection ringing in her voice.

"Very true," Louisa agreed, and the sisters continued to discuss the ball, now only a few hours away. Plans were made and gentlemen discussed. What allowed Christopher to not lose his mind was that Juliet remained rather quiet throughout the whole conversation, a most unwilling participant. Could it be that it was because of him? She loved him, did she not? Did it mean that she was considering marriage despite everything he had confessed to her?

Christopher frowned, realizing rather belatedly that she could not possibly know his intentions as he had never declared them.

Not outright.

Not to her.

Not with words that left no doubt.

A grave oversight. One that ought to be corrected without delay.

Christopher paused. "As should another," he mumbled under his breath, then quietly turned upon his heel and walked down the corridor that led to the study, the place where Troy could be found at any hour of the day. It seemed his old friend did little else lately but pour over ledgers detailing the upkeep of Whickerton Grove and other properties.

Stopping outside the door, Christopher heaved a deep breath, knowing that Troy would be furious once he learned the truth. Still, there no longer was a reason—a good reason—to keep this from him. Perhaps he ought to have told his friend long ago. Would it have eased his mind? Or would it just have brought on more torture?

Christopher did not know. Now, however, it was too late to ponder such questions. The past was what it was. All he could do now was try his best to ensure that the happiness that had been denied Troy once would perhaps find him after all.

Giving a quick knock, Christopher waited for his friend's voice to bid him to enter. Then he swung open the door and stepped across the threshold, his eyes falling on the familiar image of Troy seated behind the large desk, eyes slightly narrowed, and his forehead creased with frown lines. "Do you have a moment?" Christopher asked, closing the door behind him with a shaky hand. "There is something rather...important I need to discuss with you." Indeed, the words seemed shockingly insignificant to describe what he was about to say.

Troy regarded him carefully. He set down the quill and closed the ledger. Then he pushed to his feet, his pale blue eyes watchful. "Is it about my sister?"

Christopher stepped up to the desk, meeting his friend's eyes. "No," he said then, surprised by the steadiness he heard in his voice. "It is about mine."

Instantly, Troy's jaw hardened. He clenched his teeth, and Christopher thought he would start shaking his head vehemently at any moment, the resistance within him to discuss this matter more powerful than his need to uphold pretenses.

Yet he did not, and Christopher realized how tightly Troy controlled his emotions, never once revealing how much he suffered.

In the end, all his friend said was, "There is nothing to discuss." His eyes fell back to the ledger upon his desk as he moved from one side to the other. "I would appreciate it if you—"

"No!" At the harsh exclamation, Troy's head snapped up, and he stared at Christopher. "No, I will not remain silent any longer. There is something you need to know, something I've been meaning to tell you for years." He heaved a deep sigh. "I kept quiet before because I saw your reluctance and knew that even if I told you, there was nothing that could be done…for either one of you."

A muscle in Troy's jaw twitched, his eyes hard and unyielding. "Whatever you think I need to know—"

Christopher shook his head. "I will not leave this room until I've said all I need to say. I've kept quiet for too long with regard to so many things. Nothing good ever comes from not telling the truth."

A look of exhaustion came to Troy's eyes, and his shoulders slumped. "Why?" He blinked, and the hard look fell from his face. "Why now? Why can you not simply leave it be?"

"Because things have changed," Christopher insisted, stepping closer until the tips of his fingers came to rest upon the desk. He held his friend's gaze, willing him to listen, to open his mind and not shut out this chance for happiness. "She's no longer married, and I believe she cares for you as you care for—"

Troy's fist came down hard on the desk, his face contorted into a snarl. "It does not matter!" he growled, and his hands shook with anger. "Whatever you think I need to know will not change that she—"

"I never gave her your letter!"

At Christopher's words, Troy all but reeled backwards as though he had received a punch to the jaw. His face went white, and his eyes opened so wide, revealed such shock that Christopher cringed at the sight of it.

"I'm so sorry," Christopher said, knowing that words could never describe how awful he felt, how awful he had felt ever since realizing what his oversight, his distraction had done to people he cared for deeply. "Please let me explain. I never meant for this to happen."

Staring at him, Troy slowly sank back into his chair, his expression still blank. Yet Christopher could not help but think that he saw the occasional spark of something, some deeper emotion light up his eyes every so often. As much as Troy had tried his best to silence all he felt, some remnant seemed to have remained.

Taking his friend's silence as encouragement, Christopher cleared his throat. "When you handed me the letter and asked me to give it to Nora, I had no idea what it said."

Troy's eyes snapped up, the glower of accusation in them.

"I did not read it! I assure you," Christopher clarified quickly. "I don't know what it says even now, but from what I have observed, I assume—"

"Why?" Troy growled; his eyes hard as they glared at Christopher. "Why did you—?" His voice broke off, his lips sealing shut as though the words simply would not make it past them.

"I assure you I had every intention of giving it to her," Christopher continued his story, remembering with haunting clarity the commotion that had lingered upon the house that day, Nora's wedding day. "I was on my way to see her, but then a servant approached me with some problem. Apparently, my mother had failed to give specific instructions and now they were uncertain how to—"

"Get to the point!"

Christopher nodded. "Anyhow, I spoke to my mother, and when she went off to see to matters, I glimpsed...something on her writing desk." Christopher still wondered now and then if his mother would have ever told him about his son if he had not found out on his own. "It was a letter informing her of my son's birth. It was dated a few weeks back, and yet I had never seen it." Pleadingly, he looked at Troy, wanting nothing more but his friend's forgiveness and understanding, knowing equally well that it would be almost impossible for Troy to give. "Everything changed for me in that moment. All I could think about was that...I had to see him."

Raking his hand through his hair, Christopher walked over to the window, his gaze drawn to the gardens where he had spent most of his childhood and youth. "I almost ran out of the house then and there, my only thought for him, my son." He swallowed hard. "As fate would have it, it was my mother who spotted me hastening through the foyer. She called out to me, and...I confronted her." He scoffed, shaking his head at the memory of her incomprehensible face. "She could not understand why it bothered me, why I would want to see him. She told me not to be foolish, berating me for my poor judgment and flawed behavior. But I didn't care. I knew I needed to go. I needed to see him." He turned back around to face his friend, finding Troy's wide gaze locked upon his. "She tried to stop me, and the only thing that gave me pause was the reminder of my sister's wedding."

Troy's jaw tensed, and his fingers dug into the chair's armrests.

"I left the moment she was married," Christopher concluded his recounting of that day. "Your letter completely slipped my mind. I did not know how urgent it was or what you wished to tell her. At least not at that point. Later, much later, when I returned home and learned of your disappearance, how you had vanished the day of Nora's wedding, when I saw her face upon my next visit, the pieces slowly began to come together. All of a sudden, I remembered your letter, and I realized what it must contain." Christopher threw up his hands in a helpless gesture. "But what was I to do? She was married, and any chance you might've had was lost. I wanted to tell you, but I wondered if perhaps it would simply make things worse for you. For the both of you. So...I never said a word, not to you or to her." He inhaled a deep breath and once again stepped toward the desk, his eyes fixed on Troy's. "Until now."

Troy's head sank, and his eyes closed. He rested his head in his hands and sighed, a sound that revealed all the regret and pain and anger and longing he had held bottled up all these years.

Leaning forward, Christopher braced his hands upon the desk. "So, you see? Things have changed in a way that matters. She never refused you. She never chose another over you. This truly is a chance for the two of you to find out what you could have." He shook his head. "I don't know what happened between you both. I don't know how you suddenly...I never saw you be anything else but friends and never for a second thought that that could change one day." In that moment, Christopher could not help but wonder if perhaps Troy had looked at him and Juliet the same way. Had they all been blind to the truth? "But if you care for her, as I suspect she cares for you, don't let this chance slip through your fingers. Go to her. Tell her everything you wanted her to know that day all those years ago."

Troy's eyes were expressionless as he stared at Christopher, stared at him without seeing him. For a long moment, silence lingered, and Christopher wondered if his friend would ever forgive him. Yet that was not what mattered. What mattered was that Troy and Nora might receive a second chance. Just as he and Juliet had found. And he would not waste it. No, this time, he would fight for her. He would do what he could to make her understand how much she meant to him.

Christopher could only hope that Troy would do the same.

CHAPTER TWENTY-SEVEN

KIT & JULES

Once again, Juliet found herself laced into this monstrosity of a dress, her hair fancifully styled and gems glittering around her neck. It felt wrong. It looked wrong.

Not like herself.

As though she was pretending to be another.

As though the woman she was, simply was not good enough.

Was that true? Would she only ever have a suitor if she pretended to be someone she was not?

What about Christopher? Would he like her like this?

As much as Juliet wanted to ignore tonight's ball, her sisters would not be swayed. They seemed incapable of hearing her objections—as feeble as they were—themselves too eager to see her as happily matched as they were, insisting on dolling her up until Juliet no longer recognized herself. She wanted to protest with more vehemence, to argue against their plans, but she could not.

Not without revealing too much.

Most of all, she needed to speak to Christopher. Yet the day had passed, and she had not caught more than a few glimpses of him. The entire house was abuzz with preparations. She, herself, had spent all day assisting her mother, then found herself drawn into one conversation after another about who could possibly be a suitable match for her and how she was to procure his attentions. Juliet's head spun by the time evening fell and her sisters drew her upstairs to dress. If only she could feign a headache; however, Juliet was fairly certain that her sisters would never fall for that.

Still, their insistence felt odd. Why now? Why the sudden desire to see her matched? Was it simply because they themselves were now married? Juliet could not recall her sisters making such an effort ever before. Certainly, they had commented upon their grandmother's insistence on keeping Juliet by her side. They had wondered and speculated, but they had never shown such efforts to interfere.

A knock sounded on her door, and Juliet flinched, afraid that her sisters had returned, determined to add yet another shiny trinket to her appearance.

"Jules?" came a whispered voice through the door, and Juliet recognized it instantly, her heart speeding up as she hastened toward the door.

A moment later, Christopher pushed into the room, casting another careful look over his shoulder before he closed it again. "I'm sorry. I know I shouldn't be here, but I had to—" His voice broke off as his eyes fell on her, first widening in something resembling surprise before they narrowed once more, squinting at her as though she were an odd specimen and he the scientist completely caught off guard by what he saw.

"What are you wearing?" Christopher asked as his gaze swept over her from head to toe.

"A dress," Juliet replied simply, momentarily confused by his reaction. Was he—like herself—merely confused by this unusual choice in wardrobe that her sisters pressured on her? Was that his only objection?

Never in her life had Juliet desired to be beautiful. Never had something so superficial mattered to her. Yet, here in this moment, she wanted Christopher to look at her and...think her beautiful.

Christopher cocked an eyebrow at her as he searched her eyes. "It was not your choice, was it?"

Juliet smiled, delighted that he knew her so well, could see upon her face how she felt. "It was not. Yet how would you know?"

Christopher shrugged; yet his teeth ground together for a brief moment. "I might have overheard your sisters...urging you to contemplate taking a husband." His gaze drilled into hers. "They seem very invested in this new project of theirs."

Juliet could not help but notice that Christopher had not asked her a question. Yet the look in his eyes told her all she needed to know. "Are you jealous?" she whispered boldly, surprising even herself.

A sharp breath rushed from Christopher's lips as he stepped forward, his hands seizing her waist. "You're m—" He broke off, swallowed hard and then began again, his brown eyes almost black in their intensity. "I want you to be mine." His hands tightened upon her waist, and Juliet drew in a shaky breath as her knees threatened to turn to water. "As I have always been yours." He held her gaze, perhaps to let his words sink in or to receive a reply.

Juliet, however, could not muster a single word. Her hands reached out and grasped his arms as her world began to spin. Her heart was pounding against her ribs, and her breath came fast. She would not faint again, would she? Never had she known herself to have such a weak constitution.

"Are you all right?" Christopher asked, urgency and concern in his voice as he grasped her chin and looked deep into her eyes. "You look as though you might faint again."

Juliet chuckled. "It only happens around you."

A slow smile came to Christopher's face, and his arm around her middle urged her closer against him. "Is that a reproach?" he asked with a chuckle. "Do you want me to stay away?"

"Never," Juliet whispered, surprised to find her arms snake around his neck. "I want you to stay close."

"How close?" Christopher murmured as he lowered his head down to hers, his breath fanning against her lips. "Like this? Or...closer?"

"Closer," Juliet replied without a moment of hesitation. How she had remained nothing but friends with Christopher for years was beyond her now. All of a sudden, close was not nearly close enough.

His hand slipped to the back of her head, his fingers brushing against her skin as he pressed closer still. "Look at me," Christopher whispered, his dark gaze filled with such longing that it brought tears to Juliet's eyes. "I love you, and I want you to be my wife. I know there is more to be said, and I'm not expecting an answer right now. I will ask you again and I will do it right. I promise." He cast her a quick smile, knowing that any moment now they might be interrupted. "I simply...needed you to know."

Juliet felt her head begin to spin again, wondering if it could possibly be a sign of happiness. Odd that she had never felt it before, at least not like this.

Christopher glanced at the door. "I know your sisters are planning something, and I..." He swallowed, and his gaze darted to her lips. Then he suddenly dipped his head and kissed her.

Juliet's fingers curled into his coat sleeves, not caring if they also dug into flesh underneath. She needed to hold on to something as her knees threatened to buckle. She did not need to worry though, for Christopher held her safely cradled in his arms as he kissed her with the same longing she had felt in his kiss before.

Again, his words echoed through her head, no longer fleeting sounds without meaning. Now, she managed to grasp hold of them, look at them and examine them until their significance washed over her with a clarity Juliet had never known.

Christopher loved her. He loved her as she loved him, and he wished to marry her. Of course, he was right. A lot more needed to be said, but what mattered most no longer remained unspoken.

"I love you as well," Juliet replied on a gasp as she looked up into Christopher's beloved face. "I've loved you all my life. First as a friend, and now..." Tears rose in her eyes, and she quickly blinked them away.

"Are you saying you will marry me?" Christopher asked with a smile, gently brushing a tear from her cheek.

Unable to speak, Juliet nodded. Then she reached up and pulled him down into another kiss. Words failed her, yet there were other ways to make him understand that he had always held her heart and always would.

CHAPTER TWENTY-EIGHT

THE AUTUMN BALL

Christopher was almost deliriously happy. For the first time in his life, everything seemed to come together the way it should. Of course, he had known moments of happiness before; however, what he felt right here in this moment after Juliet had consented to become his wife was...indescribable.

Like Troy, he had been a fool not to act sooner, allowing his doubts to dissuade him from a course he ought to have taken years ago. Indeed, nothing good ever came from hiding the truth. Deep down, he had known so; yet doubts were a powerful obstacle, not easily mastered.

But no more.

Now, more than ever before, Christopher was determined to get everything out into the open, to speak honestly and tell the truth. Surely, consequences would follow, not all of which would be pleasant to bear; yet the alternative was not acceptable. He needed to speak to Juliet again, share his thoughts, his wishes and hopes. However, first they somehow needed to get through this ball.

Christopher's eyes narrowed slightly as he watched Juliet set foot into the ballroom, surrounded by a swarm of sisters. Again, Christopher could not help but notice how eager they seemed, whispering to her as well as each other, occasionally pointing or nodding toward a gentleman and then whispering some more. Clearly, they had a design to see Juliet catch the eye of a gentleman who might one day become her husband.

Gritting his teeth, Christopher squared his shoulders. He had designs of his own, and he would see them realized no matter what it might take.

The ballroom was a flurry of movements, people dancing and conversing, hurrying across from one end to the other, greeting acquaintances and sharing secrets behind fans. Candles in chandeliers and sconces cast a warm glow over the large room as the orchestra played, a lively melody drifting to Christopher's ears.

Juliet still wore the brilliantly green gown he had seen on her only moments earlier; however, she had removed the emeralds from around her neck and replaced them with a thin gold necklace, elegant and simple. Her hair, too, seemed less forced into a certain style, but rather swept up, still falling in waves as tendrils danced down to her shoulders. She looked beautiful.

She looked like herself, the way Christopher had always seen her. That shy look in her eyes as she lifted them off the floor, then looked across the ballroom and saw him. A small smile came to her face, and he watched it brighten, bit by bit, the effect sending sparks of delight through his being.

"You are still here," a familiar voice exclaimed beside him, and Christopher turned around to find Juliet's brother-in-law, Lord Barrington—Phineas—standing there.

Christopher nodded. "I am. There are...unresolved matters as of yet." He was uncertain how to respond; after all, he hardly knew the man.

Lord Barrington, however, was not the least bit put out. Instead, a wide grin came to his face, and he chuckled. "I quite know what you mean. The Whickertons are a habit that is difficult to break, is that not so?" Something teasing flashed in his eyes.

Christopher frowned, wondering what the man was referring to. "I've known them all my life," he replied honestly, "but only recently I realized that they mean more to me than I even thought possible."

Lord Barrington nodded, then chuckled again. "It seems you are in high demand," he remarked, then turned, his gaze moving over the crowd toward the other side of the ballroom.

Frowning, Christopher followed his gaze and was surprised to see little Samantha on her father's arm hastening toward him, skipping in her steps as she went. For a moment, Christopher was surprised to find her gaze fall on him, a bright smile upon her young face as she tugged her father onward. Then, however, he remembered that he had promised her a dance.

"Good evening." Mr. Sharpe, Christina's new husband and Samantha's father, greeted them before his gaze moved from Lord Barrington to Christopher. "I hear you promised my daughter a dance." Amusement lay in his gaze, but he smiled warmly as he looked down at his child.

Christopher felt a sudden pinch in his heart as he looked down at the adorable young girl. She was perhaps a little older than Sebastian, and a wave of longing washed over him. As much as he loved being here, with Juliet, with the Whickertons, he needed to return to his son soon.

Bowing low, Christopher smiled at her and held out his hand. "Will you grant me the honor of this dance, Miss Sharpe?"

Little Samantha giggled, then took his hand. "It would be my pleasure," she said, carefully pronouncing each word.

Christopher was well aware of the confused and surprised whispers as he escorted Samantha onto the dance floor. Yet he did not care. He loved how the Whickertons had welcomed Samantha into their family and into their lives, including her on this special night and granting the girl her heart's wish. Would they do so for Sebastian as well? If Christopher got his wish and one day found himself married to Juliet, would Sebastian be equally welcomed here?

Christopher did not doubt it. After all, the Whickertons were not like his own parents. They had never put reputation and standing above their children's happiness. It had taken Christopher a long time to realize that his parents simply were the people they were. Their decisions had nothing to do with him or what he had done or not done. All he could do was choose according to his own conscience, his own heart.

"You are a most remarkable dancer, Miss Sharpe," Christopher complimented the young girl, surprised to see her follow the steps with such ease, her eyes shining with utter delight.

"Thank you, my lord," she giggled, then waved to her mother and father, their eyes aglow with parental pride as they watched their young daughter. The rest of the Whickertons bore similar expressions.

Christopher wished he could tell Sam about his son; but the time had not come yet.

Soon though.

When the dance ended, Christopher escorted his future niece—hopefully!—back to her parents, who welcomed her with open arms and showered her with words of praise. "Grandfather, did you see how I danced?" the girl exclaimed as her father set her back on her feet.

Lord Whickerton nodded, a deep smile upon his face. "I certainly did." He held out his hand to her. "Would you grant me the honor of the next one?"

"Certainly, my lord," Samantha exclaimed with great poise, dropping into a perfect curtesy. "It would be my pleasure."

Everyone smiled, oohing and aahing as Lord Whickerton led his granddaughter onto the dance floor. Christopher looked up and met Juliet's gaze, a longing smile upon her face as she watched the little girl go. Then she sighed and her gaze moved to meet his.

"What about him?" Harriet asked all of a sudden, tugging upon Juliet's arm and nodding across the room. "His name is...Lord Parkhurst, I believe. Does he appeal to you?"

Christopher tensed as he watched Juliet heave a deep sigh. "I'm afraid not," she replied in a rather fatigued tone, then cast a tentative look in his direction.

Harriet huffed out an exasperated breath and exchanged a meaningful look with Christina. "I must say you don't seem the least bit interested in catching the eye of anyone."

Juliet shrugged. "Well, I suppose I'm not."

Leaning on her cane, Grandma Edie watched the exchange with equal interest before Christopher realized that the dowager was not watching her two granddaughters at all, but him and Juliet as they continued to glance at one another.

"How are you this fine evening?" Christopher addressed her with a smile, wondering if the dowager suspected more than she had been told.

The knowing smile that came to her face suggested that she did. "I see my efforts have already born fruit," she chuckled, sidling closer so as not to be overheard.

Christopher frowned. "Your efforts?"

"Am I correct in assuming that matters have progressed between you and my granddaughter?" Her brows rose meaningfully. "If so, her sisters can save their breath."

Still frowning, Christopher looked up, for the first time noting the way Juliet's sisters seemed to act as one. It almost appeared as though they were taking turns pointing out eligible bachelors or asking her what kind of gentleman would suit her.

"What are you talking about?" Christopher asked, eyeing the dowager curiously. "I thought you wanted to see Juliet matched with Mr. MacKinnear." His gaze briefly darted to the tall Scot, who stood across the room, looking mildly bored.

Grandma Edie laughed wickedly. "What gave you that idea?"

Christopher huffed out an annoyed breath. "You told me so!" He cleared his throat as two of the sisters turned to look at him following his outburst.

"Did I?" the dowager surmised with a furrowed brow. "I cannot quite recall..." Her voice trailed off as though she truly did not remember; the shrewd look in her eyes, however, spoke loud and clear.

Christopher shook his head. "Why would you tell me Mr. MacKinnear was intended for her when—?"

"Because the fear of losing someone we love is a powerful motivator," the dowager replied, her pale eyes looking up into his. "Would you not agree?"

Christopher swallowed. "You knew that I...and so you...?"

Grandma Edie nodded, then reached out and patted his arm. "You looked like you could use some help deciding, dear boy."

"And so, you let me believe that she—?" Closing his eyes, Christopher inhaled a deep breath. "And Juliet? What is the point of having her sisters parade one gentleman after another in front of her?"

The dowagers shrugged. "Sometimes realizing what we don't want helps us understand what it is we do want."

Stunned by the dowager's words, Christopher turned to look at Juliet. It was as though she could feel his gaze upon her and turned to look. Her green eyes sparkled as they looked into his, and Christopher felt his heart skip a beat as his breath shuddered past his lips. She was breathtaking!

Quite literally!

"Go and ask the girl for a dance," Grandma Edie instructed with a nod of her head. "I've been chasing away suitors for the past six years, and frankly, I'm tired of it."

Chuckling, Christopher looked at the dowager, only now realizing what she had done for him. If it weren't for her, he probably would have found Juliet married upon his return to England. "Th-Thank you," he stammered, unable to find the words to express how utterly grateful he was for her interference.

Smiling, she patted his arm. "I knew you'd eventually come to your senses, dear boy." A bit of a glower came to her pale eyes. "Took you long enough, though."

Christopher wanted to hug her. Instead, he bowed low before turning around, eyes fixed upon the woman he loved, and took a step into his future.

CHAPTER TWENTY-NINE

THE LADY DANCES

With her hand on Christopher's arm, Juliet moved onto the dance floor. It was an odd feeling, and she half expected her grandmother to interfere, to ask her to bring her some lemonade or assist her into a chair. After all, whenever a gentleman had asked for a dance over the past few years —as seldom as it had happened—her grandmother had always interfered.

Each and every time.

"You look confused?" Christopher remarked as he pulled her into his arms. "Do you not wish to dance? If not, we can—"

"No, I do wish to dance," Juliet assured him, realizing how much she longed for it. Before, it had never mattered to her because the ones who had asked had been nothing more than mere acquaintances. But this was Christopher! And she wanted to dance with him. "With you. Only with you."

The smile that came to Christopher's face made her feel weak in the knees, and his hands instantly held her tighter, as though he knew.

Perhaps he did.

"I saw you dance with Samantha," Juliet remarked, remembering the warmth that had swept through her at the sight, the way he had spoken to the girl, twirled her around, the joy in his eyes as well as the longing, no doubt for his own child.

"She's adorable."

Juliet nodded. "So are you. You are a wonderful father. I can tell." Despite her lack of practice, in Christopher's arms, she moved effortlessly across the dance floor. "You miss him terribly, do you not?"

Swallowing, Christopher nodded. "I need to return to Ireland," he replied earnestly, "but first, I need to speak to you." He glanced past her toward her family. "Do you think we can sneak away?"

Happiness surged through Juliet, and she smiled. "Oh, please, let's! Before my sisters drag over another gentleman. If only I knew who they wish to match me with; yet there seems to be no one in particular. Do they not care who—?" She broke off as she saw a wickedly enchanting glow come to Christopher's face. "What is it?"

Smiling, Christopher once more glanced beyond her shoulder. "I know who they are trying to match you with."

A shudder went through Juliet, and her hand tensed upon his. "Who?" she asked breathlessly, uncertain whether she wanted to hear the answer.

A wide grin came to Christopher's face as he lowered his head to hers another fraction. His warm brown eyes looked into hers, and Juliet could not help but feel that whatever he was about to say...would be welcome news after all. "Me," he finally said, a disbelieving chuckle rumbling in his throat. "They're trying to match you with me."

Stunned, Juliet stared up at him. "No, that can't be true. Not once did they suggest..." She shook her head, still staring at him. "But you said that grandmother told you that..." Confusion entangled her thoughts, and Juliet no longer knew how to express them.

"It was a ploy," Christopher explained, amusement dancing in his eyes. "It seems your grandmother has known for years how I feel about you, how you feel about me. She was determined to ensure you would not marry another until I finally realized that you belonged with me."

Juliet felt her jaw drop, remembering all those times when her grandmother had prevented her from stepping out into the world, from dancing and conversing with potential suitors. "Are you certain?"

Christopher nodded. "She confessed it to me herself. Apparently, she recently even enlisted the help of your sisters to ensure that this time around we would finally realize that we belong together."

Christopher's words once more conjured her sisters' discussion about matching Sarah with a good man, a man who conveniently had been Christopher. Juliet still recalled how her heart had ached at the possibility of losing Christopher to another, even to a friend. "They wanted to make me jealous," she exclaimed in a whisper, disbelief flooding her being. "They spoke of matching you to a friend of ours and I...I..."

Christopher grinned. "You were jealous?" Delight stood upon his face.

Juliet sighed. "Yes, I was. Does that surprise you?"

"It pleases me," he whispered the moment the music faded away, and the dance came to an end. "Come with me. Now." He grasped her arm, and together, they hurried out of the ballroom and along a darkened corridor.

Juliet felt her heart beat wildly in her chest, reveling in the receding voices coming from the ballroom. Shadows wrapped around them, guiding them onward, the only sound now the echo of their footsteps. Then Christopher threw open the door to the library and drew her inside.

Fortunately, a fire burned in the grate, its orange flames dancing like the guests in the ballroom and its waves of warmth chasing away the night's chill. Juliet was about to move toward it when Christopher's hand on her arm pulled her back and into his embrace.

Pushing her against the door, he moved closer, his eyes almost black in the dim light. "I cannot stop thinking about kissing you," he whispered, his voice hoarse as he leaned his forehead against hers.

Juliet reached to touch his face, feeling the tantalizing warmth of his breath against her lips. "I feel the same," she replied with a gasp as he tenderly grasped her chin and tilted up her head.

"May I?" Christopher asked, the yearning look in his eyes stealing the breath from her lungs.

"Always," was all Juliet managed to say before his mouth claimed hers. Never would she tire of this feeling, and the thought that she might never have known it twisted and turned her insides painfully.

Only a few weeks ago, Juliet had been certain of her path. She had been certain she would never be a wife and mother, urging herself to be content with being an aunt and a daughter. She remembered well how her sisters had discussed their first kisses. Had that already been part of her grandmother's plan? Had she sought to make Juliet realize her own lies?

Indeed, it had been that day that Juliet had blurted out her request to Christopher, that day that she had asked him for a kiss. It had set everything in motion, had it not?

Clinging to the man she loved, Juliet remembered her sisters' words, their recounting of their first kisses with their husbands. Yes, Juliet had been forced to be patient, to wait until she had all but given up hope.

But it had been worth it.

When it had finally come, their first kiss had been achingly beautiful. They had just confessed their love for each other, and the way they had fallen into each other's arms had whispered of the separation that circumstances had forced upon them. Yes, they had lost time, but perhaps they had needed that time to become the people they were today, only now realizing how deeply they cared for one another.

"I love the way you kiss," Christopher whispered against her lips, the tips of his fingers grazing her skin as he brushed a curl behind her ear.

Feeling herself blush, Juliet chuckled. "You're an awful tease." With her teeth digging into her lower lip, she looked up at him.

"I mean every word," Christopher rasped, then dipped his head and kissed her again. "I don't ever want to see you from my arms."

Juliet smiled against his lips. "I'm happy to stay where I am until the end of my days." She pulled him closer.

"That sounds like an impeccable plan."

"I'm very proud of it," Juliet managed to reply before another kiss claimed her lips. Holding him close, she could have happily died in that moment.

CHAPTER THIRTY

A PROPOSAL

Christopher could have kissed Juliet for the rest of the night, but he knew that unresolved matters still existed between them. Matters he needed to address before he could formally ask for her hand in marriage.

Breaking their kiss, Christopher moved his hands from her soft curves to the unyielding door in her back. "As much as I want to continue," he whispered, looking down into her sparkling green eyes, "there is something we need to talk about."

Drawing in a steadying breath, Juliet nodded. "I know."

Removing his hands from the door, Christopher stepped back, then gently took her hand and guided her over to the fire. There, they sat down upon the settee. "I love you, Jules," Christopher said without preamble, delighting in the smile that came to her face, "and I wish to marry you, but..." He swallowed, then heaved a deep sigh, his insides tensing. "I cannot place my happiness above my son's." His eyes sought hers. "I hope you can understand that."

Juliet reached to grasp his hands. "Of course. Of course, you cannot. I would never ask that of you."

"I know." He cast her a tentative smile. "I know I hurt you, and for that, I am deeply sorry." He squeezed her hands tightly. "Do you think...? Is there any chance you could...?" Christopher could not find the words or perhaps the courage to ask the question that might separate them once again.

A gentle smile blossomed on Juliet's lips, and the look in her eyes held something almost wise. "I know what you're asking, and I need to tell you honestly that a part of me is...upset," she swallowed, "that you have a child that is not mine as well."

Christopher nodded. "I would be as well," he admitted, the mere thought of Juliet bearing another's child a torture he was not strong enough to endure. "I do not blame you if you cannot—"

"What about...Alice?" Juliet asked, her features tense. "Is she still a part of your life?"

Christopher shook his head. "I have not seen her in years. She received...fair compensation and then disappeared."

Juliet inhaled a slow breath, and, for a moment, her eyes became distant. Then she blinked and her eyes found his once more. "I want to be Sebastian's mother."

Christopher stilled, uncertain if he had heard her correctly. "You...?"

Juliet nodded. "He is your son, and I want him to be mine as well. I want him to be ours. It is my only condition. Can you agree to it?"

Pulling her into his arms, Christopher closed his eyes. "Yes," he murmured into her hair. "Yes, I agree." He sat back and looked into her eyes. "It is what I want as well." He frowned. "Are you certain?"

Placing a gentle kiss upon his lips, Juliet nodded. "Seeing you tonight with Samantha made me realize that I would be a fool to refuse your son, a precious little child who deserves happiness more than anyone else in this world." She took his hand. "I want you to bring him back here."

Christopher stilled. "What?" In all honesty, he had yet to think of where they would go from here—geographically speaking. Always had he seen his future in Ireland. But now?

Juliet nodded. "I remember well how your parents' disapproval and rejection hurt you, Kit. It made you feel unwanted and unloved, and you did not deserve to feel like that." Gently, she cupped her hand to his cheek. "Neither does he." The softness in her voice vanished, replaced by something fierce. "I do not want him to feel rejected. Yes, I know society will frown upon his existence, but that is all the more reason for us not to hide him away. He is a child now, but he will grow up, and one day, he might come to think that we are ashamed of him." She shook her head, her jaw set in determination. "There are always people who disapprove." A faint chuckle left her lips. "Heaven knows that my family has pushed the boundaries, even leaped over them, more than once. Yet nothing people say or do matters so long as we stand as one."

Touched by her words, Christopher nodded, belatedly realizing that tears stood in his eyes. "You're right," he murmured. "You're absolutely right." Then he sank down onto one knee and took her hands in his. "Jules, my Jules, will you do me the honor of accepting my hand?" He had meant to say more, but his throat closed up with the emotions her heartfelt declaration had roused.

Blinking back tears of her own, Juliet all but threw herself into his arms, almost knocking him over. "Yes," she sobbed. "Yes."

Half-sitting, half-kneeling on the floor in front of the fireplace, Christopher held his betrothed crushed in his arms as the joy of that moment brought more tears to his eyes. Only days ago, he had thought all hope lost, and now, here he was, with a future as bright as the most wonderful summer day ahead of him.

Yes, he would bring Sebastian home, and to hell with his mother. If she said one wrong word to his son—her grandson!—he would send her from the house. Juliet was right. Family stood together.

Now and always.

CHAPTER THIRTY-ONE

A BROTHER'S PAIN

Juliet flinched when she heard the distinct sound of a door sliding open drift to her ears. She was all but sitting in Christopher's lap and did not revel in the idea of a guest happening upon them like this.

Quickly, Juliet scrambled to her feet, her eyes meeting Christopher's as he, too, pushed off the floor. Tears still misted his eyes, and Juliet could see the emotional upheaval the previous moment had brought them both plainly upon his face. Indeed, it seemed he had never thought it possible that happiness could one day be theirs. Juliet knew what that felt like, for she, too, had all but given up hope, believing herself content—or perhaps simply convincing herself of it!

Now she knew better.

Squeezing Christopher's hand, Juliet turned toward the door and found none other but her own brother standing there, staring at them. Although Juliet would have expected Troy to be surprised, perhaps shocked even, the look of fury she saw on his face confused her. Why would he be this angry? After all, Christopher was his oldest friend. Long ago, they had been as close as brothers.

"Troy," came Christopher's strained voice from behind her, "please, let me explain."

As Christopher stepped up to her, Juliet looked over her shoulder at his face, surprised to see a glimmer of understanding in his eyes, as though he had fully expected Troy to react in this way.

"What did you do?" Troy growled as he moved into the room, his eyes flashing with anger as his teeth ground together, as though he had to fight for control.

Juliet felt as though her brother did not even see her, his gaze fixed upon Christopher. Anger—outrage even—rolled off him in waves, and belatedly Juliet realized that something had to have happened between them, something she was not aware of.

Christopher swallowed hard, a guilty expression on his face. "Nothing untoward happened, I assure you. We were merely talking and—"

Troy's lips thinned. "You'll excuse me," he spat, "if I do not take your word for it."

Behind her, Juliet felt Christopher shatter beneath Troy's hateful words and so she stepped toward her brother, placing her hands upon his rigid arms and looked up into his face. "Troy," she whispered, trying to make him see her through his anger as she looked to find the kind and caring brother she had always known. "Please, do not place blame on Christopher. He speaks the truth. Nothing happened." Despite the tension in the room, a small smile tugged upon Juliet's lips. "Well, perhaps that is not entirely true." Her smile widened, broadened. "We are betrothed. We truly are. Will you not give us your blessing?"

Beneath her hands, her brother's arms tensed, his muscles tightening as though he had just received life-shattering news. His pale blue eyes looked thunderous in the dim light of the room as his gaze fell from Christopher and dropped to look at her face. "You accepted him?"

Confused, Juliet searched Troy's face. "Of course, I did. I...I love him." Even though they had never spoken about this, Juliet had always thought that on some level, Troy knew how deeply she cared for his friend. Had he not seen how Christopher's departure from all their lives had shattered her? Somehow, Juliet had always thought that he had.

Troy's shoulders rose and fell with a deep breath as he stared at her, as though she had suddenly proclaimed the desire to join their armed forces on the continent. "You cannot marry him," he growled then, something untamed and wild flaring in his eyes. Gone was the calm and collected gentleman Troy had always been. He no longer spoke with reason and consideration; his words fueled by a rage that made no sense to Juliet.

"What happened between you?" Juliet asked, glancing over her shoulder at Christopher, seeing that guilty expression still on his face. "Why are you so angry?"

A muscle in Troy's jaw twitched. "He has a child. Did you know that? A son." The look in his eyes clearly told Juliet that his words were meant to shock her, to convince her to end this betrothal before it had even truly begun.

"I know," Juliet said quietly, confused by the disappointment that came to her brother's eyes; disappointment to see her remain at Christopher's side.

"You know?" he demanded, an aghast look upon his face.

"I told her everything," Christopher interjected as he stepped forward, his gaze touching upon Juliet's for a split second before he redirected his attention back to her brother. "She knows what happened, what I did." He sighed. "No more secrets."

"How can you forgive him for what he did?" Troy snarled, ignoring Christopher's attempt to mend fences.

Juliet grasped her brother's arm more tightly. "We all make mistakes," she said softly, praying that somehow her brother would understand. "I'm aware of what happened, of the circumstances back then, and I cannot hold what happened against him." Her eyes pleaded with him to hear her. "I love him, and I know he loves me as well. This is our chance to be happy...finally after all this time. Please, Brother, can you not be happy for me? For us?"

The blazing anger in Troy's eyes seemed to subside a little as confusion clawed to the forefront. His eyes searched her face, incomprehension visible in the frown that touched upon his forehead. "After everything he did," he hissed, the look in his eyes suddenly distant as though he was not even seeing her, "you still want him?"

Juliet sighed deeply. "I never forgot him. I tried, but I never could.

Whether or not we love is not our choice." She reached up and cupped her hand to his cheek. "But this, here, now is my choice. I want him. He is my choice, and I need you to be happy for me."

Suddenly, only sadness rested in Troy's eyes, deep, soul-crushing sadness. He heaved a deep sigh, then closed his eyes as though it were too painful for him to look at her.

Never had Juliet seen her brother like this. He had always been composed and in control, no unruly emotions sparking in his eyes, his voice even and calm. She had always thought of him as a rational man. Of course, he was not cold-hearted, far from it; however, she had always received the impression that he did not place much stock in emotions, thinking them less important somehow.

Perhaps she had been wrong.

"You should return to the ball," Troy gritted out through clenched teeth as he took a step away from her, her hand falling from his face. The look in his eyes now held nothing but resignation. It broke Juliet's heart to see her beloved brother like this. What had done this to him? Or perhaps rather...who?

"Troy," she called after him as he stepped up to the door, "have you...have you ever been in love?"

Troy stilled, and for a long moment, he said nothing. He barely moved, except for his shoulders moving with each breath he forced down into his lungs. Juliet did not know why, but she could not shake the feeling that he was in pain somehow. Then his hand settled on the door handle, and without turning around, he once more said, "You should return to the ball." Then he disappeared.

A deep breath rushed from Juliet's lungs, her earlier happiness darkened by the questions and concerns that now settled in her heart. She spun around, her hands reaching for Christopher's. His face still held that same guilty expression, now mingling with the same sorrow she herself felt. "What happened between the two of you?" she asked, searching his eyes. "I've never seen him like this. Something hurt him deeply." Her eyebrows rose as she looked deeper into Christopher's eyes. "Or was it someone? Not you," she murmured, thinking out loud. "He's furious with you, but you are not the one who hurt him. You're not the one who broke his—"

Juliet's heart seized with a sudden realization. "Nora!" she exclaimed, gripping Christopher's hands more tightly. "It's Nora, is it not?"

Sighing deeply, Christopher nodded. "I failed your brother," he admitted in a subdued voice, full of regret and self-reproach, "as I failed my sister." He heaved a deep sigh, then straightened his shoulders. "Years ago, it was the day of Nora's wedding, Troy came to me out of the blue and handed me a letter. He didn't tell me anything else, but just urged me to give it to her right away. I asked him what this was about, but he wouldn't say."

Juliet frowned. "You didn't, though, did you? What happened?"

Christopher cleared his throat. "Only moments after Troy handed me the letter and left, I all but stumbled upon another upon my mother's writing desk. Only this one announced my son's birth." He closed his eyes, his head shaking from side to side. "After that, my thoughts circled around only one thing: seeing my son." His eyes looked pleadingly into hers. "I never meant to forget Troy's letter. It..." He shrugged. "It slipped my mind. I was already on the road by the time I rediscovered it in my pocket. Had I known what it said, I would've...I would've..."

Juliet nodded, needing him to know that she believed him, that she did not blame him for anything. "Was it a letter confessing his love to her?"

"I assume so. However, I never read it. I only figured it did once I returned and learned of Troy's odd behavior following my sister's wedding." He heaved a deep sigh. "I still have it," he glanced toward the door through which Troy had left, "and now I wonder if perhaps I should give it to Nora after all."

"Perhaps you should," Juliet replied in a shaky voice. "Perhaps it is not too late yet. They lost their chance all those years ago...as did we." She smiled up at him, sadness mixing with happiness as she considered their rocky path. "Yet here we are."

A deeply emotional smile came to Christopher's face before he pulled her into his arms. "Yes, here we are," he whispered, dipping his head and placing a gentle kiss upon her lips. "Betrothed, and soon to be married."

Smiling, Juliet nodded. "Soon."

"When shall we tell your family? Now?" He frowned. "Perhaps we should wait until tomorrow." Again, he glanced toward the door. "I think I will try and speak to Troy again."

"Thank you," Juliet said, snuggling closer into his embrace. "It pains me to see him like this."

Christopher's arms tightened around her as he rested his chin on top of her head. "It pains me as well."

"When will you leave for Ireland?"

Christopher heaved a deep sigh, his embrace tightening upon her, as though every fiber of his being was unwilling to let her go so soon. "Tomorrow. Tomorrow after we tell them." He stepped back and looked down at her. "Come with me."

Juliet was tempted to agree. "I think you should go alone, prepare your son, tell him who awaits him here." She smiled up at him. "I think I need a little time to prepare myself as well."

Christopher nodded in understanding. "Well then, shall we return to the ball?"

Nodding, Juliet accepted his arm, and they left the library. Indeed, something else needed preparing before their son returned home. Never had Juliet been one to confront others, to stand tall and speak up. Now, however, she would be a mother and she would not fail her son as Christopher's mother had failed him. No, while Christopher went to fetch their child, she would go and visit Lady Lockhart and set her straight about how a grandmother—let alone a mother!—should be.

It was about time someone did.

CHAPTER THIRTY-TWO

OLD FRIENDS

Morning was not far off when the ball finally ended, and silence fell over Whickerton Grove. Yet Christopher did not feel the least bit tired. His body hummed with energy, and he knew even if he went to bed, sleep would not find him. So instead, he stepped out of doors, hoping that the chilled night air might clear his head.

His heart felt torn in two different directions once again. He felt happiness over his future with Juliet and his son but also sorrow and regret about his friend's suffering. Did Nora also suffer?

Of course, Christopher could not be sure. He had never spoken to either of them about what might have happened all those years ago, what had compelled Troy to write that letter. To this day, he did not know what it said. Yet from the way Troy had reacted, Christopher was reasonably certain that it held a declaration of love. Had Troy hoped that Nora would call off her wedding? Had he hoped that she would return his love?

Christopher could not imagine it being any different. It made sense, and yet he had never once seen Troy and Nora together in a way that caused him to believe that something deeper than friendship connected them. Had he been truly blind? Or had whatever happened between them happened only shortly before Nora's wedding? Was that why Troy had only given him the letter the very morning she was to be wed? Or was it one-sided?

Hanging his head, Christopher stepped off the terrace and walked down to the gardens, his gaze sweeping over the starlit sky. He prayed it was not one-sided. He wanted to see them both happy, and now, finally, it appeared that chance was within their grasp. They only needed to seize it, but what if they would not?

Only a few days ago, Christopher, himself, had been on the brink of returning to Ireland, thinking that a future with Juliet was impossible. Yet he had been wrong. Christopher could only hope that Troy would not allow this chance to pass them by.

Earlier, Christopher had stopped by Troy's chamber. His friend, however, had been absent. Perhaps it was that absence which kept Christopher wide-awake. How could he close his eyes without speaking to his friend first?

Nearing the stables, Christopher frowned when he heard an odd sound echo through the night. It was a rhythmic *thwack, thwack, thwack*.

Intrigued, Christopher rounded the stables, his feet carrying him past a large stack of firewood alongside the eastern wall. An orange glow beckoned him onward, and he was wondering who was out here in the middle of the night when his eyes fell upon a torch thrust into the ground.

Another step carried him around the stables' corner and his eyes fell upon none other than his oldest friend.

Dressed only in shirt and breeches, his boots caked in mud, Troy stood in the torch's shine, an axe in his hands. His features were hardened, tense, his eyes focused on the log in front of him. Then he moved, his arms raising the axe before bringing it down with a precise and forceful swing, splitting the log in two.

Without looking up, Troy kicked the two pieces aside and reached for another log, positioned it and brought the axe down upon it yet again.

For a long time, Christopher simply stood there and watched, the anguish on his friend's face painful to behold. Sweat trickled down

Troy's temples, and he occasionally brought up an arm to wipe his forehead.

Christopher was afraid to disturb him, and yet after a while he could not bear the sight much longer. Carefully, he moved forward, worried that he might startle Troy.

"I know you're there," his friend suddenly growled without taking his eyes off the log before him. Then he brought the axe down once more with a satisfying thwack. "What do you want?"

Exhaling deeply, Christopher stepped closer, feeling the chilled night air wash over him as he moved, considering what to say. "I came to speak with you," he finally muttered on a deep sigh. "I came to apologize."

"It is too late for apologies," Troy grumbled as his hands tightened on the axe. Then he swung it over his head, a soft whistle drifting to Christopher's ears as it whirred through the air.

Thwack.

Christopher threw up his hands. "Bloody hell, Troy, talk to me! Don't pretend that—"

His eyes wide and raging, Troy spun to face him. "You ruined my life!" he roared, advancing menacingly, the hand that gripped the axe turning pale with the pressure. "You ruined everything!"

Christopher heaved a deep sigh, his friend's words like a stab to the heart; yet he rejoiced to see Troy finally vent his anger and express the pain he had kept hidden for the past five years.

"And now," Troy growled, his hands still tightening upon the axe's handle, "you come here after all these years and want my blessing to marry my sister?" His face contorted into a snarl as he shook his head. "Well, you cannot have it." He tossed the axe to the side, and it landed with a dull thud. "Never." He shook his head slowly, vehemently, his gaze hard, almost challenging, as he glared at Christopher.

Christopher swallowed hard, shocked by his friend's hateful words...yet not surprised. "You would truly withhold your blessing?" he asked almost breathlessly. "You would deny us that? You would deny *her* that?" He shook his head. "Juliet has done nothing wrong. She loves you and has been a loyal and devoted sister all these years."

Troy raked a tense hand through his tousled hair, a spark of doubt coming to his eyes, quickly masked by another surge of anger. "And you?" he demanded in a hard voice. "What have you done?"

Christopher heaved a deep breath, then slowly approached his friend. "I didn't know. Why did you not tell me? Had I known I..." He shook his head, exhaling. "I still have the letter."

Troy's head snapped up, his eyes wide. "Did you read it?"

"Of course not! I told you that."

Troy's teeth ground together. "Then hand it back so I can burn it."

Christopher shook his head as Troy held out his hand. "No, even if it is years too late, I will give it to my sister. She deserves to know how you—"

"No!" Troy roared, then charged toward him. "You will not!" He grasped Christopher by the front of his coat, his blue eyes wild as they stared into his. "You will not! Do you hear? You will not!"

Trying to remain calm, Christopher lifted his hands in appeasement. "Why not? She is no longer married," he pointed out, praying that his friend's enraged mind was capable of hearing him. "You are both free to do as you please, to love whom you ch—"

"No!" Troy roared before he drew back his arm, and Christopher watched in a rather detached fashion as his friend's fist came flying toward him.

In the next moment, a sharp pain shot through Christopher's jaw and he found himself flying backward before landing with a dull thud on the hard ground. His ears rang and bright spots danced before his eyes as a dull pain shot through his head and shoulders. He groaned, pinched his eyes shut and lay otherwise completely still, breathing in and out slowly.

"Are you...Are you all right?" came Troy's voice, still hard but now laced with regret and concern.

Sitting up, Christopher groaned as he reached to touch his jaw. He moved it from side to side, wincing as another stab of pain found him. "More or less," he gritted out, then looked up at his friend standing above him.

Troy had a contrite look on his face. There was still anger in his eyes; yet a glimpse of the man he had always been shone through. "I'm sorry." He stepped forward and held out his hand to Christopher.

Christopher nodded, then grasped his friend's hand and allowed him to pull him back onto his feet. He met Troy's gaze. "I'm not angry with you," he told him, stepping in his friend's path when he made to turn away. "Whether or not you want to admit it, I know you care for her and I know that the past few years have been hell for you."

For a brief moment, Troy closed his eyes, his jaw tensing to the point of breaking.

"Believe me, I know what that feels like." Christopher stepped closer and placed his hands upon his friend's shoulders, looking him straight in the eye. "I hesitated far, far too long, held back by doubts and fears I should never have allowed to dictate my actions. I regret that today because I will never get back the years I've lost." He sighed, then stepped back, still holding his friend's gaze. "If you care for her as I believe you do, then...do something about it." He looked at Troy compassionately.

Raking a hand through his hair, Troy stared back at him, the look in his eyes no longer fueled by anger alone. Christopher saw something contemplative in his gaze and hoped that his friend was truly considering a different course of action. Standing back and letting the world pass one by was never a good choice. Whether Troy and Nora had a future together remained to be seen; however, that future would never come to pass unless one of them took a chance.

"You never once spoke to her, did you?" The look on Troy's face spoke volumes. "You should. Think about it," Christopher urged his friend anew before he stepped back, turned and walked away. He had said what needed to be said. Now it was up to Troy.

Still, the events of the night continued to linger in Christopher's mind. Fatigue began to pulse in his veins, weighing down his limbs. Yet his mind was wide-awake, racing from one thought to another, reliving everything that had happened today. And so, he was still awake, standing in his bedchamber, eyes directed out the window at the dark world surrounding Whickerton Grove, when he saw a lone rider charge down the drive, away from the house and toward Fartherington Hall.

For a moment, concern sparked in Christopher's veins. Concern for his sister. After all, Troy seemed far from in his right mind this night. Then, however, Christopher wondered if perhaps it was about time that his friend lost control. Perhaps it would be that impulsive and untamed side of him that would allow Troy to confront how he felt about Nora.

With all his heart, Christopher hoped that one day he would see them happy again.

CHAPTER THIRTY-THREE

AN ANNOUNCEMENT LONG AWAITED

Juliet barely slept a wink that night, excitement mingling with concern over everything that had happened the night before. Yet she felt far from tired but eager to begin the day. Christopher seemed to feel the same, for when she opened the door to leave her chamber, she found him standing right in front of her.

For a short moment, they simply looked at one another, the same hint of disbelief on his face that she felt must be upon her own. "Did last night truly happen?" Juliet whispered, a tentative smile tugging on the corners of her lips. "Are we truly betrothed?"

Casting a careful glance up and down the corridor, Christopher quickly stepped inside, then closed the door. "If not, then I had the same dream," he whispered with a wide smile, pulling her into his arms. "I thought of little else but you."

Juliet wanted to dance with joy; yet a single dark cloud remained. "Did you speak to Troy?"

Christopher nodded. "I tried," he replied, and then turned so that the early morning light fell upon the other side of his face, revealing a slowly darkening bruise.

Juliet gasped. "Did my brother...?" Her eyes flickered up to meet his before they returned to fall upon the angry bruise he had retained

—no doubt—from his conversation with Troy. "What happened?" She gently touched her fingers to his jaw.

Christopher winced. "It was nothing," he replied, and she latched onto that spark of hope she saw in his eyes. "We spoke, and...I think he heard me. At least I hope he did."

Juliet nodded, then she sighed. "Shall we head downstairs to breakfast then and...?" Her teeth sank into her lower lip as she smiled at her betrothed.

A wide grin came to Christopher's face before he placed a kiss upon her forehead. "And tell them," he finished for her.

Juliet all but bounced on her feet. "I admit I can hardly wait. This... this still seems surreal somehow. Perhaps once we tell them, it will feel..." She shrugged, unable to put into words how she felt, equally unable to explain the fear she felt that the man she loved could be snatched from her arms once again.

"I know what you mean," Christopher whispered, the look in his brown eyes proving his words true. "I feel as though I'm still dreaming. Will you pinch me?" He grinned.

Instead of pinching him, Juliet pulled him down into a kiss, overwhelmed to be able to do so. Only days ago, she would never have dared and now...it seemed perfectly natural.

He was hers to kiss, was he not?

And she had to admit she liked that.

A lot.

His arms held her tighter, his kiss growing more urgent. "If this is how you pinch me, then please do so every day for the rest of my life," he murmured against her lips before claiming them once more in a searing kiss that left Juliet breathless.

"I can't believe I'll have to say goodbye to you today," she whispered, feeling tears prick the backs of her eyes at the thought.

Christopher cupped her face in his hands, gently tilting up her chin until his eyes looked down into hers. "Come with me," he murmured, tenderly brushing his mouth against hers. "Please."

"I want to," Juliet assured him as her hands slid around his neck, her fingers twirling in his hair. "But you need time alone with your son. He will have missed you." She smiled up at him. "You will come back," she said, more to herself than him. "You will come back, and then you will not leave again."

Christopher nodded, his right hand clasping her chin, his brown eyes unwavering as they looked into hers. "I promise you. I will never leave your side again. This is the last time. Never again."

"Never again," Juliet agreed, nodding her head as she fought the tears that stood in her eyes. A moment later, his mouth came down onto hers once more, sealing their vow with a life-altering kiss.

"Juliet?" came Harriet's voice through the closed door, followed by a quick knock. "Are you up?"

Shocked, Juliet and Christopher jerked apart, staring at one another for a heartbeat or two before wide smiles came to their faces, and they had to fight the urge to laugh out loud. "Yes, I'm up," Juliet called, leaning her back against the door just in case. "I'll be downstairs in a minute. You go ahead."

For a moment, silence greeted her words before Harriet asked, "Are you certain?"

"Yes!" Juliet exclaimed with a bit too much enthusiasm before she clamped her hands over her mouth as another bout of laughter threatened to undo her.

"Very well." At the sound of receding footsteps, Juliet sagged against the door before she could not hold in her laughter any longer.

Christopher joined her, his hands reaching for her as they sank to the floor together, tears leaking from their eyes as laughter fell from their lips. "Do you think she knows?" he wondered out loud. "Do you think she knows I am in here?"

Wiping tears from her cheeks, Juliet shrugged. "I don't know. Honestly, sometimes I don't know who knows what or not."

"Of course, your grandmother knows," Christopher threw in with a grin. "The woman knows everything."

Juliet nodded. "It would seem so." She grinned at him, then scooted closer, her shoulder bumping against his. "My sisters and I used to make up stories about her." She giggled, remembering those innocent childhood days. "Do you remember? One theory was that she had once been a spy."

Christopher slapped a hand to his forehead, his shoulders shaking with laughter. "It would not surprise me if that were true."

Once the laughter had finally stopped and they had dried their tears, Juliet and Christopher headed downstairs toward the breakfast parlor. Despite the ball lasting well into the early hours of the morning, her family was already wide awake and exchanging theories of their own.

"Truly, did you see them after they danced together?" Harriet inquired as Juliet and Christopher stopped just outside the doorway, exchanging a glance. "Did you?"

"But that doesn't mean that they..." Christina's voice trailed off with a meaningful chuckle.

"Well, we shall know soon," Louisa remarked with confidence.

"You don't...plan on simply asking them, do you?" Anne inquired, a doubtful tone in her voice.

Juliet heard Phineas snort with laughter, which quickly turned into a pained gasp. No doubt, Louisa had elbowed her beloved husband for speaking his mind so directly.

"Perhaps we should wait until they decide to share—" suggested Leonora, but she was quickly interrupted.

"We've been waiting long enough!" Louisa exclaimed impatiently. "Honestly, I wanted to ask her the day of your wedding." She was no doubt looking at Harriet. "Do you remember how we opened the door, and they both toppled to the floor?" A wickedly delighted grin could be heard in her voice.

Blushing, Juliet looked at Christopher, remembering the day she had asked him to kiss her. "I wanted you to kiss me even then," she whispered as he pulled her into his arms, his back against the wall separating the hallway from the parlor. "I meant what I said."

He nodded, lowering his head to hers. "I wanted it as well." He closed his eyes. "You do not know how much I wanted to kiss you that day." Then his eyes flashed open, and his head swooped down to kiss her as thoroughly as never before.

Juliet's head spun when her grandmother's voice suddenly rang out loud and clear. "Don't make an old woman wait for her breakfast. Quit hiding in the hallway and come inside. There'll be time for kisses later."

Juliet and Christopher froze before they broke out laughing once more. Then, with her hand upon his arm, they rounded the corner and stepped into the breakfast parlor where Juliet's entire family—including a tall Scotsman with a rather self-satisfied, but genuinely joyous look in his eyes—stood assembled. Everyone, that was...except for Troy.

"Have you been eavesdropping?" Harriet asked with a teasing grin, her green eyes sparkling as she exchanged a meaningful look with her new husband.

Christopher shrugged, then looked from one of Juliet's sisters to the next before his gaze came to settle upon her grandmother. "Have you been meddling?" he challenged with a grin. "Or rather matchmaking?"

For a moment, silence fell over the room as everyone stared at them. While Anne and Leonora blushed slightly, a hint of shame coming to their eyes, Louisa and Harriet grinned with delight and no small hint of triumph. "Well, is it official, then?" Juliet's mother asked, exchanging a deeply affectionate look with her husband.

"Indeed," exclaimed Grandma Edie, thumping her cane onto the floor for emphasis. "Can I sit and eat?"

Everyone broke out laughing, and Harriet pulled out a chair for their grandmother. The rest of the family followed suit, settling around the large table, husbands seated next to wives with little Samantha seated between her parents. "Well?" the girl asked, looking from Juliet to Christopher. "Are you going to be my uncle?"

Everyone at the table held their breaths, all eyes trained on them expectantly.

Meeting Juliet's gaze, Christopher smiled. "I am," was all he said, and the room erupted in cheers.

Juliet had never been happier.

CHAPTER THIRTY-FOUR

TO STAND TALL

Christopher wanted nothing more than to rush back to Liverpool and find his way to Ireland as quickly as possible. However, he knew he could not leave without exchanging a few words with his mother. And so, he directed his mount back to Fartherington Hall, his shoulders tense and his hands clenched upon the reins. For even though his mother's reaction would not change his plans, Christopher could not deny that he still wished for her approval.

More than that, for her affection.

Was he a bloody fool? Did he perhaps secretly delight in her rejection? As much as he wished she would simply turn over a new leaf, suggest that they forget the past and begin again, deep down, Christopher knew wishes like these were rarely granted. Why then did he keep hoping? Only to be disappointed again?

After handing his steed to a stable boy, he slowly ascended the steps to the front door and then stepped inside. The large house felt... empty, not like Whickerton Grove at all. There was no life here, no family, no love. Sebastian and his father were gone, and only his mother and Nora remained, both of whom had not laughed or smiled in...

He could not even say.

Striding across the hall, Christopher entered the drawing room, knowing that his mother preferred to sit here in the mornings, appreciating the light that shone in through the east-facing windows. He found her seated upon the settee near the fireplace, another piece of embroidery in her hands, her head bent in concentration.

"I see you have returned," his mother remarked in a stern voice, not even bothering to look up.

Christopher heaved a deep sigh and moved farther into the room before seating himself in an armchair across from her. "I've come to inform you of a recent development."

That, at least, made her react. Her eyes rose from the fine stitches her hands were executing and met his. "A recent development?" she asked, her voice strained as though she expected the worst. Would it forever be thus? Christopher wondered. Would she never see him in a favorable light? What on earth could he have done to deserve such mistrust?

Shaking his head, Christopher pushed back all these thoughts of his childhood. He was not here today to confront his mother about anything that had happened, about the way she had been treating him all his life. No, that part was behind him. Now, he was looking to the future.

The future with his son and with Juliet.

The thought brought a smile to his face, and Christopher saw a slight frown descend upon his mother's forehead as she saw it. "I am betrothed," he said simply, holding her gaze and noting the way she seemed to still even more. He could see her eyes narrow incrementally, suspicion and a hint of annoyance sneaking into her expression.

Christopher sighed. Indeed, it seemed it would forever be thus.

"May I ask who your bride-to-be is?" his mother inquired, a haughty expression upon her face, as she set aside her embroidery and folded her hands in her lap.

Leaning forward, Christopher braced his elbows upon his legs. "It is Jules," he said, all but whispering her name affectionately and delighting in the way the mere mention of her name filled him with joy.

His mother rolled her eyes at him. "You should know better than to speak of the lady so informally," she chided him; yet a hint of relief seemed to linger upon her face, as though she had feared his choice of a wife would displease her. For once, it seemed he had failed to disappoint his mother.

Christopher was uncertain how he felt about that. "To me, she's Jules and will always be Jules," he said, straightening as he sat back. "I am well aware that you disapprove; however, I no longer care."

His mother's eyes narrowed in surprise at his sharp tone. For a moment, it appeared she would once again reprimand him, make her displeasure unmistakably clear; yet she did not. "Have you already set a date?" she inquired, a rather indifferent look in her eyes. "After all, a wedding requires careful preparations. However, I assure you, Fartherington Hall shall be splendid for its new countess."

A tentative smile stole onto Christopher's face as he thought of Jules and the Whickertons as well as Harriet's recent wedding. Indeed, they had not spoken of a date yet, but Christopher was determined to make Juliet his wife as soon as possible. "That won't be necessary, Mother," he said slowly, enjoying the confused look on her face. Perhaps it was petty of him or even vindictive, but he could not help enjoying making her feel ill at ease. "We shall be married at Whickerton Grove."

The serene look fell from his mother's face, her eyes going wide as she stared at him. "You cannot!" she exclaimed, anger flashing in her eyes for a second before she managed to subdue it. "You are the Earl of Lockhart and it is your duty to—"

"I do not care," Christopher interrupted his mother. Again, he leaned forward, resting his elbows upon his legs, his eyes fixed upon hers. "This is my life, and you have no say in it. I will do what I deem right."

"Right?" Shaking her head, his mother stared at him, a rather dumbfounded expression upon her face, one Christopher could not recall ever having seen before. "What you say makes no sense!" Again, she shook her head. "No, no, no. You shall be married here at Fartherington Hall. Is that understood?"

A dark chuckle left Christopher's throat. "I know well that you are used to dictating everyone's lives; however, from now on, you will have no say in mine."

Her features froze, and she swallowed hard.

"I merely came here as a courtesy," Christopher continued, the look in his eyes unrelenting as hers had always been, "to inform you of my impending nuptials as well as of another decision that was long overdue."

His mother's hands tensed in her lap as she watched him suspiciously.

Christopher swallowed, feeling his hands tremble at the thought of what lay ahead. "I am on my way to Ireland," he told his mother, and with each word to leave his lips, his heart began to warm, "to fetch my son."

His mother's eyes opened in utter shock. "You cannot!" She shot to her feet, her cheeks paling as she stared at him. "What is this nonsense? You are about to marry a woman of the peerage, an earl's daughter, and you intend to make her suffer through the humiliation of parading your bastard in front of everyone?"

Surging to his feet, Christopher glared at his mother. "Don't you dare speak of him in this way!" he snarled, shame washing over him because he knew his words came far too late. He should have spoken them years ago. "He is my son, and he will soon be ours, Juliet's and mine."

A scoff left his mother's lips. "Your new bride will want nothing to do with your errors in judgment." She took a step toward him. "Be reasonable and—"

Pressing his lips into a thin line, Christopher shook his head. "You're wrong," he told her slowly, almost menacingly. "Juliet is not like you. She will not see a mistake when she looks upon my son, our son. She will see an innocent, sweet little boy, and she will be proud to be his mother."

His mother closed her eyes, a heavy sigh leaving her lips. "Don't be a fool, Christopher. The moment she finds out about the child, she will—"

"She already knows!" Watching his mother's jaw drop, Christopher smiled. "She already knows, and it was her idea to bring Sebastian home."

A frown came to his mother's face, and her cheeks paled even further. "S-Sebastian?" For the first time, sadness washed over her face, and Christopher could not help but wonder if she would have shed a tear had he been the one to die that day and not his brother.

"Yes, I named my son after my brother. You never even knew because you never cared." He heaved a heavy sigh, no longer feeling angry but deeply regretful of all those painful and wasted years. "I have no wish to quarrel with you, Mother. I came here today to inform you of my impending marriage and of my intention to bring my son home. We shall be a family, and if you wish, you may be a part of our lives," he lifted a finger in warning, his gaze fixed upon hers, "if you bury this hatred you have within yourself. One word against my son, and I will send you from this house."

Her eyes widened, yet her lips pressed into a tight line. "You cannot do that," she hissed under her breath. Still, Christopher heard doubt in her voice.

"I can, and I will," he assured her. "You will not poison my son's life the way you poisoned mine."

For a second, Christopher thought to see shock and pain flash over her face; however, those emotions quickly vanished, once again replaced by a look of deepest indignation. "Christopher, he is a bastard. He can never inherit. He—"

"I don't care!" Christopher growled into her face. "He is my son, and he means more to me than your silly notions of standing and reputation." He gritted his teeth and looked down into his mother's face, shocked to see incomprehension resting in her eyes. "But you've never been able to understand that, have you?" Sighing deeply, he shook his head. "A son is more than an heir, and, yes, I was a fool to ever hide him away. He deserves better as I deserved better." He straightened, squaring his shoulders. "I've made my choice, Mother. What is yours? If you cannot accept him, me, then I suggest you leave before we return."

For a moment, his mother looked as though she was about to respond, anger and outrage flashing in her eyes, her lips contorted into a snarl. Then, however, she clamped her hands together and sealed her lips before spinning upon her heel and rushing from the room.

Christopher heaved a deep sigh. Deep down, he had known that his mother would never relent. She was who she was and nothing he said or did would ever change that. Nevertheless, it hurt—as much as he despised admitting it.

"Bravo!"

Christopher's head snapped up, and he spotted Nora standing in the doorway, a wide smile upon her face. Her deep brown eyes seemed to sparkle in a way Christopher had not seen in a long time, and he wondered if just perhaps it had something to do with Troy. Had his friend come here last night? Had he spoken to Nora?

"It was about time," his sister remarked with a curl to her lips as she strode toward him. "I feared you never would." Her smile deepened as she looked up into his face. "I'm happy to be proven wrong."

Christopher nodded, realizing that it did feel good to have said the things he had. It had not changed anything, not between him and his mother; however, it had been the right thing to do for him as well as his new family. "You overheard?"

Nora chuckled. "It was hard not to." She regarded him curiously. "I've never seen you so angry. It suits you."

Christopher laughed. "Anger suits me?"

"Not anger," Nora marveled as her eyes swept over his face, her brows drawing down, as though she were trying to grasp something eluding her. "It's that...that fire I see in your eyes." She placed a hand upon his arm affectionately. "You look as though you've woken up from a long sleep, Christopher. Before, you never seemed quite here, you know?" A deep sigh left her lips. "You do now, though." She chuckled. "It appears Jules kissed you awake."

Christopher laughed, pulling his sister into his arms. "Thank you," he murmured, holding her tightly.

"For what?"

He sighed, then stood back. "For being you. For being happy for me." He paused, his eyes narrowing as they searched her face. "I wish I could see the same fire in your eyes."

Tensing, Nora dropped her gaze. Still, Christopher thought to have seen the hint of a smile tease the corners of her lips. Was she hiding something? What had happened last night?

As much as Christopher would like to pry for more information, he did not have time. He needed to catch the next ship to Ireland. Still...

Inhaling a deep breath, Christopher reached inside his jacket and pulled out the letter. Troy had demanded he burn it; however, Christopher was willing to risk his friend's wrath, hoping that, perhaps, one day, Troy would forgive him. "This is for you."

Nora looked up, a slight curl coming to her lips as she looked from the letter in his hand to him. "Whatever you have to say to me you can just say it now," she said teasingly. "There is no need for formalities."

Christopher smiled, overwhelmed by the sudden change he saw in her. How long had it been since she had smiled and joked like this? Of course, he had spent most of his time in Ireland these past few years; however, upon his return only a few weeks ago, Nora had seemed very different from the way she stood before him today. Had that been Troy's doing? Was there hope for the two of them after all?

"No, the letter is not from me," he told her, wondering if perhaps Troy had already spoken to her of his affections. "The truth is, I was to deliver it to you...five years ago."

However, instead of understanding, Christopher saw confusion come into her eyes. "Five years ago?" she asked, laughing. "What delayed you?" Humor stood in her eyes, and Christopher wished he could stay and speak with her some more.

Christopher bowed his head. "I am deeply sorry for not giving this to you sooner. I know I should have. I had every intention of doing so, but..."

Stepping closer, Nora placed a comforting hand on his arm, her brown eyes soft as they searched his. "What is this about? It is only a letter, nothing that ought to concern you this deeply."

Christopher closed his eyes, breathed in deeply, and then looked down at his sister. "Troy gave it to me the day of your wedding."

Her features froze as she stared up at him.

"He asked me to give it to you as soon as possible," he told her honestly, praying that she would be able to forgive him, "but then I learned of my son's birth and the letter slipped my mind." He grasped her hands, hers now limp and chilled. "Back then, I did not know what this letter contained. Neither do I now; however, I have my suspicions and I think you should read it." He held the letter out to her.

Swallowing, Nora looked up into his eyes before her gaze dropped to the letter in his hand. She moved slowly, her hand extending as though she was uncertain whether she truly wanted it.

"Read it," Christopher urged her as she turned the letter carefully, almost reverently, in her hands, "and make of it what you will. I simply thought you should know." He placed a hand on her shoulder, giving it a slight squeeze. "I shall see you soon, Nora. Be well." Then he strode from the room, eager to leave and even more eager to return.

CHAPTER THIRTY-FIVE

A WOMAN'S RESPONSIBILITY

Christopher had only been gone two days and already Juliet missed him. She missed the way he looked at her, his warm brown eyes tracing the lines of her face, easily understanding everything that went through her head. She missed the way he smiled at her, as though delighted with every second they had together. She missed the feel of him, the soft way he would trace his fingertips along the line of her jaw, the urgency with which he pulled her into his arms, and the tender and yet passionate way he kissed her at every possible opportunity.

Juliet sighed longingly, all but counting the days until he would return.

With their son.

A slight tremble went through Juliet at the thought of little Sebastian. She longed to see him, to look into his eyes, and yet she could not help but worry: would he like her? Would he even want her to be his mother?

Wringing her hands, Juliet closed her eyes, trying her best to picture the little boy. Did he look like Christopher? Did he have brown eyes? What would it feel like to look into his eyes and know that they were his mother's? To see the woman who had given him life in his face whenever Juliet would gaze upon him?

Standing by the drawing room windows, Juliet inhaled a deep breath, then leaned her head against the cool windowpane. Oh, how she hated waiting! If only the days would pass quicker!

Yet there was something she still needed to do. Right now, Juliet's emotions were still a bit too raw. However, she knew she could not hesitate too long. She needed to go to Fartherington Hall and speak to Christopher's mother before his return.

Frowning, Juliet stilled when the sound of carriage wheels suddenly drifted to her ears. It could not be her siblings departing; indeed, they had all decided to remain at Whickerton Grove a while longer—to meet little Bash and, eventually, see Juliet and Christopher married. In fact, this was not a carriage departing, was it? Instead, it sounded like one arriving. Lifting her head, Juliet looked out the window, and the breath lodged in her throat when she saw the Lockhart coat-of-arms upon the carriage that arrived.

"Christopher?" Juliet whispered, but then quickly shook her head. No, it could not be him. He was on his way to Ireland. Then who? It could not possibly be his mother, could it?

Trying to swallow the lump in her throat, Juliet hastened out into the hall, quick steps carrying her toward the front door. However, the moment it opened, she saw it was not Christopher's mother stepping over the threshold but Nora instead.

"Nora?" Juliet exclaimed with a frown as her eyes fell upon her old friend. Of course, Leo had been the one closest to Christopher's sister as they were of the same age; however, more than one summer had been spent in blissful companionship, all of them together.

Hearing her name called, Nora almost flinched. Her eyes widened, and the distracted look disappeared from her face. "Jules!" The word rushed from her lips in one quick breath, and her left hand fluttered to her chest as though seeking to calm her heart. "Oh, you surprised me," Nora said then, a tentative smile coming to her face that seemed not quite genuine. "Of course, I shouldn't have been. After all, I'm the one coming to your home." She chuckled distractedly, closing and opening her eyes and then shaking her head. Her lady's maid remained by the door, maintaining a respectful distance.

Juliet frowned. "Are you all right? What brings you here today?" Juliet could not shake the feeling that something was wrong.

For a long moment, Nora simply looked at her, her mouth opening and closing a few times, as though she wished to speak but did not know how to find the words.

"Is it about Christopher?" Juliet asked, concerned that something might have happened. "He said he wanted to speak to his mother before leaving for Ireland. Did he?" She wrung her hands.

Nora nodded. "He did." A proud smile touched her lips. "He told her off. I've never seen him like that." Her left hand reached out to grasp Juliet's. "You've made him very happy. Thank you."

Smiling with relief, Juliet nodded. "He has made me very happy as well." And then she noticed that Nora's right hand was clenched around what seemed to be a letter that she held pressed to her heart.

Juliet's heart skipped a beat. A letter? It couldn't possibly be—?

"Is...Is your brother here?" Nora asked in a trembling voice, and her hand tightened upon the parchment clenched in her fist.

Stunned, Juliet nodded. "He's in the study," she told Nora, wishing she knew what was going on or what had happened. Clearly, Christopher had finally delivered the letter Troy had handed him all these years ago. Did Troy know? "You still know your way around, do you not?"

Nora nodded, a grateful look coming to her eyes. "Yes, I believe I do." Her gaze swept over the large foyer, and a bit of a wistful smile came to her face. "It has been some time, but I remember this place well."

Watching Nora walk away, her lady's maid following at her heels, Juliet clasped her hands together, hoping with every fiber of her being that somehow Nora and Troy would find their own happily ever after. Not that Juliet had already found hers. Of course, before she could consider herself that happy, there was more to be done. Still, it was within reach.

Close.

So close.

Turning on her heel, Juliet hurried in the opposite direction and headed toward the library, knowing that her grandmother liked to sit there and rest this time of day. She did not wish to wait any longer. She needed to speak to Christopher's mother soon. Before, however, she thought it would be wise to ask for counsel from a woman who seemed to possess wisdom in spades.

"Is she here?" came Grandma Edie's voice the moment Juliet stepped into the library. Seated near the enormous fireplace, with a blanket tucked around her legs, the old woman looked far from old and fragile, something formidable and dauntless shining in those pale eyes of hers.

Juliet momentarily paused in her step. "Who?"

Grandma Edie chuckled. "Our dear Nora, of course."

Closing her eyes in disbelief, Juliet sank into a chair across from her grandmother. "How can you possibly know it is her? These windows do not allow for a look of the drive. How did you know?"

Grandma Edie merely shrugged. "Why have you come? Clearly, there is something on your mind. Out with it."

Knowing she would never extract information from her grandmother that the woman did not wish to share, Juliet sighed and settled more comfortably in her chair. "Very well. I came here to ask for your advice."

"That is obvious," her grandmother chuckled deviously. "Advice on what, however?"

After Christopher's departure, Juliet had sat down with her family and explained to them all what had happened six years ago, why Christopher had left and what had kept him away. She had told them about the little boy in Ireland, who was to be her son, and she had told them how nervous she was about being a mother.

"Oh, don't worry," Christina had counseled, wrapping an arm around Juliet's shoulders. "The moment he smiles at you, you'll be lost." She looked across the room at her husband, who nodded in agreement. They had both lost their hearts to a little girl who was not their flesh and blood.

And yet, little Samantha was as much a part of them all as she possibly could have been. Juliet knew that. She loved the little girl with all her heart. But Samantha was her niece, while Sebastian would be her son. Would it be different then? Christina assured her it would not, admitting to having had the same doubts upon first finding herself a mother so unexpectedly.

Juliet's own mother and father had nodded encouragingly. "Children are so easy to love," her mother had murmured with tears in her eyes. "You know this little boy is yours, and the moment you see him, you'll feel it. Trust me." She had looked up at her husband, his eyes misted with tears as well, as he had smiled at her.

Meeting her grandmother's gaze, Juliet inhaled a steadying breath. "I am determined to go and speak to Christopher's mother."

"About?" Grandma Edie urged; yet Juliet could not shake the feeling that once again the woman knew.

Juliet sighed, remembering the many times throughout their childhood she had seen a deeply disheartened look on Christopher's face. "It hurt Christopher to be rejected by her, by them both." She shook her head. "I cannot leave it at that. She needs to know what she did to him. Not only for...for our son's sake, but for Christopher's as well." She leaned forward, looking into her grandmother's eyes. "He puts on a brave face, but I can see how much it still pains him. Even if he's not aware of it, he believes himself unworthy of love. I can see it in his eyes. He doubts me. He doubts my love, afraid one day I'll...come to my senses and take it away." She scoffed at the ludicrous thought. "Somehow, he needs to make his peace with the past or it will forever overshadow his future. Our future."

Grandma Edie nodded. "What will you say to her?"

Juliet threw up her hands. "I don't know. That is precisely why I'm here." She cast her grandmother a tentative smile. "Any advice?"

A thoughtful look came to Grandma Edie's face before she finally nodded, as though having made a decision. "Nothing happens without reason," she finally said, her voice oddly serious, even laced with a bit of anger. "We may not be aware of it, but it is there, nonetheless."

Juliet frowned. "What are you saying? I should...uncover the reason for his mother's, his parents' rejection?"

Grandma Edie nodded. "Did you never wonder why they only singled out him? Not Sebastian or Nora but him?"

"Of course, I did," Juliet replied, remembering the many times she had done her utmost to contain the damage his parents' words had caused. "As did Christopher. Countless times I heard him ask himself that question, what he could have possibly done or said to disappoint them." She threw up her hands. "Even as a child, he blamed himself."

Grandma Edie's lips thinned. "You know as well as I do it was not his fault. He did nothing." Her weathered hand tightened upon the armrest of her chair, and Juliet was surprised to see such anger in her kind, old grandmother. It passed quickly, though, and soon, that shrewd look was back in the old woman's eyes.

"What reason could there be?" Juliet wondered out loud. "I know some parents care very little for their children, only seeing the next in line, an heir to carry on the family name. Yet..."

"Yet they treated Sebastian and Nora differently, did they not?"

Juliet nodded. "Why?" She frowned. "Do you know?"

Grandma Edie shook her head. "I'm afraid not. However, the way they always looked at him does not stem from nothing. There is a reason, one you must uncover, one his mother must admit to if you hope to give Christopher any peace of mind."

Juliet closed her eyes and exhaled loudly. "I don't know if I can do that," she whispered, then she looked at her grandmother again. "I'm not like you...or Harriet or Louisa. I'm not brave. I'm not—"

Leaning forward, Grandma Edie grasped her hand, a warm smile upon her face. "Do not tell yourself lies, sweet child. We all are brave in our own ways. You can do this. I have every faith that you can. For yourself as well as for your family. Protect them. They need you to."

With tears in her eyes, Juliet nodded, her own hand tightening on her grandmother's. "Thank you." Perhaps her grandmother was right. Perhaps she could be strong. Strong enough to confront her future mother-in-law, a woman who knew how to put others in their place, how to look at them in a way that made one want to sink into a hole in the ground.

Yet, Juliet could all but feel something deep inside her grow stronger. Protect them, her grandmother had said.

And she would.

CHAPTER THIRTY-SIX

FATHER & SON

Christopher arrived in Ireland only a few days after All Hallows' Eve. Though cold, the day was bright and cheerful, and the sea air tugged upon his hair as he thundered along the road, his mount eager to move. Impatience hummed in his veins as his eyes took in the wind-swept countryside, greens mingling with the golden colors of autumn. He breathed in deeply, his chest expanding, and a smile came to his face that deepened with each step closer to home.

Soon, home would be a different place. Now, however, Christopher still felt the familiar sense of returning to a place he loved. The place where his son had grown up. The place where he had learned to walk. The place where they had laughed together and played together.

Cresting a small hill, Christopher looked down at the snug manor house nestled in a small valley surrounded by fields of green. He spotted the swing he had hung in the tall oak tree on the western side, as well as the pond in the back where Sebastian always fed the ducks. Smoke swirled out of the chimneys, and Christopher caught the faint aroma of meat cooking.

Indeed, it felt like coming home.

Urging his mount onward, Christopher kept his gaze upon the

house, all but holding his breath, impatient for the first moment his eyes would fall upon his son.

It had been too long.

As Christopher rode up to the door, it flew open, revealing not his son, but Mrs. O'Brien instead. Her gray hair was braided in a circle atop her head, its color, as always, a perfect match to that of her dress. She seemed utterly colorless...until a smile came to her face.

Oh, for all her colorlessness, Mrs. O'Brien knew how to smile. She smiled in a way that felt warm and safe and wonderful. It had been that smile that had made Christopher hire her as Sebastian's nurse. He wanted his son to feel loved and treasured, and Mrs. O'Brien knew how to do that better than anyone.

"Lord Lockhart," she exclaimed, hastening down the few steps to the gravel drive, "how wonderful to see ye return." Her green eyes sparkled like the hills in the distance.

Jumping to the ground, Christopher returned her smile, feeling his chest expand even further. "I've asked you a thousand times to call me Christopher."

Mrs. O'Brien chuckled. "And I've told ye a thousand times that I will not." Then she embraced him in a way Christopher's own mother never had. "It's good to have ye back home, me lord." She looked up at him and patted his arm. "Good to have ye back."

Christopher sighed deeply. "It is good to be back." His eyes swept over the house and the small overgrown arch that led into the garden beyond.

"He's in the barn," Mrs. O'Brien answered his silent question. "Mrs. Whiskerson had another litter."

Christopher cast her a grateful smile and then hurried to the back of the house as fast as his legs could carry him. The scent of hay lingered in the air as he stepped toward the open barn door. When Mr. Brady stepped out, tipping his hat in greeting, Christopher put a finger to his lips to silence any reply. The old man grinned and nodded toward the inside.

Feeling his heart beat in his chest, Christopher stepped into the dim world inside, beams of light filtering through the boards and casting a warm glow over the barn. Up ahead, a ladder led up to the hayloft, from where a soft voice drifted down. "You're a wonderful mother, Mrs. Whiskerson," Sebastian's sweet voice whispered, a tinge of longing in it that made Christopher's heart clench painfully. "But now you need rest. I promise I shall watch over you and your babies." After a pause, he added solemnly, "You have my word."

Touched by his son's vow, Christopher moved closer and then quietly climbed up the ladder. The moment his head peeked over the edge, his son's eyes grew round, such open joy in them that Christopher almost lost his hold upon the ladder.

"Father," Sebastian mouthed quietly, the grin on his face almost blinding. Christopher could see that he wanted to jump to his feet, but in the last moment, he held himself back, his blue eyes drifting down to the sleeping mother cat curled up in the straw beside him, her front paws draped over his leg.

"I'll come to you," Christopher whispered as he climbed onto the hayloft. Then he shrugged out of his coat and draped it like a blanket over his son's legs. He sat down next to Sebastian, and then finally, after endless long weeks, Christopher gently pulled his son back into his arms, careful not to wake Mrs. Whiskerson in the process. Although the tabby cat yawned and stretched, she did not wake but snuggled closer, her four kittens curled up against her belly.

Sebastian's little hands reached for him as his head fell to Christopher's shoulder. "I've missed you, Father. You were gone for so long." With his head still resting against Christopher's shoulder, Sebastian looked up, his blue eyes wide and so very innocent. "But I knew you would return. Mrs. Whiskerson was worried, but I told her there was no need. I told her you would always return."

"Of course," Christopher replied, sensing the need in his son's voice. "Of course, I'll always return." He pulled him tighter into his embrace, needing his son to know that there was no one more important in the world than him. "In fact, the next time I travel I want you to come with me."

Sebastian's little face lit up. "Truly?"

Ruffling his son's light brown hair affectionately, Christopher smiled at him. "Truly. I, too, missed you terribly and I don't wish to be apart from you for that long again." He looked into his son's eyes. "We belong together, you and I, do we not?"

Sebastian's little head bobbed up and down eagerly. "Of course, Father." And then he threw himself into Christopher's arms all over again, and father and son held each other close, savoring the moment after weeks of separation. "Where will we go?" Sebastian eventually asked, sitting back and looking up into Christopher's face.

Eagerness rested in his young eyes, and Christopher smiled. "To England." He watched as his son's eyes widened even farther, a spark of adventure lighting them up. "There is someone I want you to meet." Christopher could feel his heart thudding wildly in his chest, for he knew that as much as he loved Juliet, he wanted Sebastian to love her as well. Was that possible?

An image of little Samantha in her parents' arms flashed through his mind, and Christopher knew that it was. It might take time, but perhaps nothing was truly impossible in this world.

"Who?" Sebastian asked, casting one watchful glance at Mrs. Whiskerson and her kittens. "Who do you want me to meet, Father?"

Christopher inhaled a deep breath. "Her name is Juliet, and I've known her all my life. We grew up together, and she was my dearest friend."

A small frown came to Sebastian's forehead. "Then what happened? Are you no longer friends?"

"We are," Christopher assured him with a smile, utter relief spreading through his chest about how everything had turned out. After all, they had come quite close to losing each other all over again. "We are still friends."

A questioning look remained on Sebastian's face.

"A...A misunderstanding kept us apart these past few years," Christopher said vaguely, not wishing to burden his son with too many details. "However, when I traveled back to England, we met again and finally talked to each other. I still love her as much as I loved her the day we parted ways."

"You love her?" Sebastian's little hand tightened on Christopher's, something almost hopeful shining in his blue eyes.

Brushing a hand over his son's cheek, Christopher nodded. "Yes, I love her, and I would like to marry her."

A jolt went through Sebastian. His jaw dropped, and his eyes opened wide. "Will she...Will she be my new mother?"

The longing that appeared upon his son's face almost broke Christopher's heart. Of course, Sebastian had asked after his mother and Christopher had not lied to him. It was something he had learned from the Whickertons. One might upon occasion stretch the truth or refrain from mentioning something, certainly; however, one did not lie to those one loved. Especially not about such important matters.

And so, Christopher had always spoken truthfully to his son about how he had come to be and where his mother was, why she was not with them. Christopher had often seen doubt in Sebastian's eyes. He had known that his son could not help but wonder why his mother was not there, why she did not love him enough to be in his life. In these moments, Christopher had seen the same sadness and regret and insecurity he himself had experienced throughout his own childhood. He could not recall how often he had wondered what might be wrong with him, why his parents felt no affection, no love for him, at least not the way they did for his siblings. Sebastian had done the same. Perhaps it was only natural to ask oneself these questions. However, Christopher had always done his utmost to assure his son that he was loved. More than that, that he was worthy of love. And yet doubts had remained, had they not?

Christopher looked deep into his son's eyes, needing him to hear every word he was about to say. "I told Juliet about you, and she would like that very much. What do you think?"

A tentative smile came to Sebastian's face. "Truly?" He swallowed, eagerness lighting up his blue eyes. "Do you...Do you think she will like me?"

Fighting the tears that threatened to pool in his eyes, Christopher looked down at his son. "Oh, little Bash, she will love you. I have no doubt. None at all."

A relieved sigh left Sebastian's lips, and as he snuggled closer into his father's embrace, Christopher told him about little Samantha, how she had come into this world and how she had found her way to her parents. It, too, had been an unusual path; and yet it seemed meant to be.

"You see, little Bash," Christopher concluded, wanting more than anything for his son to understand this, "she was not born to her parents; and yet she is their daughter now in every way that matters. They love her more than life itself, and that is something that will never change."

Blinking, Sebastian looked up at him. "Do you think she will like me?"

Christopher laughed. "I am absolutely certain you shall be the best of friends." Indeed, a new generation of Whickertons—fiercely loyal and shockingly dauntless—was a beautiful thought, one far from being impossible.

CHAPTER THIRTY-SEVEN

A DARK SECRET

Juliet's hands were trembling as she alighted from the carriage. An almost icy wind threatened to blow the hood from her head, and she pulled her cloak tighter around her. Yet it was not the season's cold that made her limbs tremble.

With a deep sigh, she let her gaze sweep over Fartherington Hall, knowing that somewhere inside, Christopher's mother awaited her.

"Will you assist an old woman to the door?" Grandma Edie asked with a chuckle a moment before her weathered hand descended upon Juliet's arm. "With each passing day, stairs like these look more and more daunting." A disapproving scoff left her lips as she looked at the few steps leading up to the front door.

Juliet smiled at her grandmother. "Of course, it will be my pleasure." Yet she could not help but wonder whether her grandmother's words had merely been spoken for Juliet's benefit as an attempt to distract her, perhaps. After all, her grandmother often moaned and lamented about her old age and failing body when in truth Juliet often witnessed how capable her aging grandmother still was.

Without a hitch, they made it to the front door and were then shown inside to the drawing room, where a warming fire burned in the grate. Once again, Juliet assisted her grandmother into a comfortable-looking armchair near the fire before seating herself on the settee.

Fortunately, they did not have to wait long for Christopher's mother to greet them. Only moments later, the tall, somewhat stern-looking woman Juliet remembered from her childhood stepped over the threshold, Nora only a step behind her. While Lady Lockhart greeted them with the utmost politeness, it was Nora's smile that felt warm and welcoming.

"I am truly glad to see you again, Lady Juliet," Lady Lockhart said kindly as she and her daughter seated themselves. "Indeed, I do believe it's a good idea for us to speak. My son told me of your betrothal." Her eyebrows went up ever so slightly as she looked at Juliet.

After casting a glance at Grandma Edie, Juliet met the other woman's eyes. "I am glad to hear it. I assume you were quite surprised to receive the news." She cast a smile at Nora, wondering what had happened the day her old friend had come to visit Troy at Whickerton Grove. Unfortunately, her brother had been rather tightlipped about it.

"Surprised, certainly," Lady Lockhart replied with one of those polite smiles that said very little about her true feelings, "but also pleased. Indeed, I am delighted to see our two noble families united through marriage." She paused, and a hint of caution came to her eyes. "However, there is something of which I feel obligated to inform you." She cleared her throat, and out of the corner of her eye, Juliet could see Nora roll her eyes.

"Well," Lady Lockhart began, wetting her lips as she searched for the right words to express whatever concern was on her mind, "my son spoke to me of your approval to return his...his..."

"His son," Juliet offered helpfully; however, at her words, Lady Lockhart's jaw dropped rather shockingly, and she stared at her guest in a way that Juliet momentarily feared the woman might faint. "Are you all right?"

Lady Lockhart swallowed hard. "It's true then," she gasped, staring at Juliet as though she had grown another head. "You do not object to him bringing...bringing..."

Inhaling a deep breath, Juliet met Lady Lockhart's gaze. "Of course not," she said, careful to keep her voice steady and determined so as not to inspire doubt in her future mother-in-law. "In fact, it was I who urged Christopher to bring his son back home. A child belongs with his family, do you not agree?"

For a long moment, Lady Lockhart said not a word. Her face seemed paler than before, and her hands were clamped together in her lap. "But…But he's a bastard!" she finally exclaimed when it became clear that Juliet had no intention of offering more of an explanation; outrage mingled with utter incomprehension in her voice. "You cannot truly wish to…to have another woman's child in your home." Staring at Juliet, she shook her head as though that might convince Juliet to see the error of her ways.

Grandma Edie watched their conversation with rapt attention—as did Nora—but Juliet knew she would not interfere. No, this was Juliet's battle and her grandmother trusted her to fight it.

To win it.

"Lady Lockhart," Juliet began, meeting the other woman's eyes, "I am aware of your opinion in this matter; however, Christopher and I disagree." She sighed deeply, allowing her thoughts to travel to the little boy across the sea. "Children—all children—are a blessing. They fill life with joy and laughter, and they deserve to be loved no matter how they came into this world. That is what family is, would you not agree?"

A frown descended upon the other woman's face. "You cannot be serious. Are you truly contemplating the idea of raising that…that boy alongside your own children?" She shook her head as though to rid herself of such a vile thought.

Anger sparked in Juliet's heart, not the kind one felt at becoming aware of some wrongdoing not directly linked to oneself, but the kind that was one's own. "The boy you speak of," she said, something sharp coming to her voice, "is Christopher's son as well as mine, and I will love Sebastian no differently than any other child that might be born to us." Although Juliet had had doubts before, the powerful emotions growing in her chest at this very moment proved that there was no need to feel concern.

Yes, she would be Sebastian's mother, and she would love him. How could she not? He was an innocent child, much like Samantha, and

Juliet had lost her heart to the little girl within moments of meeting her. And now, she would be the boy's mother!

"Let me make this perfectly clear, Lady Lockhart," Juliet told her future mother-in-law with a stern look. "If you reject Sebastian, if you treat him without respect, we cannot permit you to be a part of our lives." Lady Lockhart's eyes widened. "I will not allow an innocent child to be subjected to the kind of treatment you have bestowed upon your own son since the day he was born." There, she'd said it!

Lady Lockhart's gaze fell from hers, and for the first time, the woman seemed far from in control. Her hands were still clamped together, but she fidgeted in her seat as though she wished to rise and rush from the room.

"Mother," Nora spoke up with a sideways glance at Juliet, "you should think this through carefully." Her hands trembled as she spoke, and Juliet thought to see a flicker of hesitation in her eyes. "You know that Christopher's children will be your only grandchildren." Juliet frowned. "Do you truly wish to spend the remainder of your life alone? Would you not rather be part of a loud and loving family?" Tears glistened in Nora's eyes, but she quickly blinked them away.

Juliet felt her heart go out to her friend. Indeed, at least a year had passed since they had last spoken, not since she and Christopher had come for a short visit the year before, so that Juliet knew very little about Nora's life. Was it possible that Nora could not have children? After all, Lord Hayward had died without an heir. Or were her words merely intended to remind her mother that she had no intention of ever marrying again? Not even Troy? Juliet could not help but wonder, wishing she knew what had happened between them...

...five years ago...

...and only days earlier.

Lady Lockhart looked to her daughter; her lips pressed together in a tight line.

Nora sighed, then lifted her right hand to brush a tear from her cheek. "How happy has striving for things like fortune and reputation made any of us? Christopher and Juliet are in love," she glanced at Juliet, a tentative smile upon her lips, "and they will be happy together...with their children, with all their children. The only decision that remains yours is whether you become a part of their family."

Casting Nora a grateful smile, Juliet nodded. "I have no intention of keeping you from your son or your grandchildren. However, as a wife and mother, it will be my duty as well as my heart's desire to ensure their safety, their well-being, their happiness." Sighing, she looked at Lady Lockhart. "Is that not how you feel about your own children as well?"

A tremor went through Lady Lockhart, and her hands clamped together even more tightly.

"Nora, dear," Grandma Edie spoke up suddenly, "I need to move my old bones. Will you accompany me?"

Although clearly surprised, Nora nodded, then she rose from her seat and offered Juliet's grandmother her arm. Together, they walked out of the room. Still, before they vanished, Juliet caught her grandmother's eye...

...and what she saw there made her wonder.

Waiting for the door to close behind them, Juliet looked across the small space at Lady Lockhart. The woman's icy exterior had vanished, and her gaze was distant, as though she was no longer aware of Juliet's presence. Her hands clawed into one another, and her jaw looked so tense that Juliet feared it might break from the strain. Yet tears glistened in her eyes and sadness lingered upon her face.

Uncertain where to begin, Juliet rose to her feet and then moved to seat herself beside her future mother-in-law. She thought about what to say, where to begin, when the question Christopher had always asked himself simply tumbled from her tongue. "Why can you not love him?"

Lady Lockhart flinched at her words. Her eyes opened and closed and then settled upon hers.

"Christopher," Juliet clarified, for the look in Lady Lockhart's eyes made her wonder if the woman had even heard her, "why can you not love him? You've always treated him differently. It is not as though you and your late husband were not the kind of people to bestow love on their children. You did on Sebastian and Nora. But not Christopher, why?"

Lady Lockhart's eyes closed, and she hung her head, as though a weight that had been resting upon her for years had now finally become too much to bear.

"He blames himself," Juliet continued, wondering what it would take for the woman to finally understand what she had done to her son. "For as long as I have known him, he has been trying time and time again to please you, to gain your love and respect." Sighing, she shook her head. "Yet he never could. Why? I know it was nothing he did or said. It couldn't have been." She reached out and placed her hands upon Lady Lockhart's. They were ice-cold. "Please, tell me why you could not love him, why you cannot open your heart to his son now."

Tears fell from Lady Lockhart's eyes onto Juliet's hands; yet no sound emerged from the woman's lips.

A sudden thought flashed through Juliet's mind, and without thinking, she spoke it out loud, "Is he not yours?" Lady Lockhart's head snapped up, wide eyes staring into Juliet's. "Is Christopher not your son?"

Slowly, that sense of detachedness fell from Lady Lockhart's face, and she licked her lips. "He...He..." Her voice was only a whisper, hoarse and burdened. "He...He is my son," she swallowed, "but my husband was not his father."

"What?" Juliet's eyes went wide. That she had not expected. "Lord Lockhart was not..." She shook her head, unable to make sense of everything.

The expression upon Lady Lockhart's face grew less rigid. Where before there had been stoic determination, like a wall erected to keep others out and her secret safely concealed, there now was a crack in her defenses. And slowly, with each breath she took, that crack grew wider, allowing Juliet a clearer view of the woman she had known almost all her life.

Indeed, Lady Lockhart had always possessed a rather stern expression, something unapproachable in the way she looked at those around her. Yet suddenly, the look in her eyes spoke neither of indifference nor disapproval but of pain instead.

"Tell me what happened," Juliet urged gently, wondering for how long her future mother-in-law had been keeping this secret. "Did your husband know?" The moment the words left her lips, Juliet knew the answer. Of course, he had known, for he, too, had always treated Christopher...as though he were not his.

Yes, it all made sense now, and Juliet wondered how she had not seen it before.

Lady Lockhart's eyes closed, and she nodded. "Yes, he did. He always knew."

Juliet felt a shudder go through her, for the look upon the other woman's face led her to believe that Lady Lockhart had not merely... had an affair. No, the anguish in the woman's eyes spoke of someone who had suffered...greatly. In fact, it reminded her of the pain Juliet had occasionally glimpsed in Leonora's eyes after the attack on her. "What happened?" Juliet urged once more, uncertain if she truly wanted to know.

Yet, for Christopher's sake, she needed to.

Lady Lockhart lowered her head, and Juliet felt the woman's hands shiver below her own. "I don't know if you knew," she whispered, her voice wistful, "but long ago, my husband and I were very much in love." The ghost of a smile flitted over her face as her mind drifted back to times long gone. "And then everything changed." Her jaw clenched, and she inhaled a deep breath, then slowly released it. "We had just become parents, and when Sebastian was barely two years old, we decided to spend some time in a remote cabin. It was supposed to be only the three of us. No servants. No meddling parents. No one but us. We wanted time alone, and my husband had always loved the outdoors, hunting and hiking." She blinked and then looked up, tear-misted eyes meeting Juliet's. "We thought it was a good idea. We thought..."

Juliet felt every fiber of her being tense, for the look in Lady Lockhart's eyes broke her heart. Once, she, too, had been a young woman in love, full of hope and dreams for the future. And then life had taken an awful turn.

"One night," Lady Lockhart continued as her hands squeezed Juliet's painfully, "a...a group of highwaymen happened upon the cabin." Her eyes closed, and Juliet could see the reluctance to speak upon her face. "Before we knew what was happening, we had pistols pointed at our heads. They ransacked the cabin, gathered whatever valuables they could find." She shook her head. "Of course, there wasn't much, and they soon became angry. They started yelling at my husband. They struck him." She flinched at the memory. "And then they...looked at me."

A sickening sensation rolled through Juliet, and she closed her eyes, praying it would shut out the images that formed in her mind. "You don't have to—" she began, but Lady Lockhart did not hear her.

"My husband tried to protect me," she went on, her gaze distant, fixed on something on the other side of the room. "They shot him. At first, I thought he was dead, but then I heard him moan. Fortunately, the bullet had only hit him in the shoulder. I heard my son crying." She cringed. "I will never forget his wails as he called out for us, and...and we couldn't go to him."

Her eyes closed once more, and she bowed her head in defeat. "After that, I did not fight them any longer. I simply closed my eyes and waited for it to be over." Frowning, she shook her head. "I think I might have passed out at some point because I remember coming to and realizing that they were gone. My son was still screaming. and my husband was slowly bleeding-out, and so I had to..." Her eyes rose and met Juliet's. "I had to...see to them. I had to be strong. I had to..." Her jaw trembled. "I couldn't... I had to be strong."

Juliet nodded, tears rolling down her cheeks as she held her future mother-in-law's hands tightly within her own. "You protected them as best as you could."

Lady Lockhart nodded, the look upon her face still oddly distant. "I did," she mumbled. "I did try."

"Were they caught?" Juliet asked to fill the silence that slowly spread between them like a black void.

Her future mother-in-law nodded. "They were caught, and they were hanged for their crimes." Something hard came to her jaw, tensing her muscles.

"You never told anyone what happened to you, did you?" Juliet asked softly. "They...They were hanged for what they had done to your husband, but..."

"I knew if I...admitted to what had truly happened, it would ruin my family." Tears stood in her eyes as she looked up at Juliet. "Yet I wanted to. I..." She swallowed hard. "People called me fortunate to have escaped without a scratch. They called my husband brave, and his wound was like a badge of honor. I remember that for a long time, I was never quite certain if I was truly awake. Nothing seemed to make sense. Everything felt...wrong."

Juliet could not imagine what Lady Lockhart had gone through. "Did your husband blame you?"

Lady Lockhart's head snapped up, and she shook her head vehemently. "No, he did not. He was...kind to me and considerate. That night haunted him, too, and we had a silent understanding to put it behind us and never speak of it."

Juliet nodded. "And then...you found yourself with child."

"I wanted to forget it," Lady Lockhart sobbed suddenly, all anguish and pain bursting out of her, and she buried her face in her hands. "My husband and I, we both knew that it was unlikely that he was the father. Sebastian had had trouble sleeping in the cabin, and he had clung to us rather tightly, leaving little chance for us to...." She broke off and forced in another breath. "We knew this child would forever remind us of that night." She lifted her head, her cheeks tear stained. "I tried to...rid myself of the child, but..." she shrugged helplessly, "but it didn't work. I tried but..."

Helplessness washed over Juliet as she looked into her future mother-in-law's anguished face. After suffering such an atrocity, she had been at the end of her tether, all hope to ever recover from this nightmare gone.

And then there was Christopher, who had lived his whole life with this shadow over his head, not knowing why his parents had never been able to love him, always doubting himself.

Inhaling deeply, Juliet pulled Lady Lockhart into her arms, holding her tightly. "I'm so sorry for what happened to you, for what you had to go through," she said gently, well-aware that words were frighteningly insignificant in moments like these. "You confided in me, and I wish to tell you something as well." She could feel her future mother-in-law still. "I hope I'm not betraying my sister's confidence, but I think if she were here right now, she would not hesitate to share her own story." She swallowed. "A little more than a year ago, Leonora was attacked at a masked ball. It haunted her, and in the weeks and months after, she retreated from the world, convinced she would never heal."

Lady Lockhart sat up. "I'm sorry to hear it," she said in a hoarse voice before a hint of confusion darkened her face. "Was she not recently married?"

Nodding, Juliet smiled at her. "She was. In fact, the way Leo tells it, it was her husband who helped her face that night, face those fears and lingering memories. She finally spoke to us, told us what happened, and I think that helped her feel like herself again." She met Lady Lockhart's gaze. "You've kept this a secret for far too long; I understand why, but it kept you from truly moving forward." She grasped the older woman's hands. "You were brave to tell me. Be brave again and tell Nora, tell Christopher."

Lady Lockhart's eyes went wide. "I cannot! I—"

"They will understand," Juliet exclaimed with vehemence. "They will. I promise. They will not blame you. They will finally understand, and they will help you. It will bring you all closer."

Lady Lockhart's lips pressed tightly together, doubt and fear darkening her pale eyes. "He will never forgive me," she choked out. "I know he won't. I don't deserve it."

Juliet knew without a doubt that she was speaking of Christopher. "Do you want him to?"

After a moment of hesitation, Lady Lockhart nodded. "I never let myself realize it, but, yes, I know I did wrong by him. I failed him. He deserved better."

"It is not too late," Juliet urged her. "Christopher is a kind and compassionate man. He went against everyone to do right by his son."

A small smile tugged upon Lady Lockhart's lips. "You mean, he went against me."

Juliet nodded. "Yes, he did what he thought right. He is a good man. Whoever his father was does not matter. He is not him. He is himself."

A deep sigh left Lady Lockhart's lips, and she nodded. "I know. He's always been such a sweet boy," she mumbled wistfully, yet her hands were clamped tightly together. "I would look at him and see how much he wanted me to love him. I could see it in his eyes. I..."

"He still does," Juliet whispered as fresh tears spilled down her cheeks. Never in her life had she felt such turmoil, such anguish. "Give us all a chance. Please."

Lady Lockhart turned to look at her. "Will you not forever see the boy's mother when you look at the child?" She sighed. "Sebastian." A soft smile touched her lips. "He truly named him Sebastian?"

Juliet nodded. "He did because he loved his brother very much. And I admit I wondered if I'd be able to love him." Smiling, she shook her head. "Yet somehow all doubts are gone now. In a way, even though I've yet to even lay eyes on him, I already do."

"Good," Lady Lockhart mumbled despite the spark of disbelief that remained in her eyes. "I'm glad he found you." She patted Juliet's hand. "You'll be good for him, for them both."

Juliet smiled at her future mother-in-law. "What will you do?" she asked then, raising a questioning brow. "Will you continue to run? Or will you stand and fight to reclaim your life?"

A soft chuckle left the other woman's lips. "You're not one to give up easily, are you?"

"Never," Juliet exclaimed with a laugh. "We Whickertons don't even know the meaning of that word. We're stubborn and mule-headed and we do what we must to protect those we love." She squeezed her mother-in-law's hand. "And that includes you."

A spark of hope lit up Lady Lockhart's eyes, and Juliet rejoiced inwardly, knowing that somewhere down the line, their family would be whole again.

CHAPTER THIRTY-EIGHT

A NEW WORLD

Christopher watched as his son stared at the world around him with wide eyes. His little mouth hung a little bit open, and his eyes darted from tree to tree as though he had never in his life seen trees. The carriage rumbled along the road, swaying gently despite the harsh winds that howled like wolves on the hunt. The sky was overhung with dark clouds, promising rain in the near future and casting a shadow over the world.

Yet, to Sebastian, it seemed the world held nothing but wonder. He sat in his seat with his little nose almost pressed up against the glass, staring and staring. Never before had he left their home in Ireland. Never before had he traveled anywhere else. And now, the world seemed to hold nothing but wonder. It was that childlike, innocent awe Christopher envied. In Sebastian's eyes, everything was beautiful and promising.

Christopher could not help but wonder if once upon a time, he, too, had felt like that. Had he ever looked at the world in such a wide-eyed manner, delighted with everything he saw? He could not recall. What he did recall were doubts and insecurities as well as the heartfelt wish to not be found wanting.

To this day, the memories of his childhood left a bitter aftertaste in his mouth. Christopher could not shake it, for the questions remained. What had he done to lose his parents' love? Had he even ever possessed it?

Indeed, it was those very memories that kept Christopher from directing the driver toward Fartherington Hall. Yes, he had grown up there, and yet it was not home. Home was where Juliet was. Home was where people awaited him with joy and longing. Home was where their son would be welcomed.

"Father, it doesn't look all that different from home, does it?" Little Bash exclaimed, prying his eyes away from the sights before him and turning to look at his father. "I like the trees. Trees are friendly and cheerful, are they not?"

Christopher chuckled. "I suppose a devoted climber such as yourself would think so."

Bash chewed on his bottom lip. "Where we are going," he began tentatively, "will there be trees there, too? Trees for climbing?"

Christopher heaved a deep sigh, knowing full well what his son was asking. After spending his whole life on a small estate in Ireland, far from anywhere, he now found himself far away from everything he knew. Of course, he would long for something familiar. "I'm sure we will be able to find one," Christopher told his son, reaching out to grasp his little hands. "A tall and thick one, with wide branches and lots of leaves to hide behind."

The smile on Sebastian's face grew wider and wider. "You think we can build a tree house? A fort perhaps?"

Christopher nodded excitedly. "Of course. I would love nothing more." Indeed, as a little boy, he, too, had dreamed of such a fortification. Yet his father had merely rolled his eyes and urged him to return to his studies.

Christopher had never asked again. "We will build it together, you and I," he promised his son, watching the boy's face light up in a way that made him catch his breath. Yes, this was it. This was what he lived for; to see this look on his son's face. It was priceless, and he would do everything within his power to keep it there for as long as possible.

"Do you think Mrs. O'Brien can come visit us?" Sebastian asked suddenly, a tentative look in his eyes and a hint of sadness lingering upon the corners of his mouth.

Sighing, Christopher reached out and pulled his son onto his lap. "You miss her dearly, do you not?"

Snuggling into his father's embrace, Bash nodded his head. "Do you think she'll miss me, too?"

Christopher wrapped his arms tightly around his son. "Oh, she will miss you every minute of every day," he said cheerfully, trying to coax a smile from his son. "She will be completely put off by finding none of her biscuits stolen from the kitchen. Indeed, she will be utterly confused to find no sticky fingerprints upon the piano and no heaps of dirt upon the floors."

Sebastian giggled. "Where we are going, will there be marmalade?"

Tousling his son's hair, Christopher pressed a kiss to his forehead. "As much as you can eat."

With his son in his arms, Christopher looked out the window, excitement beginning to course through his veins as they drew closer to Whickerton Grove. Perhaps he ought to have sent a letter ahead. Would Sebastian feel overwhelmed if the entire Whickerton clan came pouring out the doors as one?

Despite his concern, Christopher chuckled, for he would not put it past them. As kind and compassionate as they were, their curiosity often knew no bounds. Perhaps he also ought to have sent a letter to Nora. He knew that his sister would very much like to meet her nephew. Whenever he had spoken to her of Sebastian, she had listened intently, eager to know everything he could tell her. Indeed, he should not have hidden his son away for so long. It had seemed like a good idea. He had wanted to protect him. However, he had failed to see that by cutting him off from the rest of the world, from his family, he had also isolated him.

Closing his eyes, Christopher wished he could take back the past five years. If he could, he would do things differently. In retrospect, it all seemed so simple. How could he not have seen it?

"Is that it?" Little Bash asked as he leaned forward, finger pointing out the window. "Is that the house? Is that where we are going?"

Opening his eyes, Christopher found himself looking at Whickerton Grove. It stood tall and proud, yet the way the afternoon sun peeked through the heavy gray clouds here and there and seemed to dance from window to window made it appear almost magical. Tall evergreens stood everywhere, their colors mingling with the reds, browns and oranges of the fallen leaves blanketing the ground. A deep sigh escaped his lips. "Yes, son, this is it. This is home."

Once more, Sebastian sat with his eyes glued to the window, watching intently as Whickerton Grove drew closer. The carriage rumbled along, picking up leaves here and there, as the winds brushed by on its way north. Lights shone in many windows, and as they approached, the front door opened, and Christopher could see a woman step out. Her brown hair glistened in the setting sun, and although he could not see her eyes, he knew them to be the most brilliant green he had ever seen.

Juliet.

On his lap, Sebastian seemed to be holding his breath. "Who is that?" Craning his neck backward, he looked at his father. "Is that her?"

The deep smile that came to Christopher's face felt wonderful. "Yes, that is Juliet. She must be very eager to meet you."

Again, Bash's little teeth sank into his bottom lip as he nervously fidgeted in Christopher's arms. Oddly, it reminded Christopher of Juliet. "Do you think she'll like me?" he asked for at least the tenth time.

Christopher hoped that upon meeting Juliet, his son would find the assurance he so needed. "She'll love you." He tickled his son, grinning at him. "Believe me, it's like a magic spell. No one can escape it. Whoever sets eyes upon you will instantly lose their heart."

Sebastian giggled, excitement lighting up his eyes...and then the carriage pulled to a halt and his face fell.

"Courage," Christopher whispered, taking his son's hand as he alighted from the carriage, his eyes moving to meet Juliet's. He could see that she was nervous, her hands clasped together and slightly trembling. Yet the light in her eyes told him everything he needed to know. He could see her gaze moving from him as she tried to see past his shoulder, no doubt eager to glimpse the boy who was to be her son.

And then they stood there, facing each other. Christopher held his son's hand safely within his own, fully aware that neither one of them had moved yet.

Juliet's eyes swept over Sebastian's face, her own lighting up with a myriad of emotions. Her cheeks glowed rosy, and her eyes were wide. She shivered, if from the cold or the excitement Christopher did not know. However, after inhaling a deep breath, she finally stepped forward.

Slow steps carried her down to them, her eyes never falling from Sebastian's. "Welcome," she said gently, quietly, her voice trembling ever so slightly. Again, she inhaled a deep breath, and then after finally granting Christopher another look into her moss-green eyes, she kneeled in front of Sebastian and looked into his face. "You must be Sebastian. I am so happy to finally meet you. Your father has already told me the most wonderful things about you, and I must admit I'm quite eager to get to know you for myself."

Christopher watched as the tense expression on their son's face broke and the hint of a smile flitted across his features. "Father calls me Bash."

"Bash?" Juliet exclaimed with a wide smile. "Indeed, what a wonderful name! May I call you Bash as well?"

The smile on Sebastian's face grew a fraction wider, and he nodded with eager eyes.

"How wonderful!" Juliet glanced up at Christopher before once more settling her attention on Sebastian. "You know, perhaps you could help me with something. I have at least a dozen marmalade tarts sitting uneaten in the drawing room."

Christopher felt his son's hand tighten within his own, his little eyes growing round as he held his breath in excitement.

"No one is brave enough to try them," Juliet continued. "I was wondering if you would care to have one?"

Bash's little head bobbed up and down eagerly. "Yes, please."

"Do you like marmalade tarts?"

Again, his head bobbed up and down eagerly. "Yes, I do. Very much."

Juliet clasped her hands together in joy. "That is indeed marvelous."

She pushed to her feet and then slowly extended her hand to him. "Shall I show you the way?" With a mischievous grin, she glanced at Christopher. "Perhaps we will find one for your father as well. Or shall we keep them all to ourselves?"

Sebastian chuckled, and then, fraction by fraction, slid his other hand into hers.

CHAPTER THIRTY-NINE

SHARED FAMILY

Juliet thought her heart would burst into a million pieces. It was beating so fast. She felt Sebastian's warm little hand within her own and knew that she would never be able to let him go again. She had known ever since her gaze had fallen on his little face, ever since she had looked into his wide blue eyes.

His mother's eyes.

Alice.

Indeed, part of Juliet had hoped that Sebastian had inherited his father's warm brown gaze, afraid of how she might feel should that not be the case. Yet the moment she had looked into that little face, something as trivial as the color of his eyes had no longer mattered. Her heart had gone out to him. Even if she had wished it so, she would not have been able to prevent it. She wondered if this was how mothers felt the moment they were handed their babies right after birth. This overwhelming knowledge that the world had shifted off its axis and now revolved around this little life. No matter what would happen in the future, what might be put in her path, everything that now mattered was this child, his well-being, his happiness.

Blinking back tears, Juliet led Sebastian into the drawing room.

"Here we are," she exclaimed, sweeping out an arm to gesture towards the stack of marmalade tarts upon the coffee table. "I hope you're hungry."

Oh, the way Sebastian's little eyes grew round almost knocked her legs out from under her! He was so sweet and adorable and absolutely endearing. She could have stood there and stared at him for hours.

"May I take one?" Sebastian asked, his little fingers barely an inch away from one of the tarts. He seemed desperately eager to reach for one, but apparently, he had recalled his manners at the last moment.

"Help yourself," Juliet urged him, wondering when the day would come that he would feel perfectly at home with her.

"You're a natural at this," Christopher whispered in her ear as he came to stand with her, one arm snaking around her waist, pulling her closer. "I missed you."

Excited shivers danced down Juliet's back, and she turned to look at him. "I've missed you as well." She glanced at Sebastian as he wolfed down his first tart. "The both of you." Sighing, she shook her head. "I never knew I could feel like this."

Christopher's eyes were hesitant as he looked into hers. "Then... you have not changed your mind? You truly believe you can be his mother?"

"Without a doubt," Juliet replied without a second of hesitation, surprised how deeply the thought of losing this little boy unsettled her, pained her. "He is mine now, and don't you ever think about taking him away from me," she warned Christopher with a stern look.

Pulling her into his arms, Christopher laughed. "I wouldn't dream of it." Then he dipped his head and kissed her. "You do not know how much I missed you."

"Do you want one as well?" Sebastian asked, his wide blue eyes darting back and forth between Juliet and his father.

Nodding, Juliet pulled Christopher along, and they all sat down upon the settee. Then Sebastian handed each of them a marmalade tart, his little fingers already sticky and a big drop of the fruity goodness shining orange like the setting sun upon his stark white shirt.

"These are good," Sebastian remarked in a serious tone, like one who had spent his entire life tasting tarts and judging their quality. "They almost taste as good as Mrs. O'Brien's."

"Mrs. O'Brien?" Juliet asked, eager to speak to her son and learn more about him. "Who is she?"

Taking another bite, Sebastian spoke to her of his home in Ireland, of the people he had grown up with. He told her about Mrs. Whiskerson and her little kittens, about the best climbing tree in the garden beyond the house, about the biscuits he liked to sneak from the kitchen, and the piano that made the most beautiful sounds...even though he did not know how to play it.

Juliet listened intently, mesmerized by the little boy. "Did you name all her kittens?"

Sebastian bobbed his head up and down. "Of course. How will you tell them apart without names? The stripy one is—" he broke off when a knock sounded on the door.

Juliet, too, flinched. "Oh, I'd all but forgotten," she murmured to herself, then looked at Sebastian, who stared back and forth between her and the door, eyes wide and a hint of nervousness in them. "Come in," Juliet called, reaching out a hand to place upon his shoulder.

The door swung open, and in walked Samantha with Biscuit, her talking parrot, perched upon her shoulder. For a six-year-old, the girl walked with such confidence that Juliet had never once wondered who this little girl would grow up to be.

No doubt, a force to be reckoned with.

"Hello," she greeted them cheerfully. "You must be Sebastian. I'm Samantha, but you can call me Sam. And this is Biscuit." She gently traced her curved forefinger along the parrot's beak. "He chose that name himself. I think he chose it because he likes biscuits. But only almond biscuits and only if they're not burned. Oh, and he can talk!"

For a moment, Sebastian stared at Samantha, looking overwhelmed. Then, however, a fascinated smile spread across his face. "What does he say?"

Even with the bird sitting upon her shoulder, Samantha managed to shrug. "Anything. Everything. He often likes to repeat what we say."

Squawk. Squawk. "What we say. What we say," Biscuit chimed in at that moment as though to prove Samantha's point.

Sebastian giggled, then stared wide-eyed at the bird. "He truly talks!" He spun around and looked at his father. "Father, he truly talks! Did you hear that?"

Christopher laughed, clearly delighted to see his son so overjoyed. "Yes, I did. He is a marvelous creature, is he not?"

Sebastian's head bobbed up and down for what seemed like the tenth time that day. "Marvelous," he breathed in awe.

"Sebastian," Juliet addressed him, "this is my niece, Samantha." She inhaled a deep breath. "Your new cousin."

Sebastian looked from her to the little girl and then back. "Does… Does that make you, my mother?"

Before Juliet could find any words to reply, Samantha strode forward. "Of course, it does. Once she marries your father, she will be your mother. Just like Christina became my mother when she married my father." Squaring her shoulders, she looked at Sebastian with a hint of superiority in her eyes, the wisdom of one roughly a year older.

Juliet swallowed, then reached out again and placed a gentle hand upon Sebastian's shoulder. She waited until he looked at her and then asked, "Would you like me to be?"

For a long, seemingly endless moment, the little boy simply looked at her before finally his little head bobbed up and down once more.

Juliet felt tears shoot to her eyes, and she tried her best to blink them away. "I would like that, too," she told him with a wobble in her voice.

Squawk. Squawk. "Like that, too. Like that, too," Biscuit chimed in, perhaps feeling a bit neglected. In any case, it broke the soft tension that lingered upon them, for they all broke out laughing until tears streamed down their faces.

"Biscuit often makes people laugh," Samantha giggled joyfully. "Would you like to pet him?" Without waiting for an answer, she sidled closer to Sebastian. "He is very friendly. Auntie Harriet gave him to me." Her eyes suddenly widened, and her face lit up with excitement. "Perhaps we can ask her to find you a pet, too. Grandma and Grandpa always say that no matter where Auntie Harriet goes, she always finds creatures in need." Her little nose crinkled a little. "They also say that is how she met her husband; although, I'm not sure what that means."

Utterly fascinated, Sebastian stared at Samantha, then at the bird, and then at Samantha again. "Who is Auntie Harriet?" he finally asked, clearly overwhelmed by the flood of information.

Smiling, Juliet reached for his little hand. "Samantha's Auntie Harriet is my sister. Well, one of my sisters." She felt his little eyes watching her intently. "To tell you the truth, I have four sisters," his eyes grew round, "who are all married, one cousin, who is married as well, and one brother, who—"

"Is also married?" Sebastian interjected with a giggle, and Juliet delighted in the way he simply spoke his mind.

"Well..."

"Not yet," Christopher stated with a sideways glance at her, his eyes twinkling with something like hope and expectation. Indeed, before he had left, they had spoken of the possibility that Troy and Nora might be in love. Clearly, something had happened between them. Yet after visiting her future mother-in-law and hearing Nora's declaration that she would never have children, Juliet wondered what might happen down the line.

"You have a big family," Sebastian stated with a hint of envy. "A very big family. I only have Father and Mrs. O'Brien."

"Not anymore," Samantha replied, a wide grin on her face. "You're one of us now. My aunts and uncles are your aunts and uncles. My grandmother and grandfather are your grandmother and grandfather, and I think Grandma Edie," she glanced at Juliet for confirmation, "is somehow everyone's Grandma Edie."

Juliet laughed, as did Christopher. They laughed until more tears streamed down their cheeks. Sebastian looked at them with a soft, little frown before he turned to Samantha, clearly convinced that she had all the information he needed and knew what she was talking about. "Where are they?"

Samantha pointed at the closed door. "Right outside, probably with their ears pressed to the door. They don't want to frighten you by all rushing in at the same time, but they're dying to meet you. Shall I let them in?"

For a moment, Sebastian hesitated, his little hand reaching for his father's. Then, however, he nodded, an expectant smile spreading over his little face. "Yes."

In that moment, Juliet knew everything was the way it ought to be. If there had been no Alice, there would be no Sebastian.

And that would be a sad world, indeed.

CHAPTER FORTY

FINALLY HOME

Watching his son, Christopher sighed with relief. Although the boy's eyes were a bit wide as the Whickerton clan swarmed around him, there was a look of awe upon his face that spoke of finding one's dreams come true...

...and oneself unable to believe it.

Sebastian's hand tightened upon Christopher's, and he looked up for reassurance. "All is well," Christopher assured his son. "I know they're a bit loud and wild," he cast a wicked grin at the Whickertons, "but they mean well."

Laughter followed, and while Lord and Lady Whickerton as well as their sons-in-law hung back, the sisters had no such qualms. Soon, Sebastian was kneeling on the floor next to Samantha and Harriet, trying to get Biscuit to speak. Occasionally, the parrot would oblige them, whereas at other times he would lift his head rather haughtily and all but roll his eyes.

"He's a charming boy, Christopher," Lady Whickerton told him with a gentle pat of the hand, a warm smile upon her face. "We are very happy to welcome him into our midst."

"Thank you," Christopher said, pulling Juliet tighter into his arms as emotions choked his voice. Indeed, those two words did not even begin to convey what he felt. Always had he wanted this for Sebastian—a family proud to call him their own—but feared it would never come to pass.

"So," Lord Whickerton exclaimed, "when's the wedding?"

Juliet laughed, a fetching blush coming to her cheeks.

"As soon as possible," Christopher replied with a chuckle, suddenly impatient to begin this beautiful life he glimpsed upon the horizon.

"I'll have the banns read as soon as possible," Lord Whickerton replied with a knowing smile before his gaze moved to his daughter. "You do not know what it means to me," he glanced at his wife, "to us, to see you so happy."

Christopher watched Juliet's eyes dart to Sebastian. "I think I'm beginning to understand." Then she sighed and sidled closer to him, taking his hand before drawing him a few steps away from the rest of her family. "Listen, when Sebastian has settled in, there is...something I need to speak to you about."

Christopher frowned, for he could see the way Juliet's teeth dug into her lower lip. She was anxious, and yet the look in her eyes held... hope. What had happened during his absence? "What is it?"

Again, she cast a look in Sebastian's direction. "I went to speak to your mother."

Christopher felt his jaw drop. "You did what?" An icy chill traced down his spine. "Why? Why would you...?" He pulled her closer, suddenly concerned. "What did she say? I'm sorry if she was rude to you. You know that my mother has her own opinions."

Juliet nodded. "I know; however, I thought it best to clear the air before Sebastian arrived."

Christopher scoffed, rolling his eyes. "I'm grateful you tried," he whispered, placing a kiss upon her forehead. "Please do not feel bad. My mother is as stubborn as—" The slow smile that curled up the corners of Juliet's lips gave him pause; yet a hint of sorrow remained in her eyes.

Christopher was confused. Had she broken his mother's icy exterior or not? Was she glad or disappointed?

"What I need to tell you is not easily said," Juliet continued, her voice so low that he could barely understand her, especially considering the myriad of voices echoing through the room. "Perhaps tomorrow we can go outside. I'm sure Harriet will be more than happy to distract the children, and then we can talk."

Christopher watched her carefully. "Do I need to worry?" he asked the question lightly, hoping Juliet would simply laugh his concerns away.

She did not. What had she learned from his mother? What had happened? Whatever it was, Christopher doubted that life would ever be the same again once he knew.

Juliet reached up to cup his cheek. "It will not be easy to hear, but it will help you understand, for it'll answer every question you've ever asked yourself."

Christopher stared at her. "You cannot seriously say something like this and then make me wait until tomorrow," he exclaimed in a rushed whisper, grasping her left hand and holding it tightly within his own.

"I'm sorry," Juliet murmured, once more glancing past his shoulder. "I don't think Sebastian feels comfortable without you yet, and this is something he should not hear." Sighing, she frowned. "I'm sorry. I suppose I shouldn't have said anything."

Reluctantly, Christopher nodded, once more pulling her into his arms. He shifted and looked at his son, who was laughing at something Biscuit had said. Yes, they had finally come home. He could wait a day.

One day was nothing.

Now, he needed to focus on his child.

Fortunately, the rest of the day kept his thoughts well occupied, for it seemed the Whickertons were determined to make up for the years they had spent without Sebastian. They showed him around their ancestral home, pointing out all the many hiding places the sisters had found and used throughout their lives. Samantha instructed him how best to slide down the banister in the hall as well as the most opportune moment for sneaking biscuits—for Biscuit or themselves—out of the kitchen. A stroll before supper led them to the stables and then to the small pond before Samantha and Sebastian disappeared into the nearby grove in search of the perfect tree.

"You're aware that you'll have to build them a fort now," Lord

Whickerton asked Christopher, laughing as they watched the two children dart from tree to tree.

Christopher could not say that he minded. It was an adventure he longed for.

Samantha's father chuckled. "Oh, don't we all wish we could have had one?" He looked at Christopher. "I'll help you build it if you like."

Clasping his future brother-in-law's shoulder, Christopher nodded. "I'll appreciate the help."

Soon, not only Phineas but also Drake and Jack offered their assistance—the last two with a bit of a doubtful expression, though. "Hey, is this a men-only project," Harriet challenged, "or is everyone invited?"

A wide grin came over Jack's face as he looked at his wife. "I've never known you to need an invitation to do anything."

Harriet playfully punched him on the shoulder. "Yet an invitation is appreciated," she told him with a teasingly sweet smile.

Christopher laughed. "Well, then let this be a family project," he looked down and met Juliet's eyes, "for Samantha and Sebastian and all of our children yet to be born."

"Hear! Hear!" Louisa exclaimed; one hand placed gently upon her rounded belly.

Indeed, it was a moment Christopher would never forget. He breathed in deeply, felt the chilled evening air fill his lungs and let his eyes sweep over the distant horizon, streaks of red and orange and purple lighting up the world. He saw Sebastian dart in and out of the trees, Samantha close on his heels and laughter spilling from both their mouths. Harriet and Phineas chased them, pretending to be dragons and other monstrous creatures, making the children shriek with delight. By the time Sebastian broke away and ran to fling himself into Christopher's arms, he was panting hard, his face flushed and his eyes aglow in a way that melted Christopher's heart.

Yes, this was where they were meant to be. This was the family they were meant to have. It had taken them—him!—a long time; yet it had been worth it, every obstacle, every doubt, every moment of despair.

This...was home.

CHAPTER FORTY-ONE
THE ORIGIN OF A LIFE

Juliet was overjoyed and relieved and so, so happy to see Sebastian take to his new family with such natural ease. Truth be told, someone unaware of how recently the little boy had joined their family would no doubt think him born to them. It was such a delight to see him with Samantha; after only one day, the two of them were already thick as thieves. Harriet, of course, was a blessing. She had a way with children, with anyone, that was absolutely disarming. Juliet watched Sebastian laugh and giggle and smile, and she felt her heart beat with a mother's relief to see her son happy.

"I've never seen that smile on your face," Christopher whispered as they walked along the garden arm in arm, their breaths mingling in the chilled air. "It is not for me, is it?" He winked at her.

Juliet heaved a deep sigh, one she felt in every fiber of her being. "I'm afraid not," she told him with a smile that grew wider as she looked across the small expanse toward the little boy who had come to mean everything to her. "Only this morning," she whispered, her gaze never leaving Sebastian, "he asked me if I would ever leave." The longing look in his eyes was one she knew she would never forget. "When I told him I would never dream of it, that I would remain at his side until the end of my days, he took my hand and looked up at me in a way that seemed wise beyond his years." Tears shot to her eyes, and she turned to look at Christopher, a smile tickling the corners of her mouth. "He said, 'Good', and then squeezed my hand. Oh, Christopher, I feel it now. I truly do. I had not thought it possible, especially not so quickly, but now I know. It is true."

Although joy still stood upon Christopher's face, a hint of confusion came to his eyes at her words. "What is true?" he asked, reaching for her hand, and pulling her closer before she could flutter away in her excitement.

Juliet sighed deeply, her eyes looking up into his. "I am his mother," she whispered, overcome by the awe she heard in her own voice. "I truly am. I can feel it deep inside. I thought it would take months, at least weeks." She shook her head, disbelief still rushing through her every once in a while. "But I already know."

Christopher laughed, then he pulled her into his arms and spun her around in a wide circle. "You have no idea how happy it makes me to hear you say that," he murmured once he had set her back down on her feet. "The two of you," he glanced over his shoulder to where Sebastian was still playing with Samantha and Harriet, "are two halves of my life. I cannot imagine it without either of you."

Juliet nodded. "I know. Believe me, I know. But you don't have to." She sank into his arms. "Everything is coming together the way it was meant to be. I truly believe that. For so long, I doubted the course of my life, what I was meant to do, who I was meant to be, but no longer. It was not a straight path—I suppose it rarely is—however, it led me to the very spot that has always been meant for me."

Resting his forehead against hers, Christopher murmured, "I feel exactly the same way. If only we had not lost these past few years. That is my one regret."

Juliet lifted her head a fraction to look into his eyes. "Not for me," she whispered, watching the puff of her breath dance away on the cold autumn breeze.

Christopher frowned, a hint of doubt coming to his eyes, the same kind of doubt Juliet had often seen upon his face whenever his parents had been concerned. "No, you misunderstand. I do wish we could've had these past five years together; however, part of me cannot help but think that if things had been different, if your parents had been different, would Sebastian exist today?" She lifted her brows in question, looking up into his face.

Understanding dawned, and Christopher nodded. "Yes, perhaps you're right." He closed his eyes and breathed in deeply. When he opened them again, Juliet could see a question there. "Will you now tell me?"

With a glance over her shoulder, Juliet ensured Sebastian was far enough away to not be within earshot. "Yes," she finally said, trying to find the right words. However, she doubted words existed that would cushion the blow of what she was about to say. And so, she simply began at the beginning, telling him of her visit to Fartherington Hall. She spoke of his mother's objections, objections he well knew, about his mother's doubts regarding her raising another woman's child.

"It is almost exactly what she said to me," Christopher replied, sadness darkening his face. "When I stopped at Fartherington Hall on my way to Ireland, I told her what I wanted to do, what we wanted to do and...she was appalled." His hands tensed upon Juliet's. "I no longer held back, as I was no longer worried about disappointing her. At that moment, I no longer cared. I spoke my mind until I realized what she thought no longer mattered...and so, I simply left."

Juliet believed his words, and yet she could see that they pained him. Despite everything that had happened, despite all his disappointments, he still wanted his mother's affection, her respect, her devotion. And he deserved it, just as any child did.

"I did the same," Juliet told him, taking his hands, and guiding him farther away from the others. They walked to the edge of the forest and then sat down upon a fallen log, facing one another, his eyes expectant. "I think Grandma Edie saw it first. She pretended to need a walk and asked Nora to accompany her. The look she gave me when they left..." Juliet shook her head, trying to express what she had felt in that moment. "I don't know. It gave me pause. It made me think that I was overlooking something. I couldn't quite put my finger on what she wanted to tell me, and so I simply asked the very question you've been asking yourself your whole life."

Christopher's eyes fell from hers, and he bowed his head. A shuddering breath drifted from his lips before he looked up again and met her gaze. "You know, I don't know how many times I told myself to simply ask her. I don't know why I never did. It was cowardly of me but..."

Squeezing his hands, Juliet smiled at him. "It was not cowardly. There's nothing cowardly about wanting one's mother's love." She reached out to brush an errant curl from his forehead. "Of course, it was easier for me. She's not my mother, and it was not my heart to be broken."

Nodding, Christopher inhaled a deep breath. "What did she say?"

A part of Juliet shied away from voicing the truth. She knew it would hurt; however, eventually it would be a relief. "She told me that her late husband...was not your father."

For a seemingly endless moment, Christopher simply stared at her. Then, as the truth slowly sank in, his features all but derailed. She could see disbelief and confusion, as well as denial and anger. However, lurking beneath them all was relief.

Even now.

Relief to finally make sense of something that had always been shrouded in secret.

Relief to finally have one's questions answered.

Slowly, bit by bit, Juliet told her future husband everything his mother had told her. She left nothing out and spoke of the night that had changed one family's lives forever.

Not uttering a single word, Christopher listened, his face pale and his hands clamped around hers. Every once in a while, Juliet felt his hands tense almost painfully before they once more released their grip as though he suddenly remembered not to hurt her.

"Are you all right?" Juliet finally asked, knowing it to be a completely inadequate question. How on earth was he supposed to answer? Yet what else was there to say?

Christopher shrugged. Then his gaze moved out toward the horizon, and for a long time, they simply sat there, side by side, watching the chilled autumn breeze shake leaves off the trees surrounding them. They rained down upon them like snowflakes, beautiful golden snowflakes. "If I'd known," he finally whispered, his gaze still fixed upon the horizon, "I would've..." He shrugged, then shook his head, completely at a loss.

"She should have told you," Juliet murmured gently. "They should have told you. And yet I can understand why they did not, why they could not. I think they tried to do the best they could. They could not know how everything would turn out. They did not know how it would affect you. I don't think they treated you differently with intention. I think...it simply happened. It was one of those things that one cannot help, one of those things one barely realizes. It was wrong but..."

Raking a hand through his hair, Christopher turned to look at her, a weak smile coming to his face. "How am I supposed to feel about this? Am I supposed to be relieved? Angry? Disappointed?" he shrugged, something hard coming to his jaw. "I'm unsure if I should cry or rant or throw something or..." He shot to his feet and began to pace, his hands running through his hair again and again. Every once in a while, he would stop and look at her before spinning around once more and resuming his pacing.

"There is no supposed to," Juliet told him as she rose from the log. "You feel whatever it is you feel. There is no right or wrong. You don't have to choose. You can feel disappointed and angry and relieved, all at the same time. But know this," she paused and waited until he turned to look at her, "your mother regrets what happened, what she did to you, and she believes she has no right to be forgiven." Watching tears collect in the corners of his eyes, Juliet stepped forward and placing her hands upon his arms, she looked up into his face. "You do what is right for you, and no one will hold it against you. However, perhaps with time, there is a chance for the two of you to get to know one another as the people you are today. Should you wish it."

His lips pressed into a thin line as he nodded his head, then he paused and shook it from side to side. "I don't know," he forced out through gritted teeth, the look upon his face vulnerable one moment and then hardened the next. "I don't know what I want."

"You don't have to. Not now. There is time."

Sighing deeply, Christopher nodded. "Good," he said, echoing his son's earlier reply. It made Juliet smile, and she cupped a hand to his face, feeling his cool cheek against her warm skin. Then he blinked, and his gaze focused upon hers. Something urgent lay in his eyes, and he grabbed her as though afraid she would dissolve into thin air. "You're my family," he said then, vehemence in his voice. "You've always been my family, Jules. Whenever my parents broke my heart with their rejection, you were there. You've always been there." Tears rolled down his cheeks. "I was a fool not to see it sooner. I should have. I wish I had. But I know now, and I will never let you go again, do you hear me?"

Blinking back tears, Juliet nodded. "I do. I hear you, Kit."

A smile sparked on his face. "I love you and I want us to be a family. Will you marry me?"

Juliet chuckled. "You're asking me again? Did I not already say yes?"

Christopher shrugged, the look on his face softening, as it was now marked by happiness. "I find I enjoy proposing to you...and hearing your answer."

Understanding the doubts that still clawed at his heart, Juliet pushed closer, her nose almost touching his as she looked deep into his eyes. "Ask me as often as you need to but know that my answer will always be *yes*."

Swallowing, he nodded, and Juliet could see how desperately he had needed her to say those words. "Good," he mumbled once more before hauling her into his arms and kissing her soundly.

Oh, despite everything that had happened and everything that remained to be seen, Juliet had never felt more at peace.

Patience had indeed been rewarded.

More than she ever would have dared to hope.

CHAPTER FORTY-TWO

A WEDDING LONG AWAITED

"I love this idea!" Harriet exclaimed as Christopher watched her and Jack walk arm in arm through the gardens toward the pavilion. "We should have done this. Don't you think?"

Jack laughed, and Christopher wondered about Juliet's newest brother-in-law. Indeed, as stoic and stern as he sometimes seemed, the moment his fiery-haired wife was nearby, he seemed to transform. To Christopher, it almost felt as though he were watching someone come alive. It was a thought that echoed within him, for he, too, felt as though his life had only just begun.

Now.

With Juliet.

"Get married outside?" Jack asked, reaching out and twirling a fiery strand of Harriet's hair around a finger. He gazed down at her in a way that made Christopher smile, that made him feel absolutely certain that Harriet had indeed found her perfect match. It was a look of utter devotion, of awe and disbelief, one that stated loud and clear that Jack knew how lucky he was to have Harriet by his side and that he would never even dream of taking her for granted.

"Yes, this is beautiful!" Harriet replied with a wide sweep of her arm. She quickly winked at Christopher as she spotted him standing half-hidden behind the trunk of an old oak before quickly redirecting her attention toward her husband. "Whenever I sneaked away to meet you, it was in a meadow, wasn't it?" She pushed closer, her hands sliding up his shoulders and snaking around his neck. "Our meadow."

Inhaling a deep breath, Jack drew his wife closer. "Our meadow."

"We should have gotten married there. Among the wildflowers." A faraway look came to Harriet's eyes, and she sighed deeply.

Christopher grinned as his gaze swept over *their* pavilion, Juliet's and his. No, there were no wildflowers here, especially not this time of year; however, the groves of trees randomly dotting the estate's garden here and there looked all but aflame, most of their leaves colored a brilliant red, mingling with orange, brown and gold. Heaps had already fallen to the ground while others still remained upon the branches above. It was a beautiful sight, as though the world had put on its best for today's occasion.

Bash and Sam were chasing each other through the leaves, tossing them about so that it almost appeared to be raining leaves. Their laughter echoed across the garden, welcoming more and more Whickertons as they made their way outdoors. Dressed warmly against the cold, their cheeks shone rosy and their eyes glowed with joy.

"I'm so happy for you, dear brother," Nora told him when she arrived, a smile upon her lips and tears misting her eyes. "I know how long you've been waiting for this." She embraced him, and he hugged her close.

"Thank you," Christopher whispered, relieved that she had come. Mourning or not, this was his wedding day! And he needed her here!

"Mother understands," Nora murmured as she pulled back and her eyes looked up into his. "Don't worry. She understands. This is your day, and you need to do what feels right."

Swallowing the lump in his throat, Christopher nodded, uncertain how to reply. And so, he remained quiet, relieved to see Nora greet the Whickerton sisters after more than a year. There was something hesitant in her demeanor, as though she was uncertain how she would be received after her long absence. Yet Christopher was not surprised to see Harriet and Louisa pull her into their arms without a moment's hesitation.

Drawing in a deep breath, Christopher moved toward the pavilion, casting smiles at all those already gathered there. Yet his mind replayed his sister's words. Indeed, he had sent an invitation to Nora, but not to his mother. Of course, he ought to have, but he had not wanted to.

"Then don't," Juliet had said, not a hint of doubt in her brilliant green eyes. "She will understand. I promise you. Too much has happened. Staring over takes time." She had pulled him close then, enfolding him in her arms and the soft caresses of her fingers along the back of his neck had soothed away all Christopher's concerns.

And she had been right, had she not? Had Nora not just told him that his mother understood? Was it true? Perhaps it was. Perhaps she truly knew that he could not enjoy his wedding day with the reminder of all that had happened staring at him.

Perhaps.

Christopher knew that that day would come that he would speak to his mother. But that day was not today. No, today he would marry Juliet. Finally! He ought to have married her years ago, and he would not wait another day.

Not one.

Everything else simply had to wait.

Juliet could not help but pinch herself, and a chuckle drifted from her lips as she saw the red spots dotting her arm. Indeed, she had been pinching herself all morning, afraid that this day would prove to be nothing more than a dream. Oh, how often had she dreamed of this! How often had she imagined the day she would marry Christopher!

Only to wake and feel as hollow as she had the moment she had closed her eyes.

"I assure you you are awake."

Spinning around, Juliet found Leonora's husband, Drake, standing in the doorway, his gray eyes watchful as he moved closer. He was a man who rarely smiled, rarely spoke; yet he had a way of seeing things other people missed. "Is it so obvious?" Juliet asked with a bashful smile.

The corners of Drake's lips twitched. "Perhaps not. Perhaps I simply know the feeling."

Juliet regarded him curiously, knowing that he had been the one who had helped Leonora banish her demons, who had seen her pain and known exactly what she had needed. Indeed, he often appeared distant and even cold; however, beneath that reserved exterior beat a compassionate heart. "You love her very much, do you not?" Juliet heard herself ask, surprised at her boldness; yet it seemed fitting.

Drake nodded slowly. "Yet every day I wake and for a moment I cannot believe that she is mine." Awe swung in his voice, and Juliet knew Leonora had found a man like no other. "Your betrothed feels the same."

Juliet blinked, and for a second, she forgot to breathe. "Do you... Do you truly believe so?"

"It is easy to see," Drake assured her, a rare smile tugging upon his lips. "You're his dream come true, and yet there are still moments he is reluctant to open his eyes for fear of seeing it snatched away."

Inhaling a deep breath, Juliet nodded. Yes, she had observed that as well. Even more than herself, Christopher seemed fearful. Afraid to trust that she loved him, that he was worthy of love. His parents' rejection had hurt him, broken something in him that still needed time to heal.

"Thank you," Juliet said quietly, grateful for Drake's assessment. She smiled up at him, feeling a new connection to the man, who barely said two words. "Thank you."

Drake nodded in return.

"There you are!" came Leonora's voice as she rushed into the room, the look upon her face quite different from the rather serene expression she often bore. "I've been looking for you everywhere!" Her wide blue eyes moved from Juliet to her husband. "Is something wrong?"

Exchanging a look with Drake, Juliet smiled at her sister. "No, everything is wonderful."

Leonora hesitated for a moment, clearly aware that something meaningful had passed between the other two. Then she grasped Juliet's hands. "Well, then come quickly. They're about to begin."

Rather uncharacteristically, Drake chuckled. "Don't fret, love. They can't start without her. She's the bride."

Looking up at her husband, Leonora laughed. "I suppose you're right." She embraced Juliet. "Oh, I'm so happy for you."

Juliet smiled, suddenly feeling inexplicably happy, as though the meaning of this day had only just sunk in. "Thank you, Leo. Why don't you two go ahead? I'll be right out. I promise."

A knowing look came to Leonora's face. "Very well." She tugged a curl back behind Juliet's ear. "You look beautiful." Then she accepted her husband's arm and, heads bent toward one another, they stepped outside.

Exhaling a deep breath, Juliet closed her eyes. This was it! Today was it! Her wedding day! In a few short moments, she would be Christopher's wife! And he would be her husband!

Joy flooded Juliet's being, and suddenly her feet moved, unable to wait a moment longer. She flew outside, feeling the stiff wind sting her heated cheeks as she all but danced down the path toward the pavilion. She glimpsed Leonora and Drake down the path from her and past them the rest of her family. Laughter drifted to her ears, and she smiled as she saw Bash toss an armful of leaves at Sam. The girl shrieked, leaves clinging to her curls in a deeply endearing way.

Juliet sighed. This was happiness, was it not? And then her gaze met Christopher's, and she knew it to be true. This was it! The beginning of the rest of her life!

Of their life.

The smile that claimed Christopher's lips the moment he beheld her told Juliet everything she needed to know. Indeed, this was a dream; but it was one she would never wake from.

Never.

This was a dream come true.

Finally!

CHAPTER FORTY-THREE

A PEACE OFFERING

Christopher knew that as the Earl of Lockhart, he belonged at Fartherington Hall. It was his ancestral home and his duty to see to his people. He had told himself that he would return there once he was married to Juliet; however, their wedding day had come and gone and yet they remained at Whickerton Grove.

Whickerton Grove was home. It meant love and family and companionship. It held laughter and joy and hope. Whereas Fartherington Hall was like a dark cloud hanging over his head connected to all the painful memories of his past. Indeed, he ought to speak to his mother, hear her explanations for himself. Every day, Christopher told himself that the next day he would go.

He did not, though.

Juliet remained patient, as always, with him. Most days they hardly thought of anything else but their new family, enjoying blissful moments alone together as well as with Sebastian and the rest of the Whickerton clan. Yet now and then, he looked into her eyes and knew that one day he would have to face the demons of his past.

The truth Juliet had finally revealed to him after a lifetime of not knowing had completely knocked him off his feet. There was this part of him that raged with anger, wishing to yell into his mother's face and lay blame at her feet for all the dark moments of his life. Yet another, the very same part that loved and cherished the woman he had married felt compassion. The dark part of his soul did not wish to feel it, but it seemed he could not help it. It was there, tempering every thought of retribution, of returning what he had suffered.

At first, Christopher shied away from imagining that night. He had heard Juliet's words, and yet once they had been spoken, he had not returned to them, not looked at them more closely. He had not dared. Yet at night, every once in a while, they would find him in his dreams and he would see not his father and mother and older brother attacked by a band of criminals, but instead himself, Juliet and little Bash.

Indeed, it was that dream, that thought that made him feel even more deeply about what his mother had suffered. Yes, she had done wrong by him, but perhaps...it had not been her fault. What if it had been him? What if it had been Juliet? If something so heinous happened to them, would they have recovered? How would they have coped?

Christopher could not say, and it was that thought that frightened him. Yes, it could have been him. It could have been Juliet. It could have been little Bash.

And then one morning, Christopher woke up, and he knew that the time had come. Somehow, without him even saying a single word, Juliet knew as well. Those kind, patient green eyes looked into his, and she simply knew. She left Sebastian in the care of her sisters and then called for the carriage, diverting all questions as to their destination. She took his hand and led him outside, and then they were off.

Compared to Whickerton Grove, Fartherington Hall was cold and lonely, its halls dark and unwelcoming. Juliet's presence by his side was like a light in the dark, and he clung to her hand. Kindly, she bid the butler to inform the dowager countess that her son and daughter-in-law had arrived and were waiting for her in the drawing room.

The moments it took for his mother to join them were among the longest of Christopher's life. They felt like forever, and he could have sworn he was close to wearing a hole in the carpet in front of the fireplace. And then his mother suddenly stood in the doorway and his feet pulled to a sudden halt. For a second, anger surged into his heart and his mouth opened to lay accusations at her feet, as he had every right to do.

Then, however, Christopher looked into her face and...saw her. Saw the mother he had always longed for. The mother he had always hoped she would be for him one day.

Suddenly, the lines of her face were no longer hard, marked by indifference and disinterest. Her eyes had never quite lingered upon him, never quite seen him as though she could not bear to look at his face. He remembered well the tightness of her lips, the corners of her mouth slightly downturned, a clear sign of her disapproval and disappointment.

Now Christopher saw none of that. Her eyes were misted with tears and looked into his in a way they never had before. She not only saw him, but she also allowed him to see her.

Her regret.

Her pain.

Her broken heart.

"I'm still angry with you," Christopher told her, needing her to know but also to remind himself.

Swallowing, his mother nodded, then stepped closer. "As you have every right to be," she said in a voice heavy with emotions. Christopher could not recall ever having heard her speak like this. She glanced at Juliet on the settee and a smile came to her face, one that spoke of gratitude and affection. "I'm so glad you decided to come today." Her eyes returned to him. "Congratulations on your wedding. I wish you both all the best...no matter where your path might lead you."

"And our son?" Christopher growled, a challenge meant to test her, to taunt her, to see her fail.

Sighing, his mother nodded. "Yes, your son. I do hope he is well and...that you all," she smiled at Juliet once more, "will be a family from now on." Carefully, almost hesitantly, her eyes moved to look into his. "Would you...permit me to meet him?"

Christopher crossed his arms over his chest. "Why?" Indeed, a part of him wanted her to fail, to see her revealed as a liar. He wanted to yell and rant and not have her duck her head as though she truly regretted what had happened, what she had done. Her regret was taking the wind out of his sails, and he was not yet ready to watch his anger be swept away.

Taking a step toward him, his mother wrung her hands. "I…I wish I knew what he looked like. I…" She shrugged, a deeper explanation failing her. "I'm sorry I hid him from you," she whispered, a look of utter incredulity upon her face, as though she could not believe she had truly done it. Then her chin rose, and she met his eyes with a determined look. "I was wrong. What I did was wrong, and…I'm deeply sorry. There…are no words."

That was something Christopher understood. A myriad of emotions raged within him, and yet he could not find the words to do them justice, to express what it was he felt. "I'm sorry," he suddenly heard himself blurt out, for a moment uncertain if he had truly spoken.

His mother's eyes widened in surprise before a slight frown creased her forehead.

Christopher cleared his throat. "I'm sorry for…what happened to you. I wish…I had known." He felt his shoulders slump a little, the tension that had held him suddenly waning. "You should have told me."

His mother nodded. "I know." Something utterly vulnerable came to her pale eyes. "I couldn't though."

Christopher swallowed. "I know," he replied without thinking, realizing that he truly did understand. Indeed, he, too, had been hesitant to speak to Sebastian about Alice, about how the boy had been conceived, about…why his mother had left. He had not wanted Bash to feel abandoned, unwanted, unloved, and although he had known that his motives for wanting to conceal the truth from his son had been pure, he had known deep down that lies could never be the right path.

Yet he had been careful on how he phrased the truth. After all, Sebastian was an innocent little boy. How did one go about telling one's child that his mother had not wanted him without breaking his little heart?

Christopher looked into his mother's tear-misted eyes, knowing that there had been no way for her to tell him the truth without breaking his heart. What would his life have been like if he had known the truth? He could not imagine it. Indeed, his parents' choice had been an impossible one.

"You belong here at Fartherington Hall," his mother suddenly said, dabbing a handkerchief to her eyes. "You and your family." She nodded to give her words more emphasis, her jaw set determinedly. Her eyes, however, remained filled with sorrow. "I shall make arrangements and leave within a fortnight." She cast him a small smile. "It is time happiness returned to these halls. Laughter and joy." She nodded again, and the smile on her face brightened. "Yes, it will be good to have another little Sebastian roam these halls." She sighed. "I can only hope his fate will be happier than his uncle's." Inhaling a deep breath, his mother then moved toward him. Slow steps carried her closer, the look in her eyes marked by uncertainty.

More than once, Christopher thought she would stop and turn away, but she did not. She kept her feet in place, pushing them to carry her toward him. He braced himself, thrown off balance by two contradicting desires: to remain and to flee.

And then his mother stood before him, her pale, tear-misted eyes looking into his. A tentative smile made the corners of her lips twitch as she hesitantly lifted her hands and then placed them upon his chest, right above his wildly beating heart. "I'm so sorry, Christopher," she whispered as tears rolled down her cheeks. "I need you to know that you are a wonderful man. You've proven that more than once; only I was too blind to see it." Her hands tensed, and the look in her eyes became hard, yet imploring. "That man is no more your father than Alice is Sebastian's mother. Do you hear me? Do not for a second believe that anything...he did reflects upon you. Is that understood?" Her tone was hard, harsh even, and yet Christopher was surprised to realize that for the first time she spoke to him as a mother.

His mother.

Holding nothing back.

For his benefit alone and not hers.

A deep breath rushed from his lungs. "I understand," he finally said, nodding his head. It still felt odd to speak to her in such a way, to have her look at him like this, but perhaps with time, he would get used to it. Perhaps..."Stay," he finally said. "There is no need for you to leave. We are quite happy at Whickerton Grove for the time being. Perhaps...Perhaps you would like to come visit us sometime."

A sob escaped his mother's lips and for a second, Christopher thought her knees would buckle. His hands reached out to grasp her arms, but she steadied herself quickly, the look upon her face telling him how grateful she was for this chance.

"Thank you," she whispered in a choked voice. "I'd like that very much."

Over his mother's head, Christopher met Juliet's gaze. Her smile warmed his heart, and he knew that whatever lay ahead, they would be fine as long as they were together.

CHAPTER FORTY-FOUR

FULL CIRCLE

As the first snowflakes drifted down from a brilliant blue sky, Juliet stood by the terrace windows, her husband's arms wrapped around her and her head resting against his shoulder. "I love this house in winter," she murmured, snuggling closer into his embrace. "It is so peaceful and warm, cut off from the rest of the world as though it doesn't even exist."

She felt Christopher smile, then place a kiss upon her temple. "I'm fond of the sprigs of mistletoe, in particular."

Juliet laughed, glancing over to where such a piece of greenery was dangling from the ceiling. "Is that so?" She turned in his arms. "Do you need a reason to kiss your wife?" She lifted her brows teasingly.

Christopher chuckled while his arms tightened around her. Then he dipped his head and kissed her as he did often, even with no mistletoe in sight.

Sighing, Juliet melted into him, trying her best to remind herself that they were not hidden away in their chamber but in a room often frequented by the rest of her family.

Her nosy family.

"Perhaps...we shouldn't," she murmured before he kissed her again, cutting off her words.

His hands held her close to him. "Perhaps we should go upstairs," he suggested meaningfully, placing another kiss upon her lips. "I am quite fond of doors that can be locked to ward off inquisitive visitors." He chuckled.

"We can't," Juliet replied, pulling back as he tried to kiss her again.

A displeased frown came to his face. "Why not?"

Gently, Juliet brushed an unruly lock from his forehead, letting the tips of her fingers graze his skin. At her touch, his eyes narrowed, and he held his breath. "Because our visitors will be here soon. Or have you forgotten?" He tensed ever so slightly, and Juliet reached up to cup his face in her hands. "It will be fine. You'll see."

Sighing, Christopher nodded. Then he closed his eyes and lowered his head to hers, breathing in deeply. "If you say so, it must be true."

Juliet chuckled, pulling him into a tight embrace. Oh, how she loved being in his arms like this! It was more than a simple hug or kiss. It felt as though they were drifting into one another, almost breathing as one, her heart beating in tandem with his.

"Snow! Snow!" It was Samantha's voice that echoed through the closed door. "Bash, do you see that?"

"Yes! Yes! It's snowing! It's snowing!"

"Let's go outside!"

"Oh, yes! Let's!"

Pulling back, Christopher smiled down at her. "How long do you think it'll be before they burst—?"

The door flew open with a loud bang and Bash and Sam rushed inside, their eyes wide and their cheeks flushed. "It's snowing!" they cried in unison.

Juliet smiled as her husband sighed rather theatrically before he glanced out the window. "It's only a few flakes," he pointed out with a frown. "I'm afraid there'll be no snowman building today."

The children's smiles dimmed a little; yet the exuberance that had begun bubbling in their veins was not easily swept away. Within moments, they had alerted the entire house to the fact that it was snowing. Of course, Harriet immediately joined their little cries, her face flushed with excitement as she dragged her husband along. Coats, hats, gloves and scarves were donned before they flung open the door and rushed outside.

A bit more slowly, the rest of the Whickertons joined in, delighting in the children's—and Harriet's—joy. Bundled up, Juliet and Christopher walked down into the gardens watching Bash and Sam twirl in little circles, their faces lifted to the sky as they tried to catch the occasional snowflake upon their tongues.

"Do you think Harry will ever grow up?" Christina asked with a laugh as they watched their sister join the two youngsters. She grinned at her husband, then at Harriet's, who just sighed, a rather enchanted smile upon his face.

Juliet knew that Harriet's Jack did not want his wife to be any different from the way she was. She was wild and unconventional, and although they were like fire and water, day and night, they were a perfect match. Was that not what a good marriage was based on? That one loved the other precisely the way they were?

"Very well," came Louisa's slightly annoyed voice from up the path. "But only a short walk. You do not know how exhausting it is to be this..." She extended her hands around her round belly, the look upon her face making it clear that she was searching for the right words.

"Large," her husband foolishly suggested; yet the wide grin upon his face indicated he was far from foolish but rather enjoyed teasing his wife.

Louisa's eyes narrowed. "Watch it," she warned, a hard edge in her tone. "Or this one will be our last. Heir or no heir."

Completely unperturbed, Phineas pulled her into his arms and placed a deep kiss upon her lips. "Who said I wanted an heir?" He grinned, then murmured something that made Louisa blush and then laugh, not even a spark of anger remaining in her eyes. Indeed, they, too, were an unusual couple, Juliet thought. However, they were perfect for each other as well.

As her eyes swept over her sisters and their husbands as well as her mother and father, Juliet knew they were all incredibly fortunate. In all fairness, today was a rather uneventful, ordinary day—despite the snow!—and yet it felt utterly precious.

This was life, was it not? To be with the ones one held dear, to join in their joy and sadness, to simply be there and watch their lives unfold.

As though her thoughts had called them, Juliet turned to see Christopher's mother and sister head toward them in that moment. Lady Lockhart's steps seemed a bit hesitant as her eyes moved to her son...a moment before they were suddenly drawn to the children, still dancing in a swirl of snowflakes.

To the boy whom she had never met.

The boy who was her grandson.

Seeing the tense look upon her husband's face, Juliet squeezed his hand and then pulled him along. Together, they greeted his mother and sister, and Juliet could not help but notice the way Nora's gaze swept over the assembled Whickertons. Indeed, as she found Troy absent, the look in her eyes dimmed and she sighed. What had happened between them? They clearly cared for one another; why then could they not admit to it?

That, however, was a question for another day.

"Welcome to Whickerton Grove," Juliet said kindly, smiling at her mother-in-law. Clearly, the woman was nervous, a look that suited her, for it made her more approachable. "We were drawn out of the house by the first signs of snow."

Christopher's arm beneath her hand felt tense, and Juliet understood that despite the step mother and son had taken toward one another, a great distance yet remained. She glimpsed hope in her husband's eyes but also unease and a hint of concern. Did he worry for Sebastian? To see his son hurt as he himself had been? Indeed, the memories were still too fresh, too painful, years of doubt and self-reproach having taken their toll.

Remembering her grandmother's words, Juliet knew that Christopher needed her. Here. Now. He needed her to be strong and navigate their way through these stormy waters until he felt calm enough to take over the wheel once more. Yes, she would protect her family and see them safely through this storm.

With an almost imperceptible nod, Juliet answered Christopher's silent request, a reassuring smile upon her face. Then she turned to look at her new mother-in-law. "Shall we? "

Lady Lockhart smiled, and Juliet released her husband's arm, stepping forward to pull her mother-in-law's through her own. Together, they walked down the small slope to where the children—and Harriet!—were trying to catch snowflakes. "We told him you would come today," she said with a sideways glance at her mother-in-law.

Lady Lockhart swallowed, her face tense.

Juliet stopped and turned to her. "Sebastian knows nothing of what happened. It belongs to the past and has no bearing upon your relationship with him." She smiled at her. "This is a new beginning."

Relief softened Lady Lockhart's features, and she blinked back tears as her eyes moved to the little boy. "He looks just like them," she mused, tears still glistening in her eyes as she watched Bash with a mix of awe and disbelief. "When they were little, they all looked so much alike." Her gaze moved to Christopher and Nora and perhaps to the empty spot where her eldest son ought to have been. "When they grew older, they all...went their own ways, their faces taking on their distinct expressions." She sighed again, clasping her hands to her chest. "He looks so much like them."

Juliet placed a hand upon her arm. "Would you like to meet him?"

Unable to speak, Lady Lockhart nodded.

As before, Juliet slipped her arm through her mother-in-law's and urged her onward, her hesitant steps a clear sign of how deeply this moment affected her. Tears streamed down Lady Lockhart's face, and she quickly wiped them away.

"Bash," Juliet called, trying to catch his attention as he and Sam were twirling round and round, hands clasped together to keep them from being pulled apart. "Bash!"

When he finally heard her, he looked up, lost his balance and the two children flew apart, rolling across the lawn as laughter spilled from their mouths. "Juliet, did you see?" Bash asked excitedly as he jumped back onto his feet and rushed toward her. "We were twirling so fast, I thought I could not hold on a moment longer."

Grateful to see Harriet draw Sam's attention elsewhere, Juliet kneeled down in front of Bash and took his hands within her own, delighting in the little jolt she always felt when she did so. He was her son! Her son! Sometimes, she still had trouble believing her luck.

"Bash, I want you to meet someone." She glanced at Lady Lockhart, who looked ready to faint, her breath coming fast as she stared down at Bash. "This is your father's mother, your grandmother. She has come here today to meet you."

Bash's wide eyes moved to the tall and currently rather pale lady. "Another grandmother?" he asked in that innocent and absolutely endearing way children often had.

"Yes," Juliet confirmed with a reassuring squeeze of her hands. "She does not live far from here, and you will most likely see her often. Would you like to show her around? I'm certain she would love to see the tree you and Samantha picked out for your fort."

At her suggestion, Bash lit up, excitement glowing in his young eyes. Then he stepped forward, curiously peering at his new grandmother. "It's the best tree I've ever seen," he muttered under his breath, casting a careful glance around as though fearing that if he spoke too loudly someone might hear and come and snatch his tree away. "It's tall and has thick branches that don't all go straight up. It's not good if they do."

As Bash went on discussing the merits of tree growth, Lady Lockhart fell into step beside him. Her hands were still clamped together, but a small smile shone upon her face as she tentatively asked a question here and there, slowly getting to know the grandson she had tried her best to ignore.

Juliet watched them, completely entranced by the sight, her heart beating fast against her ribs as more and more pieces of her life slowly fell into place.

"Do you think she means what she says?"

At the sound of her husband's voice right beside her ear, Juliet flinched. Her heart threatened to beat out of her chest, and she drew in a deep breath as she turned to face him. "Have you always been this stealthy?" she chided with a grin, reaching out to him at the same time, well aware that he needed her close right now.

As expected, Christopher wrapped her in his arms, not for her benefit, but for his own. A tentative smile tugged at the corners of his mouth; yet his gaze remained fixed upon the two figures walking slowly side by side toward the small grove. "Do you think she means what she says?"

Juliet looked up at him. "I believe so, yes." She reached out and gently cupped a hand to his cheek, waiting patiently until his gaze fell and he looked at her. "You know as well as I do that Bash is irresistible. Even if she tries, no one is a match for that sweet smile of his."

An older, more mature version of that sweet smile spread over Christopher's face before it suddenly seemed to pause. It was like a blossom slowly opening up to the sunshine before it halted as a storm threatened to break overhead. His gaze darkened, and he swallowed hard. "No matter what I did," he murmured absentmindedly, his gaze once more traveling to the little boy and the tall woman, "nothing ever melted her heart."

"That had nothing to do with you," Juliet said in a firm voice. She grasped his chin and gave it a little pinch until he once more looked at her, his brown gaze full of sorrow and pain and regret. "Her heart was closed off then. I suppose it had to be after what happened. It was her way of protecting herself." She offered him a careful smile. "Now, however, she dares to feel again. And slowly, with time, I have no doubt that she will be as devoted a mother as you always wished she had been. Trust me."

The smile that now came to Christopher's face held no hint of hesitation or doubt. It all but lit up the world, so radiant was it in its intensity. "I always have," he whispered, holding her tightly wrapped in his arms, "and I always will. You have been the one constant in my life I could always count on, and I have never once regretted it."

Sighing, Juliet rested her head against his shoulder and closed her eyes, savoring this beautiful moment. "Thank you for coming back," she whispered, feeling his heart beat strongly in his chest. "I think deep down I always hoped you would."

And she would forever be grateful to Grandma Edie for meddling in her life, for ensuring that she did not marry another out of some foolish notion—to avoid becoming a spinster, out of duty, or a desperate wish for love. Now she knew it would never have worked. She had given her heart away a long time ago, and without it, she could not possibly have ever loved another.

Yes, they were meant to be. Was it not like this in all the great love stories? Trials and obstacles before love triumphed? Yes, perhaps it had to have happened like this. Life had certainly tested her, tested them, but they had prevailed...

...and it had been well worth it.

EPILOGUE

Whickerton Grove, Winter 1803
Less than a fortnight later

At barely one week old, Louisa's and Phineas' infant daughter lay in her mother's arms, her little hands balled into fists and her head slowly turning red as she got ready to bawl. Indeed, it seemed the little angel had inherited her mother's spirit, loud and boisterous and demanding.

Yet Juliet loved her with all her heart. She loved the few tufts of strawberry blonde hair upon the little girl's head and the wide blue eyes that looked out into the world with such impatience, as though she could not wait to explore it all. Indeed, all her sisters, their husbands as well as her parents and grandmother doted upon the little girl, completely taken with her sweet smile and mischievous grin. Not even Bash and Sam left her side for long, staring into her little face as though it held secrets they wished to uncover.

"Oh, she's about to do it again!" Louisa exclaimed in a hushed voice from where she sat nestled in an armchair by the fireplace, a warm blanket draped around her legs. Her eyes flew up and met her husband's as he all but lunged himself toward her, snatched up the little angel with the practiced efficiency of a father and then marched around the room in a half-bounce, half-skip step that looked utterly ridiculous. However, while most of the Whickertons soon had tears streaming down their cheeks as they did their utmost to suppress their laughter, the little girl decided against wailing at the top of her lungs, snuggled deeper into her father's arm and finally closed her eyes.

"As ridiculous as this looks," Thorne remarked with a wide grin as he followed Phineas around the room with his eyes, "it works like a charm." He exchanged a delighted look with his wife. "It's like magic."

All but puffing out his chest, Phineas smiled at them proudly. "Fifth day as a father, and I'm already breaking records," he remarked far from modest.

In answer, Louisa laughed, shaking her head at him. "You talk as though you invented this. It's a proven technique to calm infants."

Phineas shrugged, then grinned at her challengingly. "Then you do it."

Louisa glared at him. "I'd love to," she said in a frighteningly sweet voice. "Then let's agree that with the next one, we'll mix it up. I'll do this odd bouncy thing of yours to calm her, if you promise to carry her for nine months and then make it through labor—which is such an adorable word for a dreadful experience that I want to slap whoever came up with it." She crossed her arms over her chest. "Well? Are we in agreement?"

Wisely, Phineas refrained from answering and instead continued his rounds about the room. Juliet noticed that whomever he passed could not help but crane their neck and stare at the sleeping angel.

"Oh, I cannot wait to hold my own," Anne whispered longingly, her hands placed gently upon the slight bump under her dress. Then she looked at Tobias. "Oh, and I can't wait to see you do that!"

Her husband laughed, as did everyone else.

Juliet exchanged a meaningful look with her own husband. While the two of them did not yet have news of their own to share, they were hopeful that little Bash soon would have a brother or sister. Another Whickerton to add to the growing clan. Indeed, Juliet could hardly wait to see a bunch of little girls and boys chase each other on the lawns and climb up into the fort that was currently under construction in the perfect tree outside.

"And what about her name?" their father asked as he looked from Louisa to Phineas and then to his wife. "Have you finally settled on one?"

A meaningful look passed between the two new parents before Louisa's gaze darted to Grandma Edie, seated only a few paces beside her in an armchair of her own. "We have, yes."

"And?" Harriet demanded impatiently as everyone else seemed to draw closer, eager to hear what it was.

A smile came to Louisa's face, and for a moment, Juliet felt overwhelmed by the strong maternal glow she saw light up her sister's eyes. "Well, we've decided to name her...Edith."

Everyone looked expectantly at Grandma Edie...who failed to utter any form of reply as she was currently soundly asleep, the only sound passing her lips a deep snore.

Laughter once more echoed through the drawing room, disturbing neither the snoozing infant nor the snoring great-grandmother. "Why Edith?" Harriet inquired, her gaze darting back and forth between her grandmother and her new niece. "Not that I object. I'm merely curious."

"Well," Louisa began, "for one, I cannot deny that I, myself, possess certain meddlesome tendencies," quite a few nodded their heads in agreement, "and apparently Grandma Edie once told Phineas that he reminded her of Grandfather." Blinking back tears, Louisa shrugged. "I suppose we thought that...there should be another Edie in the world."

Now, everyone was nodding in agreement, more than one set of eyes misted with tears. "That is a wonderful thought, sweetheart," their mother said as she walked over to her daughter and placed a kiss upon Louisa's forehead. "It's a beautiful name for a beautiful little girl."

"Aye," Keir agreed, his blue eyes livelier than Juliet had ever seen them as he peeked into little Edith's face. "She's a bonny lass." His gaze moved to Phineas and a teasing grin came to his face as he clasped a hand upon his shoulder. "I promise ye, the time will come that ye wish she weren't." He laughed heartily as Phineas glared at him.

While Drake and Jack remained rather quiet, as they often

tended to, Thorne was not the kind to hold back. "Honestly, considering her namesake, I cannot help but wonder what kind of person she will grow up to be." He grinned wickedly, not only his eyes darting back and forth between the two Ediths. "A force of nature, no doubt."

Phineas nodded enthusiastically. "That is exactly what we thought." He looked down at his sleeping daughter, and the softness and devotion that came to his face made Juliet's heart ache. "I want one as well," she whispered quietly to Christopher.

He wrapped an arm around her shoulders. "Only one?" he asked with a wide grin.

Juliet chuckled. "I wouldn't mind a dozen. After all, that means we only have eleven more to go."

Christopher's grin broadened as he tugged her into his arms. "I like how you think, Wife."

"Well," Harriet exclaimed as she turned from the two Ediths and looked at their brother, who stood in a corner by the pianoforte, "six siblings and five are married." She grinned at him, wiggling her brows and completely ignoring the steel-like expression that came to his eyes. "Any marriage plans upon the horizon, Troy?"

Juliet drew in a sharp breath, for she knew her brother well. He might appear calm to most observers; however, she could see the tight control he was currently keeping upon his emotions. She saw the way his teeth ground together, the muscles in his jaw tense, as he kept his hands linked behind his back, which he always did when something unsettled him deeply. "Harry, perhaps we should not—"

Unfortunately, Harry did not hear her. "What about Nora?" she asked as everyone stared, the same question on all their minds. After all, in the previous weeks, all of them—in varying constellations—had discussed their speculations regarding Troy and Nora at great length. Of course, Troy was not aware of it and clearly had not seen this ambush coming.

Stepping forward, Troy met Harriet's gaze unflinchingly. "I would appreciate it," he said in an even, yet barely restrained voice, "if you kept your nose out of my affairs." Then he turned and marched toward the door.

Unfortunately, yet again, Harriet was not so easily swayed. "I know you care for her. We all do. Why do you deny it?"

Troy froze, and for a long time, it appeared time itself had stilled. Then, ever so slowly, Troy turned upon his heels to face his sister, his blue eyes cold and hard, revealing the depth of his emotions better than a flood of tears could have. Juliet cringed at the sight of it. "I do not care for whatever you think you know," he said with a deadly calm. "Lady Nora means nothing to me beyond an old acquaintance. In fact, I plan on searching for a suitable wife come next Season."

Juliet drew in a sharp breath as Troy held Harriet's gaze for a moment longer. Then, he once more turned to leave.

Like a dog with a bone, Harriet was about to speak up again; however, in that moment, the door opened and a rather breathless man covered in snow stumbled into the room, whom Juliet recognized as Gerald, one of the grooms at Fartherington Hall.

"Gerald!" Christopher exclaimed, exchanging a concerned look with Juliet before he strode toward the man. "What are you doing here? Is something the matter?"

Gerald drew in a deep breath and then spoke. "I'm afraid I bring bad news, my lord. Your mother bade me ride to Whickerton Grove as fast as possible."

Juliet felt an icy chill crawl down her back and knew from the expression upon her husband's face that he, too, feared to hear the messenger's next words.

"Speak!" was all Christopher said.

Gerald nodded. "This morning, Lady Nora went for a ride," he swallowed, and out of the corner of her eye, Juliet noticed Troy tense, "and she has yet to return."

Christopher's face paled. "How long has she been gone?"

"Four hours."

Shocked murmurs went through the room. "It will be dark soon," Christopher growled with a look out the window at the snow-covered countryside. Then his gaze snapped back to the messenger. "Where did she go?"

The man shrugged. "I'm afraid we do not know. Lady Nora rides out often, but she always returns after two hours. We've dispatched men to look for her, but Lady Lockhart...eh...the Dowager Lady Lockhart bid me to ask for your assistance."

"Of course," Christopher bit out, his gaze pained as he looked at Juliet. "We have to find her."

"We will join you," Juliet's father stated, and one by one, his children and their spouses rose to their feet, nodding their agreement and support. Phineas gently returned little Edie to her mother's arms before he, too, stepped forward. "When she rides out," he asked the group, "where does she go?"

Everyone shrugged, including the messenger. Juliet turned to look at her brother. "Perhaps Troy kno—" She broke off when she found the spot where he had stood only seconds before empty.

A moment later, the sound of hoofbeats could be heard outside, and as they rushed to the window, they spotted Troy charging down the drive.

Despite his words, Nora clearly meant a lot more to him than an old acquaintance. Juliet could only hope that he would find her in time.

THE END

Thank you for reading *Once Upon an Achingly Beautiful Kiss*!

Be on the lookout for the Troy's and Nora's story!

If you want to read more about the Whickerton family, make sure to check out *Once Upon a Devilishly Enchanting Kiss* (Louisa's story), *Once Upon a Temptingly Ruinous Kiss* (Leonora's story), *Once Upon an Irritatingly Magical Kiss* (Christina's story) and *Once Upon a Kiss Gone Horribly Wrong* (Anne's story).

THE WHICKERTONS IN LOVE

While waiting for Troy's story to be released, you might want to check out Bree's *USA Today* Bestselling *Love's Second Chance Series.* Or you can dive into WOLF Publishing's latest release by the wonderful **Jennifer Monroe**: *Duke of Madness*, the first book in the Sisterhood of Secrets Series!

THE SISTERHOOD OF SECRETS

ALSO BY BREE WOLF

LOVE'S SECOND CHANCE SERIES: TALES OF LORDS & LADIES

LOVE'S SECOND CHANCE SERIES: TALES OF DAMSELS & KNIGHTS

ALSO BY BREE WOLF

LOVE'S SECOND CHANCE SERIES: HIGHLAND TALES

FORBIDDEN LOVE NOVELLA SERIES

HAPPY EVER REGENCY SERIES

For more information visit www.breewolf.com

ABOUT BREE

USA Today bestselling and award-winning author, Bree Wolf has always been a language enthusiast (though not a grammarian!) and is rarely found without a book in her hand or her fingers glued to a keyboard. Trying to find her way, she has taught English as a second language, traveled abroad and worked at a translation agency as well as a law firm in Ireland. She also spent loooong years obtaining a BA in English and Education and an MA in Specialized Translation while wishing she could simply be a writer. Although there is nothing simple about being a writer, her dreams have finally come true.

"A big thanks to my fairy godmother!"

Currently, Bree has found her new home in the historical romance genre, writing Regency novels and novellas. Enjoying the mix of fact and fiction, she occasionally feels like a puppet master (or mistress? Although that sounds weird!), forcing her characters into ever-new situations that will put their strength, their beliefs, their love to the test, hoping that in the end they will triumph and get the happily-ever-after we are all looking for.

If you're an avid reader, sign up for Bree's newsletter on www.breewolf.com as she has the tendency to simply give books away. Find out about freebies, giveaways as well as occasional advance reader copies and read before the book is even on the shelves!

Connect with Bree and stay up-to-date on new releases:

facebook.com/breewolf.novels
twitter.com/breewolf_author
instagram.com/breewolf_author
amazon.com/Bree-Wolf/e/B00FJX27Z4
bookbub.com/authors/bree-wolf

Printed in Great Britain
by Amazon

25162691R10162